MW00588469

Catrina's Cowboy

By

LuAnn Nies

Published by
Melange Books, LLC
White Bear Lake, MN 55110
www.melange-books.com

Catrina's Cowboy ~ LuAnn Nies ~ Copyright © 2013

ISBN: 978-1-61235-605-1 Print

Names, characters, and incidents depicted in this book are products of the author's imagination or are used fictitiously. Any resemblance to actual events, locales, organizations, or persons, living or dead, is entirely coincidental and beyond the intent of the author or the publisher. No part of this book may be reproduced or transmitted in any form or by any means, electronic or mechanical, including photocopying, recording, or by any information storage and retrieval system, without permission in writing from the publisher.
Published in the United States of America.

Cover Art by Stephanie Bibb

Catrina's Cowboy
LuAnn Nies

Catrina Pearson accepts an invitation from her estranged maternal grandmother in hopes of learning the identity and truth about the father she never knew and why her mother took that secret to her grave. As a photographer who's travelled the world, Catrina is ready to face any challenges the rugged Utah landscape may throw at her, but she's not prepared to handle the reclusive cowboy who ropes her heart.

Betrayed by his heritage and family, Clifford White Fox is determined to purchase the acreage surrounding his ranch and build a private world safe from judgment and emotional intrusion. His lifestyle and hard-won serenity are threatened when he stumbles across a naked woman sunbathing on the last parcel of land he needs to acquire.

Bev,
Hope you enjoy.
Love,
Auntie Lu

For

The members of my critique group, Lori Ness, Denise Devine, Robin Nelson and Chad Filly who helped bring Catrina and Cliff's story to light and who have taught me so much over the years. To Bill Brown for sharing his wisdom of ranching and for letting me ride by his side. And to the gals crazy enough to attempt Bullwhacker with me.

When you share the same interest or passion with someone, there's an unspoken bond between you. It can speak volumes in just a glance. It's as if you're connected by something deep inside that has no name. These people are very special to me and I'll always treasure their friendships.

With good friends you'll never ride alone.

Chapter One
~ Black River, Utah 1993 ~

Cliff reined in the big gray quarter horse on the fringe of the rocky ledge. Raising the binoculars, he scanned the far ridge and the meadow below searching for twenty head of wayward cattle. He pushed up the brim of his weathered cowboy hat and wiped a sleeve across his sweat-covered brow. *Three days of easterly winds, storms brewing,* he thought.

Off in the distance a hawk screeched and swooped toward something hiding amongst a clump of white Sego lilies. His gaze swept across the meadow below, coming to rest on the tattered tin roof of a little house in the distance. The old homestead wasn't much more than a tarpaper shack and neglected barn. The scattered outbuildings had been empty since its owner, Millie Pearson, moved into town. It wasn't the buildings Cliff coveted but the land. If he could get his hands on this section, he could expand his ranch, his private world. He'd shut out everyone, those who judged or criticized him for being half white and half Ute Indian.

A movement alongside the house caught his attention. Raising the binoculars, he spotted a naked woman lying on a blanket. Drawing in a deep breath and holding it, he watched as the woman leisurely rolled over and settled onto her back. A sour taste rose and burned the back of his throat. Every muscle in his body stiffened with indignation. His horse, Sonny, tossed his head and pawed the earth in restless anticipation.

Who the hell is that? What's she doing on my land? Well, land that would soon enough belong to him when he finally persuaded that crotchety old woman into letting go of it. The horse sidestepped, anxious to be on the move, and that was all the encouragement Cliff needed. Irritated that someone had the nerve to be on that property without his knowledge or permission stuck in his craw. He maneuvered his horse down the narrow rocky trail that led to the deteriorating homestead.

He should have called out as he approached and moved around to the other side of the house to give the woman a moment to cover herself, but the one thing Clifford White Fox had never been accused of was being a gentleman.

With the sun at his back, he rode into the yard and halted several feet in front of the naked woman. Dark brown hair fell around her shoulders as she leaned on one elbow and attempted to shade her eyes against the bright sun.

She made no attempt to cover herself.

Typical.

His muscles twisted into painful knots.

"What are you doing here?" His dry voice growled.

The woman frowned, as her gazed darted from one side to the other. "I'm staying here while I do some work."

"Who are you?" His question slipped between clenched teeth and parched lips.

"My name's Catrina. This is my grandmother's place." Her brows furrowed into a deep crevasse. "I have permission to be here. You don't!" Her sharp response sliced through the air like a stray spark from a campfire. "And I don't have to answer any of your questions."

She stood and wrapped the blanket around herself. Her neck, shoulders and slender arms remained uncovered, and Cliff struggled to deflect his eyes from her bare flesh. His gaze shot to her full lips and flawless complexion. His groin swelled, pressing against his jeans. He shifted his weight in the saddle. The fringe of his chaps flapped, and his spurs jingled, causing the big gray to toss his head and prance in place.

Cliff learned a long time ago not to trust women, especially naked women. They were nothing but trouble, and the sooner he sent this one packing—the better.

"Are you out here alone?" he asked, cursing himself for being too distracted by her naked curves to notice if anyone else was around.

The woman's back stiffened, and her chin cinched up a notch as she adopted that all-too familiar attitude women reverted to as a defense mechanism. Silence hung heavy in the parched heat between them.

She stood her ground, yet something flashed in her dark eyes, confirming his suspicion that she was alone. It was dangerous for an inexperienced woman to be out here on her own. But then again, he'd never met a woman who had the sense God gave a newborn colt.

She glanced around and gripped the blanket tighter. Her arched neck convulsed in a strained swallow as he watched the anger in her eyes turn to fear. Good. It's not safe to be laying naked out in the open. Lord only knows what sort of dangerous creatures are sneaking around—like him.

The sight of her exposed flesh stirred up long forgotten and buried emotions. He'd let his guard down—not a smart move. He vowed a long time ago that he would never let another woman get close enough to have that kind of effect on him. An odd feeling he couldn't name slithered up his sweat-soaked spine.

Unclenching his jaw, he snarled, "Who knows you're out here?"

Her eyes narrowed, and she sidestepped closer to the weathered door of the shack. "Several people know where I am," she replied, with false bravado.

His horse pranced in place, anxious to be on the move.

"It's dangerous for you to be out here. Whatever your business is, *woman*, do it from town." He spun his horse around, but before he could sink his spurs into Sonny's flanks, the horse bolted.

Catrina gasped. One hand shot up to shield her face from flying dirt and the cloud of dust from the horse as he spun around and fled. When she shielded her eyes in hopes of getting a look at the man's face, as if on cue, his horse sidestepped, keeping the sun at his back.

Where had he come from? How long had he been watching her? She swallowed hard and slipped into the stagnant, dim interior of her grandmother's house. She thought she'd been alone. The house set back three miles from the main road. The nearest neighbor lived several miles away.

While sunbathing, she'd fantasized about a cowboy riding across the horizon toward her; someone like a young Jimmy Stewart, who sat tall in the saddle and always stood for truth and fairness, or someone like Glenn Corbett with his captivating blue eyes, broad shoulders and rugged good looks.

She had memorized the distinctive characteristics of every cowboy from the black and white B Westerns to the big screen. No one swung onto the back of a running horse like Ben Johnson, or swaggered into a saloon, his presence alone demanding attention like the Duke himself, or laughed and gimped with a slight hitch in his get-along, like Walter Brennan. They were her heroes, taking the place of a father, uncles, brothers and grandfathers she never had.

But there was something sinister and untamed about this cowboy. She shivered. His deep, rumbling voice resembled Sam Elliott's, but with a darker, deadlier edge to it. His growl had caused the hairs on the back of her neck to stand straight out.

What if he came back? This guy was no Hollywood Western hero from her childhood. He was real. He exuded danger, and she had set up camp smack-dab in the middle of his realm.

With her back pressed to the inside of the door, Cat gulped breaths of dusty air and listened to the drumbeat of pounding hooves as they faded. Realizing the thumping came from her own chest she pulled the torn lace curtain back, wiped the dirt-smeared window with a corner of the blanket and peered out through the thick glass.

The intruder was gone.

"That was a little nerve racking," she muttered. Her heart pounded in her ears. Placing a trembling hand to her chest, she closed her eyes as her legs began to buckle. She sank into a whitewashed kitchen chair and prayed the rickety thing would hold her as she tried to regain her composure.

After a few minutes, her heart slowed to its natural rhythm, and she opened her eyes. Surrounded in silence, she watched as dust motes danced in a beam of sunlight that seeped through the wide cracks in the walls. How on earth had this ramshackle place stood for this long? Even now, it looked as if the only thing holding it up was pure stubbornness.

Cat had been ten years old the last time she and her mother had driven from Los Angeles to visit her grandmother. As she glanced around the small room, it appeared nothing had been updated since. She ran a hand over the chipped, porcelain coated, steel table and thought of her mother, Cathryn. She'd been dead a year, leaving her grandmother Millie as her only known relative. Cathryn had refused to divulge the identity of Cat's father, and Cat hoped her grandmother would be able to reveal some information about him.

Cat peeked through a crack in the wall in search of the stranger. She wondered why Millie hadn't warned her about him. Maybe she didn't know about him. Maybe he was a drifter, wandering around stealing, taking whatever he wanted.

She wished she could have seen his face, but shuddered as his words of warning replayed in her head. If she ever dared wonder what the devil's voice might sound like, Catrina was sure she'd just heard him.

* * * *

For the past ten years, Cliff had rented Pearson's land. Every few months when moving cattle, he would ride in and check on the place, but today had been the first time since Millie moved into town that anyone had been there. Although he hadn't convinced her yet, and they never shook on it, he had always known that when the time came, Millie would sell out to him. He'd better head into town and find out how long this granddaughter planned on hanging around.

A vision of the young woman spread out, naked, in front of him, flooded Cliff's mind. *Just what kind of work does she think she's going to do out there? That old shack isn't fit for a pack of coyotes, let alone a woman with long tan legs...* Cliff shook his head, forcing himself to come to his senses. It would be smart to steer clear of the old place for a while and avoid running into her again.

Sonny stopped dead in his tracks, tossed his head, and pulled at the bit. Realizing he'd been tugging on the horse's head, Cliff let up on the reins. He glanced around and noticed his horse had stopped fifty yards from a group of cattle lounging in the tall grass, in the shade of a group of trees. "Sure, now you find them," he grumbled. Circling to the north, he headed the cattle back toward the ranch.

* * * *

The few miles into Black River passed like a dream played in fast-forward. No matter how diligently Cat fixated on the road, her thoughts kept returning to the mysterious cowboy who made no bones about wanting her off her grandmother's place. *What concern is it of his if I'm there?* She wondered. *Why would my being there be a problem for him?*

She reduced her speed as she neared the outskirts of town. For a small town it appeared to have everything a person needed. The first thing she saw was a church and the Wagon Wheel Motel. She chuckled at the irony and coincidence that they sat across the road from each other. There was one filling station named "Doug's", which seemed to be a favorite hangout, she judged, by the row of lawn chairs poised in the sun, a faded Coke machine and the blare of country-rock coming from a gigantic boom box balancing on a stack of tires.

The whole town was condensed to an area of two blocks. Besides a run-of-the-mill grocery store, drug store, post office and family restaurant, the main drag housed a hole-in-the-wall called "Grumpy's". Its sign promised you could wet your whistle and stuff your gut. *No doubt, a culinary delight*, she snickered. Across the road, painted on the side of a large red brick building, was "Black River Co-op". It sold an assortment of products and items from horse and chicken feed to western hats and boots.

At the end of town across from the sheriff's office, courthouse and jail sat a white vinyl sided building. In bold black lettering, the sign read "Black River Medical Building", which was short for limited medical staff, one emergency room hospital, four room medical clinic and twenty-bed nursing care unit—Millie Pearson's new home.

Cat pulled in and parked her silver, Subaru hatchback in one of the eight parking spots by the main door. Trees, bushes, and bird feeders lined the far end of the modest little building.

She peered at her appearance in the rear view mirror and sighed. She hoped her grandmother felt better today. Yesterday when she entered Millie's private room, her grandmother appeared flushed and out of breath. She slouched in her wheelchair, an afghan tucked snug over her lap, but smiled when she'd noticed Catrina.

Today when she opened the entrance door, Cat was hit with a strong smell of disinfectant, medication and the distinct odor of the sick and dying. The bottoms of her sandals squeaked on the polished, white linoleum as she strolled by the reception counter. She waved and smiled at Jeannie Porter, the young nurse's aide behind the counter. She liked the freckled-faced woman from the first moment they had met. Just a tad over five feet, Jeannie was openly friendly with a bubbly personality, and Cat was grateful a person like her was on staff to take care of her grandmother.

The first room on the left was Millie's, a corner room with windows facing both the street and overlooking a quaint and colorful courtyard. Pausing outside the closed door, Cat drew in a deep breath and gripped the door handle. The door swung open without a sound. Her frail grandmother sat in a wheelchair by the windows, facing the road. The blinds were positioned at an angle so no one passing by could look in.

"Grandma?" Cat whispered, not wanting to startle the old women. She walked closer. "Grandma?"

"Oh!" Millie lifted her face; her eyes blinked a couple of times. "Catrina? Is that you?" Her voice sounded shallow and weak.

Cat's heart ached. *Why did I wait so long to come for a visit? I've wasted so much time, and now our time together is running out.* "Yes, Grandma, it's Cat." She knelt next to her chair and patted her warm weathered age-spotted hand. "How are you feeling today?" Millie turned away and coughed into a flowered handkerchief. "You look good," Cat said, hoping her grandmother wouldn't hear the strain in her voice. "Can I get you anything?"

"No, dear. I don't need anything now that you're here." The old woman offered a whimsical smile and placed her hand on top of Cat's. "Is it nice out?" She glanced toward the street. "It's kind of hard to tell." She shook her head. "My eyes aren't what they once were." She tugged on her afghan.

Cat drew a slight smile. "It's really nice out. There's a warm breeze out of the east." She wanted to ask her about the mysterious cowboy but wondered if it would only upset her.

Millie sat up a little straighter, glanced out the window and murmured, "Rain's comin'."

"What, Grandma?" Cat leaned forward. "What did you say?"

"Nothing, dear." Millie wiped at her nose. "I was just wondering if I'll still be here in the fall to see the leaves turn color," then pointed toward a mature maple tree in front of the courthouse across the street. "Now, sit down, child." She motioned to a chair in the corner of the room. "Sit and tell me about yourself. I want to hear all about your trip to Africa." Millie settled back into her chair and folded her gnarled, arthritic hands on her lap.

Cat slid the chair up next to the wheelchair and eased into it. As she started to speak, the door opened, and Jeannie entered. She stopped in the doorway, a puzzled expression on her face.

7

"Millie? Are you feeling alright?" The little blonde marched across the room and placed her hand against Millie's forehead. "You're not overly warm? Would you like me to ask Dr. Frank to stop by before he goes home for dinner?"

Millie waved the young woman away. "I'm fine, Jeannie. Don't bother the Doc."

Jeannie glanced at Cat. "Are you going to stay and join Millie in the dining room for dinner today?" She gently massaged Millie's shoulders.

"No. Not today." Cat glanced toward her frail grandmother. "I don't want to take too much of her time." She fought back the tears that were quickly filling her eyes. "She needs her rest."

"Well, you're welcome to stay and eat anytime," Jeannie added with a big smile. "Millie," she said leaning over the older woman's shoulder, "Did you look at the menu and pick out what you'd like today?"

Millie coughed into her handkerchief and tugged on her afghan. "I'm not very hungry. Just bring a bowl of soup and some warm milk to my room when you're not too busy."

Cat glanced up at Jeannie and offered what she knew was a rueful smile.

Jeannie shook her head and patted Millie's shoulder. "I'll be back in a little while with your soup and milk."

Cat shifted in her chair. Her grandmother was dying, and she understood it was the way of life. What she couldn't deal with was the fact that Millie was the only person who might be able to help her figure out who her father was. She had gone through her mother's belongings after she passed away and found no clues other than an envelope that held pay stubs from her mother's first job in Los Angeles. When she did the math, Cat realized her mother would have been barely pregnant with her. Her mother never wanted to visit Millie or Black River, which made Cat believe her father was from here and could possibly still live here.

"What's the matter, dear? You look as if you ate a pickle that's sat in the jar too long."

"Oh." Cat forced a smile. "I was just thinking, wondering."

"Wondering what?"

"Grandma?" Cat reached for both of Millie's hands, hesitated, then asked, "Do you know who my father is?"

Millie drew in a deep breath and then slowly exhaled. She squeezed

Cat's hands and shook her head. "Your mother never spoke a word about him to me. I have no idea, sweetheart." Millie's smoky blue-gray eyes rimmed with tears. "I wish I knew."

"I know he was from here," Cat said, hoping that might help in some way.

Millie's eyes grew round. "Did she tell you that?"

"No." Cat's chest fell in surrender. "But I'm sure that's why she never wanted to come back here. I went through all of her papers and came to the conclusion that she had to have been pregnant when she left here."

Millie looked away. "Well, that would explain a few things. But I still don't have any idea who he is."

"Do you remember who she was dating right before she left?"

Millie appeared to drift off in thought. Cat held her breath; her grandmother might say the man's name, which would change Cat's life forever. She'd find him. She didn't care where he was. She'd track him down. He was probably married and had a family of his own, but she didn't care. She just wanted the chance to meet him.

Millie turned back, a doleful expression on her face. "I can't remember."

Cat exhaled. "That's okay." She forced a smile as a lump rose in the back of her throat.

"You know, there are some old pictures in the top draw of the dresser at my house," Millie stated. "If you searched through them, you might find something that would point to someone."

"Thanks, Grandma. I'd better go. Your dinner should be here soon." Cat stood and slid the chair aside.

"Are you alright, dear?" Millie reached out her hand. "You look so despondent."

"I'm fine, Grandma. Don't worry about me." She leaned forward and hugged her grandmother. Hopefully Millie would remember something or Cat would find a photo of her mother and some cute cowboy. *Cowboy!* She pulled back. "Grandma, today a cowboy rode up to the house. I couldn't get a look at his face, but he was tall, and his voice was very deep. His horse was gray with a black mane and tail. Do you know anything about him?"

Millie glanced away and wrung her hands. "White Fox," she

whispered.

"White Fox!" Cat echoed, not liking her grandmother's reaction at hearing her description of the mysterious man.

"Clifford White Fox. He runs cattle on my place."

"He's not very friendly!" Cat placed her hands on her hips. "He's rude. He told me it was too dangerous for me to be out there by myself. He even *ordered* me to move into town."

Millie chuckled. "That one's a real man, honey, like your grandfather." Millie sat a little taller, her eyes sparked as she continued. "His mother, Ester, is a full Ute and still lives on the reservation—nice woman." The softness in her face turned hard when she added, "His father, Hank Dawson, was white, and as ornery as they come. What Ester ever saw in him I'll never know." She shook her head. "Cliff keeps to himself. Does things his own way. He's very protective of what's his and what he considers to be his." She glanced up at Cat. "I reckon he feels my place is already his."

"What do you mean by already his?"

"Well, he's been after me to sell for several years now. I've been holding out as long as I can, but..."

"Grandma, has your place been tested for minerals or oil?"

"What? No. Not lately. Your grandfather did some testing years ago. Nothing out there but red dirt, cacti and a few jackrabbits."

"Then why does he want your land so badly?"

"A couple of years ago, he bought a section of land north of me. It's land-locked, and the only way to get to it without going on reservation land is across my land."

"Why can't he just go through the reservation?" That sounded simple enough to her.

"There's more to it than that."

Just then, the door opened, and Jeannie entered the room carrying a tray. "Here's your dinner, Millie," she said, setting the tray down on the table.

"I'll go so you can eat," Cat said, as she leaned down and kissed her grandmother's weathered cheek. "I'll call you in the morning and let you know if I come across any pictures. Goodnight. Goodbye, Jeannie. Take good care of her."

"Don't worry about that," Jeannie replied, folding her arms across her chest. "I'll keep a close eye on this one. Drive careful."

Swiveling her chair around, Millie watched Catrina get into her car and drive away. She glanced up at Jeannie. "What?" she said at Jeannie's questioning expression. Millie stood, tossed the afghan to the end of her bed, then settled into a velvety blue armchair. *So, Catrina and Cliff have seen each other?* Millie shook her head and chuckled. *I bet the sparks were flying. I can just see him telling her to get off his land.*

"Here's your soup and warm milk," Jeannie purred, rolling the small table over in front of Millie. One perfect blonde brow arched above the young girl's bright blue eyes.

"Get that crap away from me," Millie snapped, waving the girl away and reaching for the television remote. "It didn't take long for that old fox to sniff her out. That ex-wife of his has been out of the picture for five years. It's time he moves on."

"Just what are you up to?"

"Catrina isn't anything like Nora," Millie said. Pointing her finger at Jeannie she added, "She's strong and independent. She needs a partner who will challenge her at every opportunity. Someone who'll love her and give her the family she so desperately needs." Millie laughed and slapped her knee. "She's perfect for that boy."

Jeannie placed her hands on her hips. "If you ask me, you're sticking your nose in where it shouldn't go."

"Well, I ain't asking for your opinion. This is family business, so you never mind."

Millie knew when she was gone Catrina would have no family. If Catrina and Cliff were together, he would make her settle down, and they would build a life together and make a family they both needed.

It didn't make any difference if she sold her land to him or if he got it when he married Catrina, either way he was going to end up with it. Owning her land would enable him to connect all of his land together. But by doing that, he would never have to set foot on the reservation again or have any connection to his family. Millie frowned. She hated the fact that Cliff had turned his back on his family and his Native American ways.

Catrina would make him understand how precious family is. She could mend those fences before he destroyed them to the point where they couldn't be restored.

Catching a glimpse of Jeannie's perplexed expression, Millie snapped her fingers and added, "That boy needs a woman he can trust, can count on." Jeannie's brows rose. "Bring me some real food this time and don't be stingy with the portions." Satisfied, Millie settled back in her chair and switched on the television.

"Oh, and Jeannie," she called before the door shut. "If there's any of that chocolate cake left, be a dear and bring me a big slice."

Chapter Two

Cat awoke to a cold room and a knot the size of a pomegranate in the middle of her back. Shivering, she pulled the moth-eaten quilt tight around her head. The alarm clock on the bent-up TV tray next to the bed read nine o'clock. She had crawled into bed around two in the morning, after hours of rummaging through her grandmother's dresser drawers, searching and praying for something that would reveal the slightest hint of her father's identity.

There were photos of her grandparents, baby pictures that she assumed were of her mother, but then she'd found an old black and white photo of a young boy. Written on the back of it was Richard Benjamin Pearson, died 1950 at the age of five. Millie had had a son Cat wasn't even aware of; a would-be uncle who was just another lost family member. Although she'd come across several photos of her mother growing up, there were none of her mother pictured with a young man. Dog-tired and disappointed, Cat had fallen asleep with more questions that would never be answered.

She yawned and scratched her nose with a quilt-covered finger. *Why hadn't her mother ever told her who her father was? Had he been married? Had it been a one-night-stand? Maybe she hadn't realized she was pregnant before she left and just never found the right time to tell him.*

Planting her bare feet on the cold plank floor, she stood and padded across the room to the electric heater. Pulling the quilt up under her chin, she gave the ancient heater a swift kick and received a sore toe for her efforts. She limped to the counter and switched on what looked to be the

13

first Westinghouse electric coffee pot ever made.

Wondering if any of the hiking trails were open, she glanced through the worn curtain and smudged glass. She sure could use a change in scenery. There were millions of Bureau of Land Management acres to hike on, and she wanted to take advantage of the many trails to view Utah's wildlife. From the many pamphlets she had collected and read this area alone was a treasure trove of national parks, historical sites and monuments. Cat's heart leapt at the thought of stumbling across ancient Indian writings or some long lost rock art.

Turning, she stared at the assorted stacks of photos strewn across the table. With a sigh, she eased onto one of the kitchen chairs and plucked a snap shot of rodeo and Pow Wow photos off the pile. It was a profile shot of a man between the ages of twenty and twenty-five, dressed in full regalia. His long raven hair hung in two thick braids adorned with ribbons, beads and feathers painted in bright colors of red, yellow, blue and orange. His stance gave the impression of arrogance as he gazed into the distance. His eyes were mere slits lined with thick black lashes and heavy dark brooding brows. A large Roman-type nose extended from his wide commanding forehead. High cheekbones and full lips were positioned above a powerful square jaw. Deep frown lines etched his weathered bronzed face. His broad bare shoulders ornamented with an elaborate colored vest topped a lean athletic torso.

His intense stern expression sent a slithering chill up Cat's spine. The photo depicted him as dangerous, defiant, and domineering…but most of all *delicious.*

Who was he? Where was he now? Most importantly, how could she arrange to be alone with him for a few hours? He was the best-looking man she'd ever seen. Her palms grew damp, and her nipples tightened into hard little buds as they rubbed against the rough blanket. She shivered, and all of a sudden, she had an itch that needed to be scratched. The chair scraped across the floor as she pushed back and stood. She tossed the suffocating quilt back toward the bed.

"I need some fresh air!"

* * * *

Doug Dolloff glanced across the bench-seat of his 1972 pickup truck to where Cliff sat, his window down, his arm resting on the door.

"What's put a burr under your saddle today?" A warm breeze scattered their red dust trail across an open field. "Are you going to tell me, or do I get to guess all the way to town?"

Cliff shot the older man a slight glance and replied, "Tell me again why I need to go into town with you?"

Doug shook his head. As long as he could remember, his younger cousin would never answer a direct question, but would reply with a question of his own. "Cause after you help me load feed, I want to stop by Grumpy's and have a burger." Then he grinned and added, "Down a couple beers and whip your sorry butt in a game of pool." He glanced over to judge Cliff's reaction and laughed at the bored look he received.

"If Nora's working at the co-op today," Cliff said, kicking at a clump of hardened clay on the floorboard. "You can drop me off at Grumpy's first and load your own feed."

"Nope," Doug grinned. He knew the last person Cliff wanted to run across was his ex-wife. "I called ahead. She's off today. Sal said she drove over to Salt Lake to see her sister and pick up supplies for the store."

Cliff's grunted response was as close to an *all right* as he was going to get. Twenty minutes later Doug pulled his truck up to the co-op's loading dock and started to load the fifty-pound sacks of feed into the bed of his pickup. They left the truck parked at the co-op and moseyed across the street to Grumpy's Bar and Grill.

They entered the dimly lit bar and walked through the blue haze of tobacco smoke. The stifling air reeked of stale beer and cheap perfume.

Doug waltzed toward the bar to order a couple of burgers, Grumpy's deadly onion rings and two tall ones. He stopped, slipped his arms around the waitress and twirled the short redhead a couple of times as the jukebox played Waylon Jennings "Ramblin' Man".

Cliff's boots scraped across the worn plank floor as he ambled to a table in a cool dark corner and dropped onto one of the chairs. He wasn't sulking; he just couldn't shake thoughts of the naked woman from his mind. She not only moved into Millie's place, she'd moved into his subconscious where she had plagued him for the past twenty-four hours.

With the palm of his left hand, he stroked his mustache and pondered. He didn't like the idea that Millie hadn't told him she was moving into town or that her granddaughter was going to be staying at her place. Millie had lived there most of her life. It wasn't like her to up and leave the place she loved so much. Yet, if she was ill, she should be where people could take care of her.

He'd drop by and see how she was doing later.

The sound of a bottle hitting the table interrupted his thoughts. He glanced up and saw Doug wink at the waitress.

"Here's to old girlfriends never meeting new girlfriends," Doug said, tapping the tip of his bottle against Cliff's.

Cliff tipped his bottle and let the cold liquid gold cool his dry throat. He shook his head. The middle-aged cowboy had always had a problem with girlfriends finding out about each other. He, on the other hand, didn't have those problems, and he planned on keeping it that way. He took another long pull on his beer. But the woman with the almond shaped eyes that shot red-hot sparks, and a body that stirred the coals of a fire deep inside that he thought had been long snuffed out kept doggen' him.

"Something dead in the bottom of your bottle?" Doug asked, giving him a puzzled look. "You've been meaner than a cat with his tail caught in the tack room door."

"Now you sound like Rooster," Cliff drawled. He reclined in his chair with his knees spread wide, his bottle resting on the thin edge of his beat-up belt buckle. "That old Cayuse followed me around the barn all morning, badgered me with questions until you pulled up."

"Well?" Doug racked up the billiards on the pool table, as the scent and sounds of beef sizzling on a well-seasoned grill wafted in the air. "You gonna tell me what's been eatin' you?"

I'm not telling you nothin', Cliff thought, raising the bottle to his lips.

The door to the bar opened, and a streak of sunlight cast a white shadow across the dark interior. A woman walked in wearing skimpy gray shorts and a snug light blue tank top. A brown foot-long ponytail swayed from side to side as she stepped up to the counter.

Doug took a step forward and bumped the table with his thigh. "Who...is that?"

Cliff closed his eyes and his throat contracted like he was fighting for his last breath in a dust storm.

Doug stood, dumbfounded. "Whoo-ee! Would ya look at those

legs?"

Yeah, Cliff was looking. He had dreamed all night about being tangled up in those long tanned limbs, those full lips...

Doug bumped Cliff's shoulder with his arm and pointed his beer at the woman. "Do ya think she's got any tan lines under those little shorty-shorts?"

A sound similar to a wounded animal worked its way out of Cliff's throat. "Not a one." At Doug's surprised stare, Cliff drained his bottle and set it down hard on the table.

There was no way she could have heard their comments from across the room, but the woman's slim body stiffened. She twisted around and cast a glance their way. Cliff cringed with a stab of guilt when her expression changed from curious to apprehensive. She paid for the bottled water, snatched it from the counter and charged out of the bar as if a pack of wolves snapped at her heels.

Doug glanced out the window. After a moment, he spun a chair around and straddled it, placing his elbows on the table.

"So? What do you know that I don't?"

"A lot," Cliff replied dryly, avoiding his cousin's glare. Though he didn't want to get into it at the moment, Doug made it clear he wasn't going to let the subject rest until he knew everything. Their food arrived; Cliff ordered another tall one and then enlightened his cousin with just the facts.

He admitted to knowing her name, but omitted the fact that he'd seen more of her than he had a right to. That tidbit of information would have pushed poor Doug over the edge. Cliff's appetite vanished when he realized he didn't want Doug or any other coyotes sniffin' around Millie's place, trying to get a look at her, especially if she had a habit of running around naked. A fist-size knot tightened in his gut. Naked women were trouble, and she was the second one he wished he hadn't come across.

* * * *

"That was him—" Cat shivered as goose pimples covered her from head to toe. She darted across the sidewalk, stepped off the curb and scrambled into her car. Her heart throbbed in her ears. The fine hairs on the back of her neck and arms stuck straight out as if an electrical storm was about to hit.

Don't panic. Take a deep breath, exhale, and relax. Cat wiped her damp palms on her shorts. She knew the man sitting in the dark corner watching her was the stranger on the big gray horse. That White Fox fellow Millie had told her about. Again, she didn't get a good look at his face; his cowboy hat had been pulled down low over his eyes. Yet, she would know him anywhere. He sat his chair with the same ease and arrogance he sat his horse.

Irritated, she thought, *I should have walked over to him and...and...what?* "Give him a piece of my mind for scaring me half to death? Yeah, right!" She drew in a deep breath as she turned the key. The smartest thing she could do was stay as far away from him as possible. Grandmother said he kept to himself, did things his own way. She'd bet he was one of those cowboys she'd read about who lived by the code of the "Old West".

That thought intrigued her, and her feelings of trepidation soon subsided. He was a real cowboy, a dying breed as they say. She wondered if he would let her take some photos of him. Maybe even paint his portrait. Glancing in the rearview mirror, she sighed, "Yeah, right after he staked me over a fire ant hill." She shifted her Subaru into reverse and pulled away from the curb. A little voice in the back of her head whispered, there must be a way to photograph him without his knowledge.

Cat headed north out of town toward the Uintas Mountains. She cleared her mind and concentrated on the rugged peaks of the orange-red mountains in the distance. Today is about hiking and taking pictures, she thought. No sick grandmother, no untamed cowboys and no wondering if the next guy she met on the sidewalk was her father. She would worry about that stuff later.

Up ahead the mountainside gorges were still covered in snow. She couldn't wait to see the lakes and valleys. She smiled and shifted in her seat with excitement.

Tapping her fingers on the steering wheel, she hummed along with the radio. She read that mountain lions and black bears were more common in the surrounding high desert basins, but that rattlesnakes and scorpions were sometimes seen in the lower elevations of the Uinta Mountains.

"Most of the mountain slopes are forested," she recited from an area pamphlet to keep her mind off him. "Coniferous trees such as Douglas fir and Engelmann spruce grow in large continuous stands. Quaking aspen occur in scattered patches throughout most of the lower elevations. Many isolated meadows resemble large parks and willow fields, which add variety to the timbered areas. Many peaks extend above the tree line."

She giggled. "There I go again, babbling like an idiot." Every time she got overly excited or her anxiety level rose, Cat found herself reciting information about her surroundings. She had been told it had something to do with her photographic memory. Yet it drove her friends and her mother crazy.

Pulling off the road, she parked by a sign posting the start of a marked hiking trail. Knowing most of the trailheads were still closed due to the time of year, she'd come prepared. Her backpack held the proper clothing for the weather and the essential gear in case of an emergency.

She unzipped her backpack, pulled out black insulated and waterproof hiking pants and slipped them on over her utility shorts. She reached into the back seat for her lightweight-hiking boots and put them on. Placing the water bottles in the side compartments of her backpack, she did a quick mental inventory, then grabbed her matching hooded jacket and camera case.

People gave her a hard time about being overly organized, but Cat never cared about that. Throughout her career, she had traveled several continents and hiked some pretty treacherous trails. She had learned along the way that it was better to be overly cautious and safe rather than caught in a dangerous situation unprepared. Although she had been known to take a risk to get the most spectacular photos, she wouldn't deliberately put herself or anyone else in harm's way.

The stranger popped into her thoughts, and she stopped in her tracks. She wondered what sort of danger she would be putting herself in if she ever got the opportunity to photograph the nearly endangered species in his own habitat. "Yep." She laughed. "I'd approach that cowboy the same way I'd approach a tiger—inconspicuously. He would never know I was lurking in the shadows watching him."

Closing the car door and placing her keys in the designated pocket on her backpack, Cat turned toward the trail and drew in a deep breath of clean air. This was just what she needed, a relaxing day of hiking.

Almost two hours later, she stooped and placed her hands on her knees. The air at this high altitude, crisp and clean, burned her lungs as she drew in a labored breath. She settled on a large rock conveniently positioned next to the trail and extracted a bottle of water from her backpack. Taking a deep swallow, she savored the cool liquid as it soothed her dry throat. Over the last hour and a half she had snapped photos of twisted Pinon pines emerging from rock formations, the towering snow covered mountains to the north and a golden eagle in search of his dinner. She took several rolls of beautiful landscapes, rocky ridges covered in delicate clumps of Blue Flax and fields of purple coneflowers. Yet, so far, the wildlife she hoped to shoot eluded her.

Placing a loose strand of hair behind her ear, she shivered as a cold wind assailed her. The warm breeze and sunshine she'd enjoyed the last few days seemed to have vanished. The temperature had dropped several degrees since this morning and just over the mountains, threatening gray-black storm clouds were rolling toward her.

She glanced back at the trail. How far was she from her car? If she went back the way she'd come, even at a quick pace, it would take her almost an hour to reach it. She took another gulp of water then tossed the backpack over her shoulder and scouted the path up ahead. She hiked several feet before coming to a fork in the trail. Pulling out her compass, she chose the path that appeared to hook around to the south—back toward the trailhead.

Scampering down the rugged path, Cat stumbled over rocks and sticks while trying to keep an eye on the towering thunderheads. At last, her car came into view. She sprinted the last few yards, as the sky opened up, and penny size raindrops assaulted her. Tossing her backpack and camera case on the front seat, she jumped in and slammed the door.

"Wow! What a storm. I'm soaked." She laughed and wiped her wet hair back from her face. She sat for several minutes, waiting out the worst of it. The wind and rain were deafening, and soon the windows steamed up. She started the engine, and when the windows cleared, she shifted the hatchback into gear.

After several miles, her headlights became ineffective as the rain intensified, drumming heavily against the windshield. She wondered if she was the only idiot driving in the severe conditions. The wipers fought to keep the windshield clear as muddy grass, twigs and rain pelting her car.

Cat clutched the wheel with a death grip as she crept along searching for a place to pull over. Water and mud covered everything around her, making it impossible to judge where the road was. She couldn't see a thing. At this speed, it was going to take her hours to get home.

All of a sudden, she felt like she was floating, as if the tires were no longer touching the pavement. White knuckled, Cat turned the wheel first one way then the other, the car merely veered to the right in slow motion. "Oh...Crap!" She scanned all the windows, but darkness engulfed her.

"What's happening?"

The car tilted sideways, bumped a hard surface, made a quarter turn to the left, then bobbed. Stiff as a mannequin, she froze with a death grip on the steering wheel.

Several seconds passed before she realized the car was floating. She heard a splash when she frantically pumped the brake. "Crap!" She glanced down; her car was filling up with water. Trying to stay calm, she drew in a labored breath and struggled to free herself from the seatbelt. "This can't be happening!"

Getting onto her knees, Cat peered over the seat. The hatchback area of her car was filled with water. Her oil paintings, which had been packed safely in a custom made, wooden crate, were half under water. All her framed photos, her notes, everything for her African exhibition next month in New York were doomed!

Frantic, she reached for her camera case and purse. Holding them over her head, she opened the driver's side window. The force of the wind sucked her breath from her lungs as she struggled to crawl out through the window. Wet hair whipped across her face, stinging her cheeks as water and debris struck her from all sides. Perched on the door, purse and camera case held above her head, Cat gaped at the side of the road as it rushed by several feet above her. She was floating in a flooded ditch.

One hand, which held her most prized possession, rested on the top of the car. With her other hand she clung to the car for dear life, her legs pressed tight against the inside of the door. She stared up the side of the bank toward the road and wondered if anyone could even see her. As the current carried her further along the ditch, the little car rocked from side to side.

What if I flip over?

The car hit something, she screamed, the passenger's side dipped down, causing her side to raise high out of the water. Then the car leveled off and continued to float further from her destination.

Cold wind and water continued to seep through her clothing. Shivering, she kept a watchful eye on the road and prayed someone would come by and see her. She glanced down at the water swirling inches below her. How long would the storm last?

How long could she hold on?

Cat raked her teeth across her lower lip and tasted blood. Her body shook from the cold and pure terror. Her gaze shot back to the road. "Flooding—water rising and overflowing its normal path. But a flash flood is a specific type of flood—appears and moves quickly across the land—little warning it's coming." She spat out a mouthful of water, coughed and whipped her head around to the other side. Lightning flashed a little too close for her liking.

Her voice quivered as she rushed on. "Many things can cause a flash flood. Generally, they're result of heavy rainfall concentrated over one area." Her fingers slipped on the wet metal, and she lost her grip. She reached for the seatbelt strap and wrapped it around her free hand. The frigid rain struck her in the face blinding her.

A loud "Bang" sounded toward the rear, and the floating car came to a halt.

Cat shrieked her scream drowned out by the booming claps of thunder. She squinted through the rain, but it was too dark to see what stopped her. It must be a driveway or a field road, she thought, instantly filled with hope. All she needed to do was get to the back and jump off onto the road. The car dipped from side to side as she struggled to crawl onto its roof. She tugged the straps of her purse and camera case over her head, with slow deliberate movements. She slipped across the cold wet metal on her knees toward the safety of the bank at the back of the car.

Then, out of the darkness, the blinding flash of headlights appeared.

* * * *

Rooster shook his head as the 1952 International pickup rattled along the treacherous road. This was a bad one, and he hoped he wouldn't lose too many calves before it ended.

"I'm getting too old for this..." Last month he'd turned seventy-two, and with the drastic drop in temperature, his body ached from injuries inflicted by sixty-some-odd-years of rodeos and ranching. Gnarled fingers gripped the steering wheel as a strong gust of wind blew the sturdy old truck to the opposite side of the road. Intense rain pelted the windshield, making it impossible to see. An image of a comfortable chair by a warm fire struck him. It's time to retire from ranching, he thought. But what would he do, take up knittin'?

He turned up the defroster and peered through the foggy windshield. "What in blue blazes?" In the ditch alongside the road, a person knelt on the roof of a car. He shook his head and eased the truck to a stop. Tugging his worn, distorted Stetson down tight against the wind and rain, he flipped up his collar and opened the truck door. The cold rain slapped against his back as he fought his way to the side of the road.

The person waved both arms in the air, but the wind stole any pleas for help. The small hatchback was lodged against the bank of a field entrance. Hidden below the surface, Rooster knew a dangerous whirlpool sucked the rushing floodwaters through a metal culvert. The person, who he could now tell was a woman, edged closer to the back of the car.

His arms shot out in front of him. "Stop! Stay there! Don't move!" He feared she couldn't hear him over the pounding rain. Turning, he yanked open the truck door and pulled a lariat off the seat. Limping to the back of the truck, he made a loop in the rope and threw it. The rope caught the wind and fell to the wet ground. He took a step closer, gathered up his rope and threw again. The rope struck the side of her car, yet still out of her reach. Concentrating on gathering up his rope, he took another step and slipped on the wet grass. His feet shot out from under him, and his bad hip hit the ground. Cursing under his breath, he crawled on his hands and knees to the bumper of the truck. A sharp pain shot down Rooster's leg as he struggled to pull himself up. Once he got to his feet, he turned, took a cautious step forward and nodded his head toward the woman. Taking a deep breath, he made another loop and sent the rope sailing through the air.

The lasso circled her; she grabbed the rope and slipped it under her arms. When she looked toward the rear of the car, he tugged hard on the rope and shook his head from side to side. If she went off the back the current would pull her under and into the culvert. He'd never get her out before she drowned.

Planting his feet far apart, he wrapped the rope around his hips for leverage and leaned into it. Prepared to support her weight, he nodded his head, and the woman crawled onto the hood and then eased off the side of her car into the water. Her feet swept out from under her, and she went under. Digging the heels of his boots into the mud Rooster held fast to the rope and inched backwards. He pulled and fought until the woman's head emerged above the rushing water.

When she reached the side of the road, he knelt down and reached out both hands. He grabbed a handful of her jacket and dragged her up the side of the bank to the road.

Hair covered her face, and she coughed water out of her lungs. "You okay, girlie?" Her head bobbed up and down in response. "Can you stand?" When she started to get up, he slipped the rope from around her, gripped her by the elbow and hauled her to her feet. He tossed the lariat into the box of his truck and opened the passenger's side door for her.

"Are *you* all right?" she asked, blinking through strands of wet hair. "Did you hurt yourself when you fell?"

"Don't you worry about this ol' Cayuse. Just get in before we both drown."

White teeth flashed through mud and hair when she smiled. "Watch your step, there's a running board," he instructed. "That a girl." He helped her into the truck. "Let's get out of here." He slammed the door. Reaching out, he braced himself against the truck and hobbled through the wind and rain to the driver's side door.

Cranking up the heat, Rooster shifted the old truck into gear and started off down the road. Glancing over, the young woman looked like a drowned rat. She shook violently and huddled against the door; two leather bags clutched to her chest. Her eyes were large and round as she stared out through the windshield.

"Name's Walter...Walter Running Bird." She didn't reply. "Everyone calls me Rooster." Still no reply. "You okay, girlie?" Should he turn around and head back toward town? The hospital? "It's just a mile or two to the ranch. You'll be safe and warm there."

"Th-thanks for st-stopping and helping me. I owe y-you my life."

"I'm just glad I happened along when I did." He didn't want to think what would have happened if she'd gotten caught under the car or sucked into the culvert.

He gripped the steering wheel tighter. Muddy water rushed over the road in front of them. The wipers flew back and forth at top speed, fighting the water, mud and debris that hit the windshield.

"What's your name, girlie?" He flashed a friendly smile. "What the douses are you doing way out here during a whopper of a storm like this?"

She wiped the hair from her face and stammered, "My na-name is Ca-Ca-Catrina." She shivered. "I've ba-been st-staying at my grandmother's-M-Millie Pearson's place."

"You don't say!" So this little drowned filly was the reason he couldn't get a straight answer out of Cliff when he returned home the other day.

"Do you know my grandmother?" She cut into his thoughts.

"Sure do. How's she doing?"

She looked down at her hands, her tone soft when she said, "She's very ill. She's moved into town."

"I hadn't heard that." The girl turned away and glanced out the side window. He'd never known Millie to be sick. She'd always been tough as nails and as ornery as a coyote with two feet caught in a snare.

"Millie invited me to Black River for a visit. She said springtime in the foothills of the mountains held an abundance of new life and a world of mystifying beauty." She rubbed her hands up and down her arms for warmth. "I registered at the motel, but she insisted that I stay out at her place."

Rooster turned off the tar onto the ranch road. The slimy, red clay clung to the tires, causing the pickup to fishtail, carving out deep ruts that filled with water. He glanced over when she yelped as her head struck the passengers window. "Sorry, gets a little rough out here. I should have warned you."

"Did you know that most flash flooding is caused by slow-moving thunderstorms?" she muttered, her eyes large and round as if in a trance. "Thunderstorms that repeatedly move over the same area or heavy rains from hurricanes and tropical storms."

Rooster fought between keeping his eyes on the road, watching her, or turning the truck around and heading back to town. After a few minutes, they pulled up to the front porch of the dark two-story log house.

When the girl gave him a questioning glance, he nodded his head. "It's open. The light switch is just inside the door on the right."

She hesitated, her big eyes staring through the dim lit interior at him.

"Go on, girlie. It's all right. It'll be safer riding out the storm here than at Millie's place. If you're hungry, help yourself. I need to check on a few things in the barn, and then I'll be in."

She shivered, and a precarious smile crossed her face. "Thanks." With a death grip on her bags, she opened the door. Rain blew in as she climbed out of the truck.

Poor thing, he thought as he watched her fight her way up the stairs and into the house. "Hope she didn't hit her head too hard." Her rambling made him nervous.

He had heard her mother, Cathryn, passed away after an auto accident last year. Millie had told him that she and the girl weren't close, and that the girl's father hadn't been a part of her life. What was she doing here? Was Millie so ill that she sent for the girl?

When the lights came on in the house, Rooster relaxed a little and drove toward the barn.

* * * *

Cat rushed across the big porch, opened the door, switched on the lights and stepped inside. The room could have been right out of one of her favorite old western movie. A half-filled kerosene lantern sat in the middle of a round oak table. Positioned at the far end of the room was an old porcelain and cast-iron wood cook stove. Next to that was a small refrigerator with some funny looking fan-thing attached to the top. Worn, wide-plank-boards made up the floor and tongue and groove cedar covered the interior walls.

A pearl handle revolver in a worn, hand-tooled gun belt hung on an elaborate antler coat rack by the door. Cat wondered if it was loaded. A braided rawhide reata rope, an old tan cowboy hat that looked as if it had seen a few too many stampedes and a faded, tattered jean jacket, which looked fifty years old, hung on the other hooks.

She set her purse and camera case on the counter by a coffee grinder with a broken crank. Her rescuer, a Native American she was sure by his rich tan and leathery features, appeared to be a successful rancher.

She leaned down and removed her hiking boots and wet socks, then shivered when her feet hit the cold floor. She roamed around the antique filled house until she found a bathroom, where she removed her hiking suit and hung it over the shower rod. Still clothed in her shorts and tank top, she glanced around and found a blue denim shirt hanging on the back of the door, but decided to wait and ask Rooster before she borrowed it.

Removing the elastic hair-binder holding what was left of her ponytail, she towel-dried her hair and combed her fingers through it. Staring at her reflection in the mirror, reality hit. Her supplies, all of her photos and paintings, everything in her car were ruined. Her career could very well be over. Weary and weak-kneed, Cat sank to the edge of the tub and placed her face into her hands.

What am I going to do? Everything is ruined. All my photos of Africa—lost. Tears burned the back of her eyes. Anxiety bubbled up inside her, and she gulped deep breaths. "Don't panic, you're not thinking straight."

A dull ache throbbed in the back of her head, and her stomach growled. She should call Millie to let her know that she was all right, but it was late, and she was probably asleep. Shivering, Cat hugged herself, yet the gesture offered little comfort. She needed hot food, a hot shower and a warm bed. She'd call Millie in the morning.

Tears streamed down her cheeks as the events of the day grouped together and hovered like gray clouds. In the morning, she would need to go over and check Millie's place, and then see about her car. "My car! What's going to happen with my car and everything in it?" Glancing around the unfamiliar room, she sobbed. What was going to happen to her?

* * * *

Clouds of smoke rose from Sonny's flared nostrils like a locomotive ascending a steep hill. Muddy water slashed against his chest and belly as he trudged toward the glowing barn lights in the distance. Hidden under a sodden, cowboy hat and a full-length oilskin duster, Cliff frowned. Where the Hell was that damn woman? She had plagued him all day. Just thinking of her made his body ache in ways that both aroused and irritated him. No matter what he did to distract himself, her face and *body* haunted him. And though she posed a threat to him in regards to getting his hands on Millie's land, the thought of her, scared and alone in that shack during the storm, twisted his gut ten ways to Sunday.

He'd pressed Sonny forward toward the old homestead, but when he topped the rise and looked down into the meadow below his heart had slammed against his ribs. The only structure that was still standing—minus half of its roof—was the old barn. Lumber, glass, and tarpaper lay strewn across the weed-infested yard. The large tree, which had shaded the small dwelling in the past, lay uprooted across what was left of the little house.

Relief washed over him when he'd realized that both the woman and her car were gone. He had ridden the three miles out to the road, then toward town, in case her car had gotten stuck. Sonny had protested when they passed the ranch road turn-off, but a jab of Cliff's spurs persuaded him to continue on.

Farther down the road he'd found her car lodged against a field entrance. Frantic, he'd crawled down into the ditch and searched inside and under the car for her. He even checked the culvert and prayed he wouldn't find her there. For several moments, he stood in the middle of the road, debating if he should ride toward town or turn back. He decided he'd head home, get the truck and drive toward town to look for her.

He surveyed the situation as he rode the big gray into his yard. The house lights were on, as were the lights in the barn, and the International pickup sat parked by the front porch. Good, Rooster was there. He would have checked and fed the young stock, and there would be hot coffee waiting on the stove in the house.

Cliff dismounted, slid the barn door open and led Sonny inside. He removed his gear and placed Sonny in his stall, where there was hay and grain waiting for him.

"Rooster, you ol' coot—God love you."

He switched off the lights, flipped his collar up and ran for the house. *How far could she have made it on foot? What if she was hurt?* He took the front steps two at a time. Pushing open the door, he stepped inside and froze.

Cat glanced up and gasped as a tall imposing figure filled the doorway, while the storm raged on in the darkness behind him. Water dripped from his wide brimmed hat and long duster. Dark eyes studied her through two slits. An icy cold breeze whipped through the room, and goose bumps covered her body.

It was White Fox, and he stood not ten feet away from her. *What was he doing here?*

Although she told herself she wasn't going to allow this guy to get to her, she stood paralyzed, like a rabbit in the tall grass, hoping the fox hadn't spotted her.

She forced herself to glance toward Rooster who sat at the table. He nodded his head, glanced toward the man in the doorway, then back to her. She noticed one corner of the old man's mouth curve up just before he turned his attention back to his plate. He obviously knew the intruder, and besides, it wasn't likely that White Fox would bother her, not with the old man sitting there.

Never taking his eyes off her, he kicked the door behind him closed. Without a sound, removed his wet hat and duster and hung them by the door. The sound of someone shuffling a handful of quarters caught her attention; she soon realized the strange sound came from the spurs strapped to his boots.

Like she had seen in a hundred westerns, he raked both hands through his damp curls, and with slow and deliberate moves, wiped his thick mustache down with one hand, his tongue darting out to lick off any moisture left by the rain.

She was sure the intimate gesture was meant to intimidate her. It worked. She stood motionless, trying to read his expression and anticipate his next move. Rooster's chair scraped across the floor, causing her to start. All of a sudden, the rank odor of sweat-soaked horse and leather assaulted her nostrils.

"Catrina Pearson, this here's Clifford White Fox," Rooster said wincing as he slowly rose to his feet. "Cliff, this here is—"

"We've met," he interrupted in a gravelly voice, sweeping a suspicious glance over the table set for two and the food cooking on the stove.

"You don't say..." With an amused expression, the old man settled back into his chair.

Cliff slid the chair back and deposited himself in front of the empty place setting. Shocked, Cat remarked with a hint of sarcasm in her voice, "Won't you join us?" This guy got the prize as the rudest man she'd ever met. Walking to the stove, she picked up the cast-iron pan and contemplated smashing him in the head with it. After emptying the contents into a bowl, she walked over and set the bowl on the table.

She had thrown together a casserole made from leftovers she found in the refrigerator, and without hesitation, Rooster filled his plate and dove in.

After the older man filled his mouth for the third time, Cliff helped himself to a heaping spoonful, and examined it. "What is it?" he asked, sliding her a sideways glance.

Wonderful, she thought. He was one of those guys, who didn't like the food on his plate to touch.

"I don't know," Rooster's fork paused halfway to his mouth. "But it's my favorite," he confessed, with a lopsided grin.

Cliff grunted and plopped the spoonful onto his plate.

She took her time walking to the cupboard for another glass and plate. Unobserved, she surveyed the intense cowboy, who was set on getting her grandmother's property.

His thick black hair brushed his collar. Dark brooding eyes were set deep above a slightly humped Roman nose and high cheekbones. A long thick mustache hid his upper lip, and she couldn't help but wonder what it would feel like to have him sweep it across her bare skin. A shiver slithered up her spine. *What's wrong with me? Pull yourself together.*

Around his neck, under a faded, tan colored, cotton shirt, hung a ragged, blue silk bandana. His long muscular legs were clad in faded muddy Wrangler jeans. Spurs strapped to mud-covered cowboy boots finished off the vision of a cowboy lost somewhere in time.

He could have walked the streets of Tombstone alongside Wyatt Earp or rode off the pages of a Zane Grey novel. There was something forbidden about this guy, something dangerous, something she definitely wanted to explore more closely. She felt the heat of a full body flush wash over her. She didn't need a hot bath...she needed a cold shower.

Cat grabbed a fork from the drawer and made her way back to the table. Both men pushed their chairs back and stood when she approached.

"No. Please, stay seated," she said, perching herself on the edge of an empty chair. Rooster smiled, nodded and winked. Mischief danced behind those wise old eyes, and she wished she knew what thoughts were knocking around in her knight-in-not-so-shinning-armor's head.

"Catrina here," Rooster pointed at her with his empty fork, "Is an artist." He grinned when Cliff's fork stalled halfway to his mouth, and he refrained from glancing up. "Yep, told me she has an art show all set up in New York at the end of the month."

Cat shifted restlessly in her chair. "That's if I have anything left to exhibit. My car was swept off the road into the ditch. It's filled with water. I'm sure everything is ruined." Her stomach rolled at the reminder of how close she came to being hurt or killed.

"You should've known better than to drive that little car in a storm like this." Cliff's voice rumbled low between them. He turned his head slightly and glared at her. Why was he angry with her? The storm had caught her off guard. She had no idea how severe it would become. He didn't look away; his stare demanded an explanation of some sort. He made her nervous. She felt a rumbling deep inside, and before she could stop, her mouth opened, and the words flowed out. "There's usually no warning before a flash flood happens. A heavy rain collects in streams, gullies, turning them instantly into a river of rushing currents."

His brows furrowed into deep lines, and she knew he thought she'd lost her mind. Unable to control herself, she continued. "There is enough power to change the course of rivers and wash away houses. Floods can move boulders, tear out trees, and destroy buildings and bridges." When Cliff blinked, she slapped a hand over her mouth.

The sound of the older man's fork hitting his empty plate drew her attention. "This is where I came in." Rooster stood, picked his hat up off the table and placed it on his head. "I'm headin' home. Thanks for the meal, girlie." He slipped his arms into his wet coat and hobbled out onto the porch then receded into the blustery darkness.

Cat stared at the closed door. What had she missed? "This isn't his place?" *Was he coming back? He wouldn't rescue me from one disaster then dump me off in the middle of another? Would he?* An alarm sounded in the back of her head, and she wondered if she should run after him.

"There isn't much left of your grandmother's place." Cat jumped at the sound of his voice. Cliff's chair scraped across the floor when he slid it back. Bracing the heel of one boot against the other, he slipped off his mud-caked boots and stood. "There's an empty room at the top of the stairs." Without waiting for a reply, he walked toward the giant stone fireplace in the next room and disappeared up the wooden staircase.

Even though he had offered her a room in his house, he hadn't appeared thrilled about having her under the same roof.

Cat slumped back in her chair. What just happened? How could everything in her life change so drastically in such a short period of time? Closing her eyes, she listened to the wind rattle the old porch windows, though the rain appeared to have died down. Every bone and muscle in her body ached. On top of being filthy and exhausted, she was the unwanted houseguest of a man who apparently didn't like her. Releasing a deep sigh, Cat rubbed her aching temples. She wanted to crawl into a hot bath and then a warm bed. Maybe if she slept long enough, she'd wake up and find it had all been just a bad dream.

She glanced around the messy kitchen. "Great, no dishwasher. How do people survive out here?" She gathered the dishes from the table, walked to the sink and made quick work of tiding up the kitchen.

Ten minutes later, Cat's damp clothes hung from every available hook in the bathroom. She sighed and slid down into a tub filled with steaming water. Though she tried to relax, her head filled with questions. *Why did Rooster pretend this was his ranch? Well, he never came right out and said it was his, but he didn't say it wasn't. Where did he call home, and why hadn't he taken me with him? I guess he wouldn't have left me here if he thought I wouldn't be safe.*

She glanced at the locked door.

Closing her eyes and resting her head against the back of the tub, she wondered what had happened in the cowboy's life that had made him so callous. Was he bitter all the way through, or did he have a soft sweet gooey center? What would it take to break through that hard shell and capture his true character with her camera? *What would I really find?*

After her bath, she didn't want to put her dirty, wet clothes back on, so she slipped into the soft blue denim shirt that hung on the back of the bathroom door. She rolled up the sleeves. Bringing one arm close to her face, she inhaled the scent of leather mixed with fresh air and soap. She switched off the bathroom light and headed for the stairs.

The old wooden treads creaked as Cat dragged her tired body up the stairs. At the top, she stopped and glanced down the hall. There were four closed doors, three on the east side facing the barn and one on the west. At the end of the hall, a painting of a boy fishing hung over a small half round table.

Cat tugged on the hem of the denim shirt, raked her teeth over her lower lip and reached for the antique glass knob. The door opened without a sound. She stepped into the room, closed the bedroom door and turned the lock. A moment later, she heard muffled footsteps outside her door that paused, then continued down the stairs.

Cat drew in a sharp breath. *Would a tiny lock like this stop a man like him?*

Chapter Three

The ancient black pickup straddled deep ruts in the road as it rambled toward the house the next morning. Catrina's gallant hero poised behind the wheel and, sporting a wide grin, came to a stop a few feet from the steps.

"Hey, girlie." Rooster greeted her through the opened driver's window. "You don't look so waterlogged today."

When a stream of tobacco juice followed his words and splattered across the ground, she cringed and shook her head. "I finally dried out," she replied, glancing down at her wrinkled and stained hiking suit. "I really do need to check on my car and see what's salvageable though I'm afraid everything is probably ruined." The knot in her stomach twisted, threatening to cause a scene. *Don't panic.* Taking a deep breath she added, "I also need to get over and check on Millie's place."

Rooster hopped out of the truck and limped toward the stairs. "Doug towed your car into town this morning." He pushed his hat to one side and scratched his head. If the bowlegged, old cowboy, with his weather-beaten black hat, sported a mustache like the one White Fox wore, he would be a twin to Yosemite Sam.

"Said it'll take a few days to wring 'er out. A few more to tell what's ailing 'er." He spit again, regarding her with wise eyes that twinkled with mischief. "You're welcome to take the International here," he nodded toward the truck. "Can you handle a stick?"

Surprised at his offer, she nodded back. "I can drive a manual. Don't you need it today?"

"Nah. There's enough work around here to last me three lifetimes."

Although he rolled on his heel and made his way back to the truck, a definite hitch in his get-along, he never complained about his obvious pain.

She descended the stairs and followed him around the wide front end of the truck with four missing hubcaps. "What year is it?" she asked and wondered if it would be wise to venture very far in a relic. He pushed the door handle down and pulled the driver's side door open.

"She's a 1952 wonder," he beamed with pride. He stepped aside so she could place her foot on the running board and slide in behind the wheel.

The interior reeked of cigar smoke, though she didn't recall detecting it the night before. Clumps of drying clay covered the worn floorboards. She slid across the faded and cracked leather seat. A lone key dangled from the dashboard on a rusty piece of wire. Thank goodness it wasn't a push button start like the ancient land rovers she'd driven in Africa and Australia.

The only instruments on the dash were a large speedometer flanked by a gas gauge and an oil gauge. Her hand settled on the ball of the gear shifter, a large metal rod protruding up from the floor.

"Reverse is to the right and down," he said, nodding toward her hand. "The lever to slide the seat forward is in front, under the seat."

Cat nodded back and then smiled. Was Cliff watching them from some hidden spot, wondering what these two bobble heads were discussing? Trying not to be too obvious, she glanced around, hoping to catch a glimpse of him.

The house had been empty when she woke up and crept down the stairs. Using his toothpaste, she brushed her teeth with her finger and then because she had no choice tugged on her dirty clothes.

"Well?" Rooster stared, expecting a reply.

"Well what?" she replied, puzzled. Could he tell she was scouting out her surrounding, looking for Cliff?

He slid his hat back and placed his weathered hands on his hips. "Well, you think you can handle her?"

She fought the urge to nod her head. "Yeah, I think so. How often do you have to pull the choke?"

"Only when she's cold."

She raked her teeth over her lower lip and asked, "Does it have four-wheel-drive? What if I get stuck?"

"No four-wheel-drive. Just put her in low." He patted the fender with affection. "With these tires, she'll walk you right out of any trouble you might get into."

"I really would like to check on Millie's place, then go into town and pick up a few things."

"She's all yours, girlie. Take your time." He took two steps and tossed back over his shoulder, "Cliff's out bringing cows in. We'll be branding in a few days." He turned, spit and then winked. "You'll want to be here for that. It's more fun than being the only man in town on girls' night out!" He chuckled at his own joke and with a slight limp moseyed toward the barn.

What a lovable old coot. She couldn't help but like the wizened cowboy. Yes, he most likely had saved her life the night before, but there was more to it than just that. Something about him put her fears to rest, made her feel safe and secure. She didn't understand it.

"Hey!" she called, leaning out through the window. Rooster stopped and peered back over his shoulder. "I'll swing by the motel and see if there are any open rooms."

"Why? There's more than enough room right here."

"But... Cliff," she hesitated.

"Don't fret over that ornery cuss. He just likes to hear himself growl." As if that settled everything, he waved a hand in the air and continued on his way. Once again, Cat wondered what the real story was behind Clifford White Fox. If she learned anything from traveling all over the world, it was that people weren't always what they appeared to be and to not judge by what people said, but by their actions. The fact that Cliff offered a perfect stranger a room in his home proved he wasn't as calloused on the inside as he wanted everyone to think.

* * * *

Cliff stood in the stirrups leaned forward and swung his lariat high above his head. He swung it three times then released the loop. It circled and landed on the thick branch that lay across the wire fence. He dallied the rope twice around the saddle horn and sat low in his saddle, as Sonny backed, his hoofs digging into the soft ground. The large branch fell from the wire fence, and Cliff dragged it far enough away so the fence could be repaired. Dismounting, he removed the rope from the branch and retied it to his saddle. He reached into his saddlebag and pulled out his fencing tools.

Glancing up at the large cedar tree, Cliff remembered the night he and his wife, Nora, lay on the grass under the same tree. They talked of starting their family. He had wanted a large family, a family of his own. He wanted to live in a place where he could be himself and not have to pretend to be something he wasn't. They had stared up at the stars and planned their future—a future that was never to be. How ironic, that the same tree which once had been strong and solid like his life now stood broken and incomplete.

Despite the fact that his heart had been latent and cold for the past couple of years, it had been jolted back to life yesterday. When he found that crazy woman's car floating in the ditch, something inside him snapped back to life. He feared she had slipped trying to get out of her car and gotten herself trapped under the vehicle and drowned. Relief washed over him when he walked in and found her standing in his kitchen. Yet knowing she was right down the hall hadn't helped him sleep any better.

Cliff's heart slammed against his ribs like it had the day before and like it did every time that woman crossed his mind. Admittedly, he was sexually attracted to her. Who wouldn't be? With those beautiful dark eyes, brown hair and a body any man would sell his soul to possess. The last thing he needed was a crazy woman in his life. He needed to figure out just how he was going to get rid of her.

With tools in hand, he ambled toward the fence. Distracted with the realization that he didn't want her to leave, he caught his foot on the branch and stumbled.

Behind him, Sonny gave a soft whinny and shook his head.

Cliff felt his jaw clench as he turned and glared at the horse. "What?" The gray tossed his head and pawed the ground with his right front hoof. Cliff sneered. "You think you're so smart. Mind your own business, you old Cayuse."

The horse put his nose in the air, lip raised and let loose with a loud whinny. Cliff snorted, "Smart ass."

* * * *

Cat maneuvered the ancient pickup around the deep ruts as it rattled down the long driveway. At the end, the old truck bounced over a cattle guard. She came to a stop where the red clay ranch road met the cracked pavement. Hanging from the ranch entrance pole that she hadn't noticed the night before was a weathered old sign.

Letting up on the brake the truck rolled forward, and she looked back through the mud-smeared window. "Circle D Ranch," she mused aloud. *Why would Clifford White Fox's ranch be called the Circle D?* She couldn't help but feel she had seen him somewhere, other than in the hole-in-the-wall bar in town. There was something about those intense eyes and the set of his jaw. Surely, she'd remember if she had met him before.

Shrugging off the feeling, she turned onto the pavement and drove to her grandmother's road. She down shifted, the old truck bounced and rattled when she turned off the main road and crossed the cattle guard. As Cat approached the dilapidated heap of weathered debris, a gasp ripped from somewhere deep inside her. The truck leaped forward, and the engine died as she viewed the carnage with a gaping stare.

An uprooted tree divided the house; the small dwelling now resembled the letter 'M'. Glass, splintered wood and broken shingles littered the muddy yard. A torn lace curtain hanging from a broken window, flapped in the wind reminding her of a surrender flag.

"Oh my God!" She couldn't believe her eyes. The truck roared back to life with a turn of the key. Shifting into first gear, she swerved around a yellow wash pail sticking out of the mud. Her stomach twisted into knots as she inched her way toward what was left of her grandmother's house.

"What am I going to tell Millie? She'll be heartbroken! She's so fragile. What will this do to her?"

Cat pulled the truck as close as she dared to the wreckage and turned off the engine. Her hiking boots sank deep into the slimy red clay. Steadying herself against the tree, she crawled over the debris and stepped up on to the kitchen floor.

As far as she could tell, the old Kelvinator refrigerator held up the roof on one side, and the only closet in the house held up the other side. Only a corner of the flattened kitchen table stuck out from under the tree. Most of her clothes and Millie's mingled in the foul smelling water, mud and broken glass that covered the floor. Bile burned the back of her throat. Shaking her head, she leaned against the large tree and closed her eyes. *What more could happen?*

The storm had ruined everything, and she wasn't even sure if her car would ever run again.

Leaning over, Cat picked up a mud-soaked red T-shirt and laid it across the tree. One by one, she extracted items from the floor. Her overnight bag was wedged in the far corner between the space heater and what was left of the outside wall. She crawled over broken furniture, and as she reached for her bag, a photo caught her attention. It was the photo of the Native American man dressed in regalia that she'd seen earlier.

She stared at the snapshot in disbelief. "Oh, this just keeps getting better!" The Native American in the photo strongly resembled Clifford White Fox. In the photo, his hair was much longer, and the mustache was gone, but it was the same strong jaw and Roman nose. She placed the photo in her jacket pocket. She had one more question she hoped Millie could answer.

Leaning down, Cat tugged her favorite blue jeans out from under a soaked quilt, took in her surroundings and sighed. "I need a dumpster. This is going to take me weeks to clean up."

Feeling overwhelmed, she collapsed on the corner of an overturned chair. "I need a plan." After a moment, she added, "I also need to get into town before it gets too late, or I get too dirty." She glanced down at the spots of dried mud that covered her wrinkled hiking suit. "I need new clothes and a hairbrush." She ran her tongue across her teeth. "A toothbrush and lots of trash bags and boxes."

Cat made her way to the edge of the house. Before jumping to the ground, she reached down and picked up a damaged photo off the floor. The photo was of her mother, Cathryn, in a party dress, around thirteen years of age. Tears filled Cat's eyes. Since her mother's death, she realized that they had been much more than just mother and daughter. They were a team, sometimes sisters, but always friends. Now the only family she had left was her grandmother who was virtually a stranger to her. And with her illness, who knew how much longer she would be around.

She stared at the photo again. Her heart ached, her breath lodged in her throat as a deep longing grew in her soul. "Why couldn't you tell me who my father was? Why was it such a big secret? I don't care if he has another family—I just want to know his name. I just want to meet him face to face."

She wiped away the tears and gazed at the destruction surrounding her. If there had been any evidence tucked away in the little house, it was long gone now.

"You can't lose what you've never had," she murmured, jumping to the ground and trudging through the mud to the old truck. Opening the door, she hopped in and kicked the mud from her shoes. She suddenly caught her reflection in the rearview mirror and winced at her windblown appearance. So much had been riding on this trip. She wanted to spend some time getting to know her grandmother Millie, hopefully learn the identity of her father and meet him before she drove across country to New York.

Now, everything had changed, and she wasn't even sure if her car would ever be drivable. *Everything happens for a reason,* she told herself. *Maybe you're not supposed to go to New York. Maybe you're supposed to stay here in Black River and spend what little time Millie has left, getting to know her.*

Taking a calming breath, she said, "You can always paint, take more photos and have other shows."

Though she said the words out loud, they didn't make her feel any better.

* * * *

Millie yanked open the bottom drawer of her dresser. "Where the hell did I put my knitting?" People on a talk show laughed and clapped on the blaring television across the room. She jumped when she heard Jeannie Porter's voice behind her.

"Can I help you find something?"

Straightening up, Millie sat back on her heels and placed a hand over her heart. She scowled up at the young woman and then held up a ball of blue yarn with two knitting needles stuck through it. "I found what I was after." Rising to her feet, Millie marched to her bed. Settling back against a stack of pillows, she crossed her ankles.

Jeannie motioned toward a tray of empty dishes. "Are you finished with your lunch?"

"What's it look like to you? I licked the plate clean as a whistle."

40

Taking the tray, Jeannie added, "Can I get you anything else from the kitchen? Maybe a bone to chew on for the afternoon?"

Millie ignored the girls comment. She liked Jeannie. The girl was the only one in the whole place who could give as good as she got. Then out of the corner of her eye, Millie saw Rooster Running Bird's pickup roll into the parking lot. The rusty old International crawled to a stop, and her granddaughter hopped out of it. "Shit."

Jeannie turned, one brow raised. "What changed your mind about the bone?"

"No. I'm sorry, Jeannie." She glanced out the window again. "Would you bring me a hot water bottle?"

"Are you all right?" Jeannie asked, puzzled and started to put the tray down.

Millie placed a hand on her hip. "My hip's been bothering me some today."

The girl nodded. "I'll be right back."

Millie shoved her knitting under her pillow before scurrying into her wheelchair. Covering her legs with a blanket, she grabbed the remote, turned the sound down and switched the station to the channel that aired an all-day church program.

* * * *

Cat hesitated outside Millie's room. How was she going to explain the damage to her place? At least she had her health and could start over. Millie had lost her home and all of her belongings, except for what she had brought with her when she moved into town. Everything her grandmother had left was behind this door in her nine by ten room.

Taking a deep breath to steady herself, she knocked twice and, with hesitant steps, entered the room. Millie sat hunched over in her wheelchair, a blanket across her frail legs. She stared at her television where a minister promised everlasting joy, and peace of mind.

"Millie?" Cat stepped into the room. "Millie," she called again, louder when she received no response. "Grandma?" She took a step closer, not wanting to startle the old woman.

Millie turned and smiled. "Catrina, how wonderful to see you. What did you think of that rain?"

"That was some storm." Cat pulled the empty chair closer to Millie.

The old woman chuckled. "You should have seen the mess we had here last night." She waved her arms around as she spoke. "The street turned into a river, and they duct taped all the entrances shut to keep the water from getting in." She clapped her hands together, and added, "What a hoot!"

Relieved Millie felt stronger Cat didn't feel so apprehensive about giving her the news about her house.

"What about you? Where were you held up when it hit?"

Cat offered a half-hearted smile. "Well, I had no idea how bad it was going to get. I'd been hiking when I spotted the clouds moving in. I reached my car just as the sky opened up. I started out for your place, but soon realized it wasn't going to let up." She paused, took a deep breath and exhaled slowly. Millie leaned forward and waited.

"My car was swept off the road and into the ditch before I made it home." Millie placed a rough calloused hand over hers. "An older man stopped and helped me. His name is..." What had he said? She could only remember him calling himself Rooster.

"Rooster?" Millie spat. "Walter Running Bird, a dried up old Ute?"

"How'd you know?" Cat searched the old woman's face. Was she psychic?

Her grandmother only grinned, and asked, "Did he take you to my place?"

All of a sudden, she felt embarrassed, but she didn't know why. She glanced down at her lap and hesitated. "No. He said he knew you and took me to the Circle D Ranch." When she glanced up, she was relieved to see Millie's wide grin. "I thought it was his ranch, but I jumped to the wrong conclusion. The ranch really belongs to that White Fox fellow." At Millie's nod, she continued with her story. "I'm only staying there until a room opens up at the Wagon Wheel Motel. This morning, Rooster said my car had been towed to the garage on the west end of town. I need to stop by there today. Hopefully, the mechanic will be able to tell me what it's going to take to get it running again."

Millie frowned and held up one hand. "Wait a minute. Back the wagon up. What's this about staying at the Wagon Wheel?"

"I'm not sure how to tell you this." She paused and prayed for strength. Maybe a doctor should be present before she told her grandmother she no longer had a house.

"Catrina, you're stalling. Spit it out," Millie demanded.

Cat reached into her pocket and pulled out a small brown paper bag. She emptied the contents, some dime store jewelry, an alarm clock and a pile of photos onto Millie's lap. At the older woman's puzzled stare, Cat's eyes filled with tears. "I'm afraid this was all I could salvage from your house."

"What? It's gone?"

"It's still there. The big shade tree is holding it down," She added, hoping she wouldn't break down and upset her grandmother more than she already was.

"Well," Millie sunk back into her chair. "The only thing that's been holding the old place up these past few years has been plain ol' stubbornness." She waved a dismissive hand in the air. "Don't fret over it. That four-eyed idiot with the funny looking haircut down the street is going to write me a big fat claims check."

Cat sighed. She hadn't even thought about her grandmother having any insurance coverage. "I'm so relieved. While I'm in town, I'll get some boxes and garbage bags. I'll clean up as much of it as I can."

Millie patted Cat's hand. "I don't know what I'd do without you. You're all I have left." She leaned back and searched Cat's eyes. "All we have left is each other. I'm so glad that you came to town."

Wanting to change the subject, Cat reached for one of the photos. "I found this picture in your dresser." She handed Millie the snapshot of the Native American dressed in full regalia. "Who is this?"

Millie gazed at the photo for a several moments. Her features softened, and a slight grin crossed her face before she glanced up. "Who do *you* think it is?"

Surprised by the woman's questions, Cat blurted out, "The first time I saw it I had no idea. But now, I'd swear it's Clifford White Fox or a brother of his."

Millie didn't answer, just nodded her head as if thoughts were swimming around in her mind, fighting to see which one would surface first. Cat settled back in her chair and waited. By the amount of time it was taking Millie to collect her thought, this story promised to be a good one. Again, she was surprised when Millie glanced up, and her eyes were rimmed with tears. Cat frowned.

"It's Cliff," she said, running an arthritic thumb over the photo. She handed the photo back to Catrina and then folded her hands on her lap.

Obviously, the man lived a totally different life at one time, and she was anxious to hear his story. "Tell me about him. Please."

Millie's intense stare seemed to peer right into Cat's soul; she paused for a few seconds before she spoke. "For the first half of Cliff's life he lived on the reservation with his mother, his younger brother Charlie and a handful of other relatives. Constant friction between Cliff and his brother forced Esther to send Cliff to live with his father. I think he was about fourteen." She paused. "His father, Hank Dawson, never married," she continued with a sarcastic snort, "The only thing that meant anything to him was land and cattle. The boy was just another hired hand that the old man didn't have to pay. Everything the boy ever did was never good enough for Dawson.

As Cliff grew older, it became apparent he was confused as to just where he belonged. He tried to live both as a white man and as an Indian. He married a pretty, young Ute girl. Of course he had no way of knowing that Charlie also loved her."

"Oh, my lord!" Catrina gasped, leaning forward in her chair. "What happened?"

"Well, the conflict between Cliff and his brother finally came to a head one day at a Pow-Wow. Both of them dressed in their finest regalia, competed in the dance competition."

On the edge of her seat, Cat waited, fearing she knew how the tale ended.

"Cliff looked so handsome in his fineries that day." Millie glanced out the window.

"Grandma! What happened? Who won?" Cat demanded.

"Charlie won the competition—and the girl's heart. Later that night, Cliff found them..." She wrung her hands together, her eyes growing misty. "He divorced her, cut his hair short and gave up all his ties to his family and his Indian way of life."

"What a terrible thing to go through," Cat said. The story tugged at her heart. "That does explain some of his strange behavior, I guess."

Millie went on to add, "Then that winter his father died of pneumonia, leaving the ranch to his only child, Cliff."

Cat leaned back in the chair. "So that's where the name *Circle D Ranch* comes from? Dawson."

Her grandmother frowned. "Yes, but I don't understand why you can't stay at the Circle D. It's a big enough place—real nice place!"

Since Millie appeared stronger, Cat felt now was as good a time as any to explain *her* situation. Sitting up straight in the chair, she took a deep breath and jumped in with both feet. "You're right. It is a nice big place. It's just that everything in my car, my photos and paintings, I'm sure are all ruined." She swallowed hard. "But there's still enough time to pull off the show in New York. I just need to fly back to Los Angeles, go through my negatives and develop the ones I want. I might even have time to repaint one."

Millie's face paled. She started to cough, closed her eyes and then a trembling hand covered her heart.

Cat jumped to her feet. "Are you all right? Do you need the doctor?"

Millie's eyes fluttered open. "Cathryn?" she whispered.

"I'm getting the doctor!"

The older woman grabbed for Cat's hand. "No! Just help me to the bed. I need to lie down for a while."

Cat moved to the bed and pulled back the covers. Then sliding her hand under Millie's arm helped her out of the wheelchair and into her bed. "How's that?" Panic boiling up inside her, she searched Millie's face. "Are you sure you don't want me to get the doctor?"

The door opened, and Cat turned to find the nurse's aide walk in. A frown marred the blonde's face. "Is everything all right?" Jeannie asked, crossing to the side by the bed.

"She didn't feel well," Cat replied, hoping the aid couldn't detect her underlying hysteria.

Millie glanced at the young girl. "I'm fine, dear. I just need to rest for a while, that's all."

Jeannie held up the hot water bottle. "Do you still want this?"

"Oh! Yes. You're a saint to remember."

Cat took in the fact that Millie's sudden flat tone didn't match her sincerity.

Jeannie lifted a corner of the blanket up. "It was your *right* hip, wasn't it?" Then she shoved the hot water bottle under the covers.

Millie's eyes rounded in surprise. "Yes. Thank you."

"I'd better go." Cat leaned over and kissed Millie's weathered cheek.

"All right, dear. You run along, and don't worry about me."

"You get some rest. I'll stop back later."

Millie closed her eyes. "If I'm still here," she replied in a frail voice.

Cat's stomach churned. She glanced at Jeannie, and together they walked out in to the hall. Lowering her voice Cat muttered, "I'd like to speak with Dr. Crawford about my grandmother's health."

Jeannie offered a slight smile. "He's out of the facility today."

"When will he be back?" Cat turned to glance back at her grandmother's door. "She seems all right one minute, and then the next..."

Reaching out, Jeannie placed a comforting hand on Cat's arm. "I'll stress your concerns with Dr. Crawford as soon as he returns and have him contact you."

She glanced over her shoulder toward Millie's door. *Should I stay, or should I leave?*

With a slight squeeze of her hand, the aid said, "You go run your errands. I'll keep an eye on your grandmother."

Cat felt embarrassed when her eyes welled up with tears.

"Go on now. Everything's going to be fine."

"Thank you, Jeannie. Millie is lucky to have you watching over her. I'll be back just as quick as I can."

"Don't rush. Take your time."

Once seated behind the wheel of the old black truck, Cat exhaled a deep breath, but it did nothing to calm her nerves. What was she going to do? How could she think of leaving town when Millie was so ill?

Her grandmother, her only *known* living relative, she couldn't—wouldn't abandon her.

* * * *

Cat swung into the filling station and parked. She had checked the Wagon Wheel Motel, but there had been no vacancies. Unfortunately, a number of homes had been damaged, and several people had found themselves in the same predicament. *Looks like I'm going to have to stay where I'm at for the time being.* She'd never liked being told what to do or being forced into something that wasn't her idea. But for the time being, it appeared she didn't have a choice.

A man stepped out of the filling station, pulled a grease rag from his back pocket, wiped his hands and walked toward her. She opened the door, stepped over the running board to the ground and greeted him. "Hi!" She glanced at the name embroidered on his work shirt and stated, "You must be Doug."

One puzzled black brow rose as the tall slim man raked his gaze over her. He stood six feet tall and couldn't have weighed over a hundred and twenty-five pounds. His thick black hair brushed his collar. Dark eyes and distinct cheekbones spoke volumes of his Ute heritage. Hours of hard work in the sun had etched his friendly face with deep lines.

"I'm sorry. My name is Catrina Pearson," she said, reaching out her hand. "I believe you towed my car in here."

"The '91 Subaru hatchback..." His voice flowed sweet and slow like molasses.

"How bad is it?" All of a sudden, she wasn't sure she wanted to know the truth.

"Well, it's not good. I've got it torn apart and drying out. Trying to figure out what still works." He nodded toward the shop, and she followed as he ambled back into the whitewashed, cement block building. "I opened it all up and pulled out everything that was removable," he said, stepping aside.

Nothing could have prepared Cat for what she saw. Clumps of stained photos, the corners curled stuck together. Water dripped from clothes that hug from shelves on makeshift hooks or lay strewn over tires and cases of oil. "Oh, my God." Could this day get any worse?

"I'm sorry I didn't have a better place to put your things," he offered. "I hope I didn't wreck anything."

She scanned the area. "Where's the wooden crate—my paintings?" Without a word, he pointed to the other side of the car.

Rounding the back of the hatchback, she found the crate covered with wet clothes and pushed them aside. One by one, she removed the four oil paintings. They were covered in stains, the canvass ruined from the muddy water. Her heart sank. They had taken months to complete. Even though she decided she couldn't leave town because of Millie's fragile heath, she had hoped that not everything in her car would be ruined.

The only thing left is to call Crystal and see if she can replace me with another artist.

"I put some of the smaller things in a box," Doug said, cutting into her thoughts.

When she turned, he pointed to the floor behind her. In a box, she found brushes, knives, tubes of oil paint and a tub of cleaner. "Thank you. I'll take these..." She picked up the box. "And the other stuff with me." Glancing around, she sighed. "Do you have a garbage can that I can put the things that are ruined in?"

He disappeared around the corner and returned with a large, dented, metal trashcan. Setting it down next to her, he offered, "There's a Laundromat on Main Street, between the grocery store and Grumpy's."

"Thanks. Will this clay wash out?" She held up a white blouse, streaked with rusty-red mud and moaned.

With the man's help, all the salvageable items were loaded into Rooster's truck.

"Where can I call you when I get this figured out," he asked, pointing back over his shoulder toward the shop.

"Humm, I'm staying at the Circle D Ranch." When his brows shot up and one corner of his mouth curved up in a lopsided grin, she added, "My grandmother's house is wrecked, and the Wagon Wheel is full." His head bobbed in agreement, and his grin widened. "There's plenty of room—it's a big place," she replied, hoping he hadn't heard the slight catch in her voice.

"Yes, ma'am."

She was sure she heard him chuckle when he turned and strolled back into the shop.

With a quick glance at her watch, she saw it was after two o'clock. Still needing to stop at the grocery store and drug store, she drove to the middle of town and parked. Deciding there was no reason to lock the truck she jumped out and slammed the door. In the store window across the street hung several brightly colored western shirts, jeans and a large display of jewelry. Oh, yes. She was definitely going in there.

Twelve minutes later, throwing her purchases from the drug store into the truck, Cat headed across the street.

The clean and organized store was a pleasant surprise. Besides clothing and jewelry, it carried books, music, and home décor items. In the rear, they sold feed and grain.

Cat headed for the clothing section, bypassing shelves lined with beautiful ceramic pots, carved ironwood statues and scented candles. There was everything from farm and work clothes to fancy western wear. Work boots, western boots and a wide assortment of jackets. There was even a wall covered in cowboy hats in any color you could imagine.

Zeroing in a display of jeans, she crossed the room and rummaged through the pile. Finding several in her size, she hung them over her arm and moved on to a rack of blouses. After selecting three brightly colored shirts, a woman's voice behind her asked if she needed any help. She turned to face a stunning Native American girl around her same age.

Long black braids framed her flawless, heart shaped face. She wore tight black jeans, a black and white western shirt trimmed in silver and black dress boots. The large silver belt-buckle adorned with a huge black onyx stone matched her necklace, earrings and bracelets. The woman's gaze took in Cat's wrinkled and mud stained hiking suit.

"As you can see, I need some new clothes," Cat said, knowing her tone revealed a hint of embarrassment. "I got caught in the storm yesterday, and all my belongings are either wet or ruined."

"Well, it looks like you've got a good start," motioning to the armload of clothes she held. "Let me take these over to the fitting room for you. Keep looking." Taking the clothing, she smiled and walked away. Within minutes, she returned, and asked, "Where are you staying?"

Cat offered a half-hearted smile. "I was staying at my grandmother's place in the country." She sighed. "Thank goodness she had already moved into the nursing care center, because there's nothing left of her house."

"Oh, that's terrible. Were you in the house when the storm hit?"

"No, I was on my way there, but my car was washed off the road and into the ditch. A nice man stopped and helped me. He took me to a nearby ranch, where I stayed last night. I checked at the motel today for a room, but they're all filled up."

"What are you going to do?"

Cat shook her head. "I don't know. I guess I'll have to stay where I am until I can figure out something else." She blushed after hearing her own words spoken.

The woman held up a pretty, turquoise shirt. "Whose ranch are you staying at?"

"The Circle D." She took the shirt and held it against her chest. "It's about fifteen miles northeast of here."

"The Circle D—with Cliff?" The woman fought to hide her surprise.

"You know him?" Cat asked, reaching for a red and pink flowered shirt.

"Yeah. I know him." She turned away and straightened the rack behind her.

"I've been invited to stay. They're going to be branding calves in a few days." She hadn't realized how excited she was at the idea of watching her first branding. Would it be like in the movies, or was it done differently now? She turned to stare at sales woman. "I have no idea what I'm supposed to wear."

After a long moment the woman turned, a wide smile crossed her face. "It's really just a big social event. There's always a lot of people and tons of food. I'm sure we can find you the perfect outfit so you'll fit right in."

* * * *

From the corner of the window, hidden behind a display, Nora had watched the girl shove three large bags into *her* grandfather's old truck. Although they had been divorced for almost five years, she still didn't like the idea of the woman being in Cliff's house.

An image of the woman walking out on branding day lightened her spirits. *Wait until he gets a load of her in her new outfit. It might be worth driving out to see his reaction first hand.* She chuckled.

"What kind of trouble are you stirring up now?"

Nora spun around at the sound of the deep voice. "I hate it when you sneak up on me like that."

He didn't move from where he leaned against the doorframe, just studied her with those golden-brown eagle eyes. The blatant passion she witnessed drove her crazy. Heart racing, she busied herself straightening up a display, but monitored him from the corner of her eye. His long hair hung loose against the back of his faded black t-shirt. His thumbs were hooked in the front pockets of worn, ripped, blue jeans so faded they looked almost white.

She'd been out of town for a few days and had a pretty good idea of what he was after. "What are you doing in town? Lost?" Her voice laced with sarcasm. She walked several feet away, needing time to think. Except it wasn't possible with him in the same room.

Over the past several months, their relationship had turned stagnant. Downright boring. She wanted excitement and a man with more than a few bucks in his pocket.

Salt Lake hadn't proved to be all that exciting; she had missed him, too. Facing him, placing her fists on her hips, Nora spat, "What do you want?"

Without a sound, his eyes locked on hers, he slunk toward her like a panther stalking its prey. Heart drumming against her ribs, Nora took a couple steps backwards and hit the corner of the fitting room. When she made the mistake of glancing behind her, he struck.

They fell into the small dressing room, the curtain concealing them from the rest of the world. "Charlie!" She screamed, close to hysterics as his mouth closed over hers.

Chapter Four

Cliff reached into the back of the red ranch pickup for the log chain. Not far away a worn out Black Angus struggled, bogged down in the middle of a thirty-foot-wide water hole. Her nose lay in a divot filled with water. With every labored breath, bubbles rose from her flared nostrils. This was one of the things he hated dealing with after a heavy rain.

"Damn cattle never learn." Cliff dragged the heavy chain; the links clinked together like wind chimes. When the watering holes were deep, the cattle could wade out into them and drink. However, as the holes dried out and only a small amount of water remained in the middle, the cattle would walk out for a drink and sink to their bellies, leaving them trapped in the mud. If the animal wasn't found and pulled out within a couple of days, it would die.

Rooster backed the truck at a ninety-degree angle to the cow's head. Cliff motioned to him with a quick wave when he reached the fringe of the bog.

Rooster jumped out of the truck and hobbled toward Cliff, one corner of his mouth cinched up with his signature grin. Since the first time Cliff had met the seasoned cowboy, it struck him that it was Roster's nature to spin any situation around and make light of it. It had made putting up with Hank's abuse a lot easier.

"Hey, pup, you need me to show you how to do this?" he teased, slapping Cliff on the shoulder.

Glancing down at the crippled-up old cowboy, Cliff suppressed a grin and replied, "You just remember to pull slow and easy, so we don't break any of her legs or pull her stifle joint out, or we'll have to shoot her."

"Don't forget who's been ridin' roughshod over you for the past twenty years." Rooster leaned back against the bumper and folded scarred, richly tanned arms across his thick chest.

The canny old coot had been more of a father to him than Hank ever had. He'd taught Cliff everything he knew about cowboying and ranching. Every time Cliff fell, the man had picked him up, dusted him off and shoved him in the correct direction. He never scolded or berated him, yet made sure he learned something from his mistake then dropped it.

"Watch her head." Cliff ignored him as he crouched down and started to crawl on his belly toward the cow. Glancing over his shoulder, he saw a stream of tobacco juice shoot from the cowboy's smirk.

Wide-eyed, the cow swung her head from side to side, as he slithered closer. "Easy, girl," he whispered, digging his elbows and the tips of his boots into the mud. He pulled the heavy log-chain along behind him as he inched nearer. The closer he drew to the frantic cow, the deeper he sunk into the bog. Hoping the cow wouldn't start thrashing and injure herself, he moved slowly and spoke to her in a gentle tone. "You're going to be all right, girl. Just don't bash my brains out while I'm trying to save your life."

Cliff recalled the first time he watched someone try to slip a chain around a bogged-in cow. The cow had swung her head and caught the man full in the face, breaking his nose, eye socket and jaw. Luckily, Rooster and another hand were there to pull the bloody, unconscious man back to the truck.

"Is this going to take long?" The old man's teasing words echoed behind him. "It's getting awfully close to dinner time."

Cliff glanced over his shoulder and sneered, only to be treated to a big belly laugh. Drawing a deep breath, he turned his attention back to the nervous cow, now three feet in front of him. Steering clear of her swinging head, he edged closer to her shoulder. "Easy now. I'm going to slip this chain around your neck, and that old Cayuse over there is going to ease you right on out of this mess."

She swung her head, intent on connecting with her predator. After ten or twelve missed attempts and Cliff's skillfully dodging the massive head and streamers of snot raining down at him, he finally slid the log-chain up over the bovine's shoulder. Flies buzzed around them as he stroked her sweat-covered side.

"Easy, girl." A guttural sound escaped from the trapped animal. "You're okay." Reaching under the bovine's neck, he grabbed the heavy hook and pulled the chain around, fastening the hook to one of the links. Tight enough to not slip off, but with enough give to avoid choking her.

The cow bellowed and started thrashing. "Hold on now, save your strength," he muttered, stroking her gently. Yet his soft touch and words of encouragement did little to pacify the terrified animal. Before Cliff could get far enough away, she swung her powerful head and caught him just above his left eye.

Sharp pain shot though his forehead. Silver and white stars swam before his eyes. Fighting to stay conscious, he leaned back against the animal's side. In the distance, he heard Rooster's voice, but the ringing in his head made it impossible to understand the old boy's words. Raising a hand, he hoped to reassure the old man that he was all right, just dazed. Blood ran into his eye. He brushed it away with the back of his hand.

Ignoring the excruciating pain that filled his head, he fixed his gaze on the red hue of his pick-up fifteen feet away. Lying on his stomach, he crawled back over the boggy ground to where Rooster waited. The old man no longer laughed or teased, as he watched Cliff's slow and painful progress.

"You all right, son?" He bent down and helped Cliff up off the ground, his hands going right to his wound.

"I'm fine," Cliff said, swatting his hands away. "Let's get her out of there." He glanced toward the U-shape welded to the frame to double check that the chain was fastened securely. He didn't need the chain coming undone, though there was always the chance of it breaking and causing harm to either man, animal or truck.

He felt the old man's eyes watching him, no doubt trying to judge the degree of his injury. He could afford to lose a little blood, but he couldn't afford to lose this cow. "You ready then, old man?" he asked, meeting the other man's stare.

Rooster shook his head and hobbled to the driver's side, slid in and started the engine. Shifting the pickup into low gear, it purred and eased forward taking up the slack in the chain. Frantic the cow bellowed as the chain grew taut around her muscular neck. Pulling her onto her side, the vacuum that held her prisoner slowly gave way. The bovine's front legs emerged from the mud with a loud sucking sound as the truck pulled her to safe ground.

Her sweat soaked flanks heaved with exhaustion. Knowing she would lay there for several hours, Cliff leaned down and eased the chain from around her neck.

"I'll come back out and check on her," Rooster said, as he stopped at Cliff's side. "And bring her some grain and water." He pushed his hat back and scratched his head. "You wanna swing into town and have the vet take a look at your head?"

Ignoring his comment, Cliff heaved the muddy log chain into the box of the ranch pickup. He opened the passenger door, swiped a dirty hand across his soiled clothes, scraped his mud-caked boots on the running board and crawled in. Resting his sweat-soaked arm on the opened window, he settled his aching body back against the seat and closed his eyes. He heard Rooster yank the driver's door open.

Tilting his head to the side, he asked, "You don't happen to have a couple cold ones hidden in here by chance?"

Reaching over the side of the truck, Rooster retrieved a clear plastic container and handed it across the seat. Cliff struggled to sit up, removed the cap and took a long swig. The warm water did little to quench his thirst, but it soothed his dry throat. He handed the container back and licked the excess moisture from his mustache. "Thanks, but it didn't quite do the trick."

Rooster laughed. "There's a couple of Coors waiting for you in the tack room fridge," he offered with a crooked grin and lumbered in behind the wheel. The pick-up roared to life, bouncing though ruts and washouts as they crossed the open field.

Cliff gazed out over the rain beaten grass where the mud had destroyed the pastureland. If the grass didn't come back, he'd be forced to buy hay and have it trucked in to keep from touching his winter supply. Tomorrow he'd ride over to Millie's to check the condition of her pasture and the section he owned north of there. Remembering the condition of Millie's house, he glanced toward Rooster and asked, "Did you have much damage to your place?" A humorless sound escaped the old man as he maneuvered the truck on to the field road that led back to the ranch.

"Lost two large trees behind the house and the area where I planned on puttin' in a garden... Well, it might be kinda' nice having a pool."

"Your house is okay then?" Cliff asked, but his gut twisted when the older man's forehead furrowed with deep frown lines.

Here comes the other shoe.

"Yeah, for the most part. Nothin' a hand full of nails won't fix. But a couple of houses south of me were hit pretty hard."

Cliff knew Rooster was referring to his mother's house, and he didn't want to hear about it. He shot the meddling old coot a warning stare and then shifted his gaze back out the window. "I'll send them a check." There would be plenty of people willing to help his mother and *Charlie* with any repairs. They neither wanted nor needed the likes of him hanging around.

Twenty minutes later, they rounded the paddock and a stack of red corral panels and drove toward the barn.

Rooster cleared his throat. "Did you know Millie was ill when she moved into town?" He pulled up to the barn and switched off the engine.

Cliff shook his head and thought back a couple of months to when he swung by her place to make her another offer. "She sure hadn't given me that impression, the way she was hauling boxes out to her car. Although I still haven't figured out what she meant by her remark that there was more at stake for both of them then just a chunk of dirt."

The old gal knew what it would mean for him to have her place, yet it seemed she was going to hold him off awhile longer.

He opened the door and as his feet hit the ground, a humbling pain slithered up his spine, exploding in his head. At that moment, he felt older than Rooster looked. He lumbered toward the cold beer waiting in the barn and wondered what would it take to persuade the ol' girl to sell out to him?

* * * *

Cat pulled up to the ranch house, the cab of the old truck filled to overflowing with her purchases. To show her appreciation for helping her and for letting her stay there, she'd picked up T-bone steaks for dinner and the makings for an apple pie. With no vacancies at the motel, she had no idea where she would go if she were asked to leave.

It took several trips before she had everything in the house. Food items and toiletries lined the counter tops, and the tiny refrigerator threatened to bust wide open. Sweat soaked and exhausted, she struggled out of her hiking boots and pants, leaving her dressed in her blue tank top and gray shorts. With a sigh, she plopped down onto a kitchen chair. "I need a shower." She leaned back against the chair and closed her eyes. "No. A long hot bath." Smiling to herself, she added, "And then put on clean, *new* clothes. Oh, how wonderful." After a moment, she glanced at her watch. It was late, and she wasn't sure what time Cliff and Rooster would come in. She wanted to bake them an apple pie and have dinner ready when they walked in. It was the least she could do.

She hauled herself up and out of the chair. First thing, she would splash some water on her face; braid her hair into two long braids to get it out of her way. Then she would throw a load into the washing machine, wash the new clothes she bought, her hiking suit and the few items salvaged from her car and grandmother's house.

Barefoot, she padded around the kitchen. She dug in the cupboards looking for pots and pans, flour and sugar and a rolling pin. Two hours later the homey scent of fried potatoes and chopped onions and the sweet aroma of hot apple pie filled the house. She enjoyed playing housewife and pretending she was cooking for her own family.

She set the last glass on the table when she heard male voices through the screen door. Rooster's words were easily understood as he confessed, "If the food tastes as good as it smells, I might be forced to take her to wife." She chuckled at his teasing, but the baritone muttering that came from Cliff made her skin cover with goose bumps. A flock of birds took flight in her stomach. She chalked it up to being hungry and wiped her sweaty palms on her shorts.

The screen door swung open, and the old cowboy lumbered in, removing his hat when he saw her. "It sure does smell good in here. Did you make apple pie, girlie? It's my favorite!" His appreciative gaze swept over the kitchen as he grinned from ear to ear. "My late wife used to make apple pie when she wanted some extra money to pick up something special for herself in town."

Cat couldn't help but grin when he winked. "I wanted to thank you both for being so helpful to me," she said, hoping her rusty cooking skills would suffice. "There were no vacancies at the motel, but I'll keep checking every day."

Rooster moved to the side and started to remove his muddy boots. A gasp slipped from her lips when Cliff strolled in. He'd removed his boots and left them on the porch. Judging by the mud caked down the front of his clothes, he should have left them out on the porch, too. By the glint in his eye, she knew he had read her mind. But then she spied the dried blood on the side of his face. "What happened to you?" She stepped forward, her hand instantly rising to brush his thick black hair away from his brow. His nostrils flared, and he leaned away from her touch. When his hand shot up and grasped her wrist, his light touch shocked her as much as his reaction. He released her just a quickly, and she stepped back. Without a word, he pushed past her into the other room and stomped up the stairs.

"What's for supper? I'm starved." Rooster rolled up his sleeves as he hobbled to the sink to wash his hands.

Cat gave herself a hard mental shake. "You can start with the salad on the table," she said, but at his frown, she added, "I've made fried potatoes, and it will only take me a couple minutes to fry up the steaks—depending on how you want yours."

"Rare." He rubbed his hands together. "Just so I don't have to rope it and hog tie it."

With a hitch in his gait, Rooster made his way back to the table. Taking his fork, he picked through the salad bowl, but smiled when he caught her watching him. The sound of the shower running pulled Cat's attention away from the old cowboy perusing the table.

Her imagination conjured up a picture of Cliff standing under the flow of hot water, steam rising up around his tanned, muscular body. *Oh, to photograph that body—naked!*

* * * *

Cliff stood with his hands braced against the ceramic tiles, but the cold water running down his back did little to sedate his intense thoughts. He couldn't get over how alluring Catrina looked in her tight little top, shorts and bare feet. Seeing her hair in braids almost pushed him over the edge. When her eyes filled with concern and she moved toward him, he knew he should have said something, anything to stop her. Instead, he did the one thing he had told himself he'd never do. He touched her, and a wave of pure lust washed over him. If that old man hadn't been standing there, right now she would be in this shower with him, and he would be living the dreams that plagued him since the first day he laid eyes on her. A knife twisted in his gut as the scene flashed before him.

Naked—stretched out on a blanket—heaven help me.

Gathering what was left of his wits, he turned off the water, toweled off and dressed. Catching his reflection in the mirror, he frowned at the cut on his forehead that had swollen and turned black and blue.

"You've had worse—you'll live."

Moments later, he strolled into the kitchen to find Rooster leaning back in his chair, rubbing his satisfied belly while Cat picked at her salad with a fork.

Noticing him, she jumped to her feet, her brows tugged into a deep frown. "Sit down," she said, sliding one of the chairs out from under the table. "I found a first-aid kit in the cupboard. There's antiseptic and some butterfly Band-Aids."

"It's fine. Don't worry about it." He wished she would sit back down or go upstairs or just disappear altogether. Sadness filled her beautiful brown eyes, and he couldn't help but do as she wished. As if his feet were chained to concrete blocks, he trudged across the room and settled into the chair. He ignored Rooster when the old cowboy chuckled and shook his head.

His skin tingled with anticipation as she moved around him.

"This will only take a second," she murmured, sidling up next to him. "Then I'll fry up your steak." She tipped the antiseptic bottle onto a cotton ball. "It might sting a little, but it'll keep you from getting an infection." She dabbed his forehead. He steeled himself against the pain, just turned to look up at her.

"I'm sorry," she said then leaned forward and blew gently on the wound. The movement placed her perfect breasts mere inches from his face. "Is that better," she asked, her sweet mouth turned up in a hopeful smile. She had no way of knowing that her kindness and gentle touch were killing him. *Good God! Was the old man ever going to leave?*

Rooster rocked back in his chair and picked at his teeth with a toothpick, his eyes glowing with amusement at Cliff's discomfort.

Rooster turned his attention to Cat and asked, "What did you find over at Millie's place this morning?"

Cliff listened as she describes the destruction she had found at the old homestead and the mess at Doug's gas station. Her voice quaked when she added that most of her clothes weren't even worth trying to save.

"I hope it was all right that I used your washing machine." Her soft voice only inches from his ear as she placed a second Band-Aid above his eye. "I can't wait to soak in the tub and put clean clothes on tonight."

Cliff shifted in his chair as he pictured her reclining in his tub, and out of the corner of his eye, he caught the wolfish grin that crossed the ol' Cayuse's face.

"There. All finished." Stepping in front of him, she asked, "How do you want your steak?"

Looking innocent with a satisfied smile on her lips, she stood patiently waiting for his reply. Steak wasn't what he hungered for, and he wondered what she would do if he threw her over his shoulder and carried her up stairs. "Don't bother, I'm not very hungry."

Frowning, she asked, "Would you like a piece of my pie?" Though he didn't reply, a spark lit in his eyes, and she knew her cheeks turned to a bright shade of pink.

* * * *

"I don't know about him," Rooster said, shoving his empty plate a side. "But you promised me a piece of hot apple pie piled high with vanilla ice cream." His eyes sparkled with anticipation.

Cliff sighed inwardly with relief and disappointment when she sidestepped away from him. He watched her move around his kitchen as she waited on the meddling old fool.

Rooster grinned like a hyena when she placed a large piece of apple pie topped with three scoops of ice cream on the table in front of him. "Thanks, girlie." He winked and raised a forkful to his mouth. Closing his eyes, the old man moaned with appreciation. After a moment, he glanced at Cliff and stated, "I think we're goin' have to find a way to keep her here."

She smothered a giggle in response to his antics.

The old man's wearing out his welcome. Cliff stifled the growl building deep in his guts.

Between forkfuls, Rooster asked, "How's Millie feeling?"

Cat perched on the edge of a chair, wrung her hands and sighed. "I wished I knew what was wrong with her. One minute she seems fine, and then the next it's as if she doesn't know who you are." She turned toward Rooster as if she expected him to have the answers. A tightness engulfed Cliff's chest when her eyes pooled with emotion.

"I've asked that Dr. Crawford call me as soon as he comes in. I'm hoping he'll be able to tell me something."

Jealousy jolted Cliff like a lightning bolt when the old cowboy reached out and placed a gnarled hand over Cat's.

"Try not to fret too much," Rooster said. "Millie's tougher than you think." He pushed back his chair. "Well, I guess I'd better go check on that cow." His joints creaked and snapped as he struggled to his feet. "Great dinner. Thanks, girlie." He tweaked her nose. "Steak and apple pie's my favorite." He hobbled to the door, slipped on his coat and hat and ambled out.

Cliff watched the woman's expression soften and a slight smile come to rest on her lips as the old man's words washed over her. What would it take to have her look at him with such affection? He gave himself a mental shake. *That cow must have hit me in the head harder than I thought. I've been down that road before, and it cost me much more than it was worth.*

Embarrassed to find her staring at him when he finally came to his senses, he stood, reached for his hat and coat and headed for the sanctuary of the dark porch.

"Now what did I do to tick him off?" Cat stared at the closed door. "He never said a word! No thanks for having dinner ready. No thanks for bandaging up his big, fat, ugly head. Nothing." Shaking her head and tossing her hands up in the air she grumbled, "Then he just disappears into the night." She started clearing off the table. "Must have been a real treat being married to *that one*."

Carrying glasses and silverware, she marched to the counter. "I just wanted to thank him for letting me stay here by fixing him a nice dinner. Then he says he's not hungry." Grabbing the dishrag she stomped back to the table "His head's split wide open. All I wanted to do was help him." She gathered the plates and bowls, swiped the dishrag across the table then threw it into the sink. "What do I care if he starves or bleeds to death?"

She had been through some hard times in her life, but today ranked right up there as one of the longest, most trying days she ever had. Breaking the news to Millie that her house was destroyed had been easier then she thought. Though her dream of finding any evidence that could tell Cat who her father was appeared washed away right along with her career.

Cat had never been one to feel sorry for herself. She knew no matter what you were up against, there were always others worse off. With a little time she could rebuild her career to what it was—maybe even better. Suds flew into the air when she dropped a couple plates into the dishwater. Millie could build a house bigger than the last if she truly wanted to. But could Clifford White Fox rebuild his life to what it had once been? And would he if he could?

No matter how much he frustrated her, she couldn't help but feel empathy for Cliff. Millie had told her about the trouble between him and his brother and about his divorce. She recalled the Native American snapshot she had found. At the time, he looked so noble and confident dressed in full regalia, his long dark braids adorned with ribbons and feathers. *It's not that he isn't noble and confident now...there's just something missing.* She paused and glanced out into the darkness. *It's almost as if his soul has been extracted, pulled out and thrown aside like his old life.*

"How different his life must have been before everything changed." Rinsing the last dish, she pulled the plug and watched the water disappear down the drain. She couldn't compare their lives, but it was funny how the events of one day could alter the rest of a person's life.

* * * *

Cliff studied the woman through the window. She confused him, fascinated him and drove him crazy all at the same time. She marched around the kitchen carrying on a conversation with herself as she cleaned. At times, she even appeared to be arguing with herself. Maybe the stress of everything was finally hitting her.

His chest tightened with guilt as he recalled her description of what she found at Millie's and Doug's. Though he tried to steer clear of her all day, he hadn't been able to avoid wondering how she was or what she was doing.

She tossed a dishtowel on the counter, and he watched her walk out of the room. Turning, he glanced off into the darkness. She shouldn't have had to face that mess alone. He didn't know why, but he should've been there for her. His stomach burned with guilt. *Should I go back inside, take her in my arms and tell her everything's going to be all right?* He shook his head at the foolish thought. No, he had no right to do that. Besides, he knew if he touched her, he wouldn't be able to control himself. He ached to hold and kiss her, to feel her bare skin against his.

Closing his eyes, Cliff leaned back in the weathered hardwood chair and let the night air cool his heated body. How long he sat like that he didn't know. A noise caught his attention. The kitchen light switched off. Twisting, he looked back through the window. Cat crossed to the stairs. His old denim shirt came to her mid-thigh, showcasing her long smooth legs. She'd rolled the sleeves half way up her arm, and her dark hair hung loose, cascaded down her back.

He wiped his damp palms across his jeans. The night before when he'd snuck down stairs to use the bathroom he found a light blue bra and matching panties hanging over the towel rack to dry. He watched her disappear up the stairs, knowing she wore nothing under the shirt. Every muscle in his body tightened. Closing his eyes, he laid back against the chair. *Great, another sleepless night, or worse, another night dreaming he was making love to her only to wake up alone again.*

He lurched to his feet and trekked crossed the porch. Reaching for the door handle, he paused. "What would she do if I kicked the bedroom door in?"

Chapter Five

Cat crept down the stairs, intent on avoiding Cliff before she left for her grandmother's place. She lay awake most of the night trying to figure him out, eventually concluding it was a lost cause. The man wasn't just a closed door—he was a locked, throw-away-the-key, welded-shut door.

The house appeared empty as she hesitated on the landing, scanning her surroundings for any sign of him. The rising sun cast streaks of crimson across the masculine room. A set of bleached out longhorns were mounted over the French doors that led out to a grand flagstone patio. She stepped off the last tread and darted across the bare hardwood floor. As she passed the massive stone fireplace, an oil painting caught her eye. Several cowboys driving a herd of longhorns hung over the split-log mantel. How had she missed seeing this before?

Tentatively she reached out and stroked the broad, dark frame. The original oil, done in shades of soft turquoise, coral and earth tones bore the signature of CM Russell. "Russell," Cat grinned and whispered in her presentation voice, "Is famous for depicting the everyday life and antics of the early cowboys, Native Americans, and Mountain Men. Both horse and rider exhibit contorted facial expressions, depicting the turn of events they've suddenly found themselves in." She sighed and shook her head. "Wonder if Cliff has any idea what this painting is worth?"

A stately, mission style grandfather clock stood guard in the far corner of the room, its pendulum quietly taking note of the house's activities. Set in the opposite corner was a well-worn, brown leather, high backed chair with an antique quilt thrown over one corner. A round antique side table and Tiffany lamp made a cozy reading corner. But she

64

was drawn to the huge bull elk that hung between the two long windows. Her nose twitched as she drew closer. Dust covered the hide of the shoulder-mount. Cobwebs stretched across the wide expanse of its trophy-sized antlers. *Had it been shot close by? What are the chances of me seeing something this size?* Her heart raced at the thought.

Turning to leave, she discovered a large oak door, which blended in with the heavily paneled wall. She shot a hesitant glance around. A rush of excitement surged through her as she reached for the handle and eased the door open. Though the shades were pulled and the room smelled musty, she could picture the large manly office belonging to cowboys like Ben Cartwright or John Chisum. "What a magnificent room," she said, stepping in and closing the door.

A massive oak desk dominated the room. Behind the desk hung a portrait of a man poised like a western hero from the silver screen. She giggled, wondering whether the size of the portrait and elaborate frame had been a compensation for something else.

Taking a step closer, she read the name etched on the large brass plaque at the bottom of the frame. "Hank Dawson!" *Cliff's father.*

Though the man in the portrait had a lighter complexion and rounder face, the similarities between Cliff and his father could be detected in their hard, unwavering stares and the arrogant lift of their chins. Judgmental, gunmetal gray eyes fixed her with a stare. In life, he would have turned the guilty into cowering rabbits.

Something brushed against her leg. Glancing down, she gasped and jumped at the sight of a ceramic-coiled rattlesnake. Its mouth stretched open, long fangs bared. Repetitive diamond shapes decorated the snake's brown, black and tan body. Cat exhaled and shivered. "I hate snakes."

She stepped back, brushed a hand across the desk and disturbed the desktop calendar. Moving away from the realistic reptile, she circled the desk and reached to straighten the calendar. Her hand froze as she read *December 1988.* "This calendar hasn't been changed for almost five years!"

Why hadn't Cliff bothered to flip his calendar over?

Her gaze scanned the dim room. The oak file cabinet in the corner and enormous gun cabinet were both covered in a thick layer of dust.

She shivered and exited the room as if Hank Dawson's icy fingers ran up her spine.

* * * *

Three hours later, Cat perched on a branch of the tree that lay crosswise through what was once her grandmother's house. She came armed with boxes, trash bags and the little bit of determination she was able to muster. She gathered up her grandmother's personal items: cards, pictures, books, muddy clothes and scraps of material. Dejected, she stared at the overflowing boxes and bulging trash bags; she found little worth saving. Brushing a loose strand of hair back with the side of one dirty hand, she heard her stomach protest her hunger by growling.

Wiping her hands across her jeans, she walked toward the truck. After retrieving an apple and a chocolate candy bar, she rounded the pickup and settled on the opened tailgate to nibble on the apple and study the hard packed soil. Eggshell cracks covered the earth where the ground started to dry, leaving standing water in only the deepest ruts.

Turning her face into the slight breeze, she spied the old barn off in the distance. She had always thought the tall barn was odd looking. She had even researched the style, but had been unable to find another one like it. Built into the side of the hill, it allowed for a hay wagon to be backed in and unloaded. The lower level permitted enough headroom to store a tractor.

Cat jumped off the tailgate, grabbed her camera and headed for the barn. She gathered wood and shingles along the way and by the time she reached the entrance to the lower level, her arms were full. Entering the old building, she stopped and stared. Several boards were missing from the far wall and the stench of wet moldy hay and rotting wood almost over powered her. An old red tractor sat in a corner, the two front tires sunk deep into the mud, one back tire flat.

She dropped the debris she collected and brushed the dirt from her chest and sleeves. Flinging the camera case back up and over her shoulder, she climbed the long narrow ladder to the hayloft. A thin layer of straw and hay covered the floor. She frowned, half of the shingles and boards were missing from the ancient roof and walls. She placed her hands on her hips. "It's a miracle it's still standing!" She approached an opening in the wall and glanced out.

From this height, I can see for miles. Without thought, she pulled her camera out, flicked open the shutter and peered through the lens. She took some shots of a small group of antelope against the red rock background. A jackrabbit hiding in a scrub of cottonwoods. A hawk perched high in a dead tree—the bright blue sky made a perfect backdrop.

Then a movement to her right caught her attention. She pivoted to catch the shot, focusing on her target with a grin. As if discovering a rare species, she steeled her excitement and photographed the man in his own element. The usual hardness and stubborn set of his jaw was absent as he easily drove the cattle. The tranquility that surrounded him even caused one corner of his mouth to turn up in a slight infectious grin. Cat couldn't help but feel his contentment and smiled. *What wicked plot is he concocting in his evil mind?*

She sidestepped to a spot where only a couple of boards were missing, where she could watch Cliff without him spotting her. It was fascinating to watch him and his horse move the small band of cattle. Suddenly, a large calf broke from the group and darted in the opposite direction. The horse spun around, and with his ears pinned flat against his head gave chase. Within seconds, the team cut in front of the calf, turning him back toward the rest of the cattle. As man and horse worked together as one entity, she rapidly snapped photo after photo.

Preoccupied with her subject, she had no idea when he had turned the small herd in her direction. When she realized they were moving closer to her hiding spot in the barn, she spun around, her glance darting around the hayloft. Needing a place to hide, she stepped back, crouched down and peered through an opening in the wall, watching as he rode past. She spied a good spot where she could take more photos and scurried across the hayloft, gambling that he wouldn't be able to see her through the missing boards.

Without warning, she heard the sound of wood cracking. A floorboard beneath her foot gave way. She bit her lip against the scream bubbling in the back of her throat as one leg plunged through the floor. The camera flew out of her hand and jerked against the strap, slapping her shoulder. Her hands slapped against the floorboards. A cloud of dust billowed up around her as a sharp pain shot up both arms.

Shifting her weight, she tried pulling her leg free and noticed her pant leg was raised, her bare leg bleeding. A scream ripped from her lungs as another portion of the floor gave way. Her hands scraped across the rough floor as her arms shot out to keep from falling all the way through. Only her arms, shoulders and head remained in the hayloft while the rest of her body dangled several feet above the hard packed earth below. Kicking like a frog, she struggled to pull herself up, but failed after several attempts. Small pieces of rotten boards fractured off around her and fell to the ground, landing with a faint thud. Instinctively, her fingers spread. If the remaining boards gave way, she knew she wouldn't get away without a broken leg, maybe a broken arm. The dust made her nose twitch, and she was afraid she might sneeze. But she froze when she noticed the camera strap around her neck had hooked on a nail in the side of a floor joist. If she fell now there was a good chance they'd find her literally swinging from the rafters.

"Don't panic." She glanced around, took a shallow breath and felt her lower lip quiver. "Dutch barns have a broad gable roof that can extend low to the ground. Crib barns were built of un-chinked logs and can be found in North Carolina, Virginia, and Kentucky."

Her eyes filled with tears, and a sob tore from her constricting throat.

"Is this some new kinda exercise? Or did you just want to hang out in here for the day?"

"I'm stuck!" Her body stiffened as his arms circled around her legs. Her thighs collided with his hard chest, and she felt his hot breath brush across her bared stomach. "What are you doing?" She yipped like a killer Pomeranian.

"Take it easy." His gentle voice soothed her bubbling hysteria as he instructed her. "You're all right. I've got you. Work your shoulders and head through the hole."

The heat from his body seeped into hers, raced through her blood stream and ascended all the way to the tips of her ears. How did he know she was trapped? She wouldn't be able to face him if he'd seen her sneaking around snapping photos of him. "I can't." Her voice cracked as she attempted to snuff out another sob before it escaped.

"It's all right, I won't let you fall." His deep reassuring voice helped her relax—just a little.

"No! The strap attached to my camera is hooked on a nail." The arms around her legs tightened, and she screeched as her body rose up through the floor several inches.

"Can you slip it off now," he asked and she felt his cheek brush against her bare side when he spoke.

She twisted to the side, and the strap tightened across her throat. "Dairy barns in the Midwest... Tobacco barns in the southeast," she recited, frantically struggling to remove the strap from the bent nail. "I got it!"

"Alright. Work your arms and shoulders through the hole, one at a time."

"No!" Panic washed over her. "Just push me up. I'll come down the ladder."

"It's not safe. You could fall through again. I've got a good hold on you."

She was well aware of that fact. She just didn't know if it was a good thing or a bad thing.

Careful not to scratch herself again, Cat worked her right arm and shoulder through the long narrow hole. She could feel her shirt rising higher as it caught on the jagged boards, and she heard herself start in again, "Round barns are cheaper than rectangular or square barns to build. Prairie barns were built for large herds and for hay and feed storage." *Damn nervous condition.*

As if in slow motion, she slid through his powerful hands as he guided her body down. Blindly, she reached down, first one hand then the other, and dug her fingers into his shoulders. Her legs spread and slid over the top of his muscular thighs, bringing them face-to-face on the saddle. A breath lodged in her throat at the intimate way she straddled his lap. Hoping to put some distance between them, she pushed against his shoulders. Her backside came up hard against the saddle horn, which caused her to thrust her hips forward. Unable to control herself, and to Cat's horror, she repeated this motion several more times until Cliff planted his hands on her hips and stopped her.

"You'd better stop doing that," he whispered deep and low.

She froze. With his hat pushed back, she could see small specks of light brown and green in his dark eyes. His entrancing stare held her paralyzed as it searched the depths of her soul. Calloused hands caressed and explored the sensitive skin under her shirt. The earthy scent of his masculinity engulfed her. Her senses buzzed with life, pushing her dangerously close to the edge of her control.

His warm breath brushed the side of her cheek when he asked in a teasing voice, "What were you taking pictures of up there?"

She blinked several times. "Nothing." Her voice shook in spite of her determination not to let her feelings show.

His thick brows rose in question as he reached for her camera. She clutched it to her chest, her heart slammed against her ribs. Being a private man, she knew he would be upset if he found out that she'd taken photos of him. Photos she would never be able to replace if he ripped the film from the camera.

The muscles in his legs flexed, and her hands grasped his shoulders as the horse started to move.

"Watch your head," he said, ducking down as they rode out of the barn. Once outside, the horse stopped. "You can let go of me now." His deep voice vibrated through her body, sending shivers up and down her spine.

A hint of amusement danced in his eyes. She pried her cramped fingers from his shoulders, and he effortlessly lifted her off his lap and set her on the ground.

She chewed her lower lip, her legs trembled, and she prayed she wouldn't collapse. This cowboy was too sexy, too mysterious, and too distracting. She needed to remember she hadn't come to Utah looking for a roll in the hay. She came to find her father.

He dismounted and opened one of the saddlebags tied behind his saddle. For a brief moment, she wondered if the horse would stand like the ones in the movies or wander away.

"Let me see your leg." Cliff knelt down on one knee in front of her. His eyes skimmed over her body like a caress, finally coming to rest upon hers.

"What?" Her voice quivered. She took a step back. "What for? I'm fine." She glanced down and saw a couple drips of blood on her shoe. The thought of his calloused hands roaming over her bare skin again caused every cell in her body to ricochet like a pinball machine. His piercing eyes held her gaze, and desire washed over her in long hot waves. What would it be like to be held in his arms—skin to skin—making love? Somehow, she knew he would be demanding yet yielding, powerful yet vulnerable. Her insides quivered. At that moment, she would take whatever he offered and give him anything he demanded.

Before she started quoting sexual techniques and positions, she took a deep breath and released it slowly, hoping to control her desire. "Thanks for saving me." She offered a friendly smile. "I appreciate it."

Cliff nodded his head once, an indication for her to lift her pant legs. "This might sting a little, but it'll keep you from getting an infection."

The exasperating man was throwing her own words back at her. "No, that's okay." If he touched her right now... "It's just a scratch. I'll be fine."

A dark shadow crept across Cliff's face. He stood and replaced the little white tube back into his saddlebag. "Don't go back in there," he said, pulling his hat down low over his brow. With one smooth gesture, he stepped into the stirrup and swung into the saddle.

"Thanks. I'll be careful." She brushed the hair out of her face, grateful that he had no idea just how much she wanted to lead him up into the haymow and thank him proper.

His eyes squinted to mere slits. "I mean it!" He spoke in a tone used for unruly children. "Stay out of that barn."

Now what did I do wrong? No man had ever spoken to her like that before, and she didn't like it. She did what she wanted, when she wanted and wherever she wanted. Cat clutched the camera to her chest and struck a defiant pose. "Don't worry, Mr. White Fox," she said, her voice laced with an undercurrent of sarcasm. "I understand the danger. I don't take unnecessary chances."

"Good." He leaned back in the saddle. The movement was slight, but the horse spun around and bolted.

Cat shook her head and watched him ride away. "This guy's disposition changes like the weather around here." Placing her hand on her hips, she shook her head. "You have to hand it to the man...he can sure make a dramatic exit."

* * * *

Cliff shifted his weight in the saddle and spurred Sonny toward the cattle he'd left grazing in a small clearing.

His heart had catapulted into his throat when he had heard a woman scream. It nearly stopped beating all together when he'd rounded the barn and found Cat dangling through a hole in the haymow floor.

Straddling him, her breasts pressed against his chest and those dark chocolate eyes fixed on his had revived a long-lost fantasy that he knew would haunt him for the rest of his life. His groin tightened, and he shifted uncomfortably in the saddle. He wanted her more than any woman before. Sonny sidestepped and tossed his head in protest to Cliff's firm hold on the reins. Loosening his grip, he offered a lame apology. "Sorry."

The woman was a dog gone distraction. What would she have done if he'd hauled her off into the tall grass, then stripped off her clothes? He shook his head and felt every muscle in his body tense. She was driving him crazy! And like every other night since she'd arrived, tonight he would dream of making love to her, and in the morning, he would be moved by just how real it had been.

She dredged up feelings long buried and a few he'd never experienced before. He needed her out of his house, out of his head and out of his life. *She's no different than Nora. Just another scatter-brained woman who doesn't think before she acts.*

He rubbed a calloused hand across the back of his neck in an attempt to ease the building tension. "They're all the same. Decide want you want, screw the consequences and charge blindly forward like a maverick calf in search of its mother."

Women...

He urged Sonny into a trot. He really needed to speak to Millie Pearson again about buying her land. If there weren't anything for Cat to stay around for, she would pack up and hit the road. The thought should have brought him some joy, but the idea of never seeing her again sat in his stomach like one of Rooster's pancakes.

* * * *

Rooster hobbled out of the barn and into the bright afternoon sun as Cat parked the International in front of the ranch house. The sweet, energetic girl had been on his mind all night. There was something strangely familiar about her, but he couldn't put his finger on it. What was it? The way she walked with her long-legged stride or the mischief that sparked in her eyes when she teased and giggled?

She jumped out of the truck, swung her camera case over her shoulder and started toward him. She grinned and waved as she approached the elderly man, her swift pace making quick work of the distance between them.

"Hi, Rooster." Her eyes twinkled with genuine affection. "Whatcha up to?"

He reached up and gave his old hat a shove back. "Hey, girlie. I need to go out to my place and pick up a headstall I've been working on. I hung it smack-dab in my way then walked right past it this morning. You're welcome to ride out there with me."

Her expression wavered, and she glanced back down the driveway. "Yeah! I'll go with you." She hooked her arm through his and gave it a little squeeze as they headed back toward the truck.

"You might find something to take pictures of while we're there." He escorted her to the passenger door where she hopped into the truck.

Holding up the battered and scratched up case, she chirped, "I've got lots of film."

As they drove past Millie's driveway, he noticed that she stiffened slightly and glanced toward the old homestead. Earlier Cliff had headed off in that direction. Had their paths crossed?

They drove in silence for several miles, the only noise coming from the old pickup as it rattled down the tarred road. By the way the girl fiddled with her camera case and her clothing, it was evident that something bothered her.

He would probably never know what it was, and he doubted that she would confide in an old coot like him. But he knew Cliff better than he had known his own son, and if Cliff suspected his world was threatened, he would charge like a bull cornered by a pack of wolves. Was that it? Had the jackass viewed her as some sort a threat? Without taking his eyes off the road, he shot a stream of tobacco juice out his window. "You know, faith is a misunderstood word," he stated dryly. "Most people think it only means to believe or loyalty and devotion." When she didn't respond he continued, his voice somewhat monotone. "To me it means trust. Sure, you gotta have faith in what you believe in, God, Spirits, whatever you want a call it. But a man needs to trust people, trust his faith, the Spirits."

He didn't turn when he felt her gaze on him. If he had, she would've been able to see his heavy heart and the pain he'd kept buried deep inside for years.

"Everyone has losses, and everything happens for a reason. We don't always get to know what that reason is or understand why." He swallowed the lump building in the back of his throat and shifted his weight off his sore hip. "You just have to believe in the Spirits and that they'll let you be around long enough to see the good that comes of it."

A couple more miles passed before Cat spoke. "I found a snapshot of Cliff when I was going through some photos at my grandmother's. He looked so different with his hair decorated with beads and feathers. Millie told me the photo was taken at a Pow Wow."

Rooster glanced her way. "Was that all she told you?"

She placed several loose strands of hair behind one ear. "No. She told me Cliff and his brother danced in competition with each other that day and that Cliff lost." Her eyes were masked with sadness. She turned in the seat to face him. "Millie also said that after that day Cliff cut his hair short and turned away from his Native American family and way of life."

The truck jounced off the blacktop on to the reservation road. What had Millie told her about his granddaughter, Nora? He glanced her way and asked, "Did she mention Cliff's wife at all?"

With her eyes downcast, the girl played with the hem of her shirt. "Nothing other than they're divorced. Is that why he's so cold and distant?"

He wasn't sure how to answer, but before he could reply, she continued. "It's almost like he hates everyone. He looks at you like… I don't know…" She waved her arms around. "Like he doesn't trust you. That he's sure you're going to do something wrong and he doesn't want to be anywhere near you when it happens."

Another stream of tobacco juice flew. That pretty much summed up the ornery-cuss. Reaching up, he scratched the stubble on his jaw. "He hasn't been happy in a handful of years," he heard himself say.

She pulled one knee up onto the seat and groaned. "I don't understand. If giving up his other life makes him so unhappy, why doesn't he just go back?"

"You can't shove the calf back in after it's been born, girlie. Don't work that way." He offered a sympathetic grin as he glanced in the mirror only to see red dust billowing behind them as they drove across the Reservation.

Rooster knew he was a dead man the minute Cliff got wind of this conversation. But it didn't matter. He'd lived a good long life. If the

Spirits decided it was his time—he was ready.

He figured he was in up to his axles already; he might as well bury himself all the way. Taking a cleansing breath, he plunged forward. "Well, Cliff and his brother were always competing with each other when Cliff lived on the res. Both boys were very proud, very Indian-*onish*." He glanced her way, and she smiled.

"Each day Cliff felt he was being tested, that he had to prove his mind and heart were that of a full-blood." Her expression went blank as she tried to absorb his words. "When his mother sent him to live with his father on the ranch, Hank Dawson expected Cliff to forget his other life, but the boy held on as long as he could. For years he walked with a foot in two worlds, though he never really felt accepted in either."

Rooster saw her wipe a hand across her damp cheek before she turned to examine the row of small houses coming into view. The tale of Cliff's troubled life had affected her more than he imagined it would. He liked the young woman who had been dropped into their laps, and a blind grizzly couldn't miss the way she and Cliff were taking the long way around the barn to evade their attraction to each other. Could she be the one to open Cliff's eyes to what was really important? Help him rope and hogtie the pieces of his life and put them back together? He was meddling in their lives like on old woman, but he didn't care. She wasn't aware that the Spirits had sent her to them or that she somehow held strong healing powers for the people.

He cleared his throat. "Cliff felt the pressures of society to choose between living the white's way or the Indian's way. He's spent the last five years building a world of his own. A place where he feels he belongs, free from judgment, free to be himself. In making this choice, he's caused himself and his family a lot of heartache."

Cat drew in her gaze and turned to stare at the old cowboy. The crooked smile and easy charm she had come to expect had vanished. His weathered features were etched with deep worry lines. She wasn't sure how to respond to everything he had just told her. She wanted to ask him about Cliff's ex-wife, what she was like, who she was and had she remarried.

Rooster painted a clear picture of Cliff—how he had become the man he was now. Yet earlier, when Cliff had teased her in the barn, she'd caught a glimpse of who he might have once been. There was a gentleness about him for a few moments. Then, as if he remembered where he was, who he was, it vanished. His features returned to stone, and once again his voice became laced with arrogance.

Though there were a few pieces missing in the Clifford White Fox puzzle, she was determined to find those pieces and uncover the true picture.

Chapter Six

Cat awoke disoriented, the blankets twisted and hanging off to one side of the lodge pole bed. She spent most of the night tossing and turning, agonizing over what to tell her agent, Crystal Robertson, about the ruined photos and paintings. Around dawn, she decided that she would put off telling her as long as she could.

Throwing the covers back, she leaped out of bed, slipped into jeans, a white tank top and a yellow and white-striped western shirt she had bought in town. As she brushed her hair, she thought about the New York art festival, which Crystal promised would launch her career. This was to be her premier show, a chance to show the art world that she was a talented artist and had an eye for photography. The amazing photos she took in Africa, along with her three oil paintings proved she had only scraped the surface of her talent.

She heaved a sigh as she placed the brush on the dresser and stared at her reflection in the antique beveled mirror. "What am I going to tell Crystal?" At the last minute, the vivacious redhead had called in a few favors and booked Cat in one of New York's largest spring art festivals. Now she had to call and inform her that five months of work had been washed away in a matter of hours, not to mention the thousands of dollars the trip cost. The fear that her agent would let her go, ending her career before it ever got started, made her stomach roll and twist with apprehension.

Cat took a deep breath, reached for the phone and smiled at her reflection in the mirror. She heard somewhere that if you put on a big smile the person on the other end of the phone would get the impression that everything was hunky-dory.

"Hello. Crystal Robertson."

"Crystal? Hi, it's Cat."

"Catrina! How are you? Are you here in New York already?"

"I'm great," she said, turning away from the mirror's knowing stare. "No. I'm still in Utah."

"How is your vacation going? Taking a lot of photos?"

Cat settled on the edge of the bed. "Actually, I took several photos one day while I was hiking."

"That's wonderful! Great news," Crystal said excitedly. "The gallery has extended your display area to sixteen feet. And I was able to contract your name on the front page of the show brochure. You're a star, Catrina Pearson! What do you think about that?"

Chewing on her lower lip, Cat knew it was time to come clean. "Great. I have a slight problem though. Well, it leans a little more toward a big problem."

Cat relayed the events of the past few days, bringing Crystal up to date on the storm and flash flood. And that the man from the only gas station for fifty miles said he wasn't sure he could get her car up and running.

"Oh my God, Catrina. Are you all right?"

"I'm fine, but I'm not sure how much longer I can stay here," she said, glancing around the rustic room. How long Cliff would put up with her intrusion—she wasn't sure. On her next trip in to town, she would go back to the Roach Motel to see if they had any openings yet.

"Are you telling me that you can't stay at your grandmother's house any longer," Crystal said, her voice laced with astonishment.

Cat laughed, despite herself. "What house? It was pretty much washed away in the storm."

Crystal gasped. "Where have you been staying?"

"I'm staying at a ranch a few miles from my grandmother's place."

"With that old cowboy?" Crystal teased, sounding relieved.

"No. With a young cowboy." Cat stood and started to pace around the small room. "But that's another story—for another day."

"I look forward to hearing about that when you get here."

Plopping back down on to the bed, Cat stared at the receiver. "You still want me to come to New York? Why?"

"Catrina! It's too late to change the show brochures, and the press releases were sent out earlier this week. You have three weeks until the show. There's plenty of time to fly to Los Angeles, collect your negatives and fly to New York. We'll make reprints here, and there might even be enough time to redo one or two of your oils before the premier."

"I could fly back after the show, pick up my car and visit with Millie for a while longer," Cat replied, thinking out loud.

"Everything will work out fine." Crystal interrupted her thoughts. "Call me as soon as you get your flights booked. I'll have a car waiting at the airport for you. I've got to run, dear. Talk to you soon. Bye!"

The line went dead. What had just happened? Crystal made it sound so easy, as though her idea would solve Cat's problem. The only question Cat had was, where was the nearest airport, and how was she going to get there?

Walking out of her room, the smell of fresh coffee drifted up the stairs from the kitchen. Cat's stomach growled. "Sounds like a polecat caught in a trap," she said and then laughed at her poor impersonation of the grizzled old cowboy she'd grown so fond of.

As Cat reached for the coffee pot warming on the wood cook-stove, the telephone rang.

"Hello..."

"Yes. May I speak with Catrina Pearson, please?" A friendly feminine voice asked.

"This is she."

"Hi, Catrina. This is Jeannie Porter from the Blake River Medical Center. Dr. Crawford would like to see you as soon as possible."

"Is something wrong? What happened?" Cat asked, fighting to control her emotions. "Did Millie fall? Is she sick?"

"I'm sorry. I didn't mean to upset you," Jeannie replied in a soothing tone. "Millie's fine. Dr. Crawford just wants to discuss her condition and some changes in her treatment."

"Oh. All right," Cat said, relaxing. "Thank you. I'll leave right now." Hanging up the phone, Cat poured a cup of coffee, grabbed two cookies from a plate on the counter and headed for the door.

She saw Cliff and Rooster constructing a large pen out of several long metal gates. The old black truck sat parked nearby like a good soldier, waiting for orders.

"Hey, girlie, thought you were going to sleep the day away!" Rooster greeted her with a wide grin. She returned the old man's smile, but couldn't help notice how Cliff kept his back toward her.

"Good morning. I have a favor to ask." She addressed both men. Rooster nodded, but Cliff continued to ignore her.

"What do you need? Just name it, and I'll rope and hogtie it for ya." One bushy eyebrow dipped in an animated wink, and he slapped his hand against his thigh.

Cat laughed at his antics. "The medical center called, and Dr. Crawford wants to discuss Millie's condition with me as soon as possible. I was wondering if I could borrow one of the pickups?"

Rooster placed an arm around her shoulders. "Yes, ma'am. You go right ahead and take your pick." He gestured with a sweep of his arm.

"Thank you," she said smiling up at the weathered old cowboy. "I shouldn't be too long. Do you need me to pick up anything in town while I'm there?" Her gaze swept from Rooster to Cliff who continued to fasten two panels together with a short piece of chain. The sleeves of his shirt were rolled up, and the sweat-soaked material clung to his muscular back. His profile showed a clenched square jaw and thick brows pulled together in a deep furrow. If he bared his teeth just then, he would resemble a huge guard dog ready to strike.

The man must wake up each morning looking for things to be mad about. No wonder he's alone.

As she drove away, she waved. Her problems were solved, and she wasn't going to let Cliff ruin her day.

* * * *

When Cat entered the medical center, Jeannie stood at the counter conversing with a middle-aged man in a long white lab coat. Pushing up his thick brown-rimmed glasses with one finger, he smiled and extended his hand as Jeannie introduced them.

"Catrina Pearson, this is Dr. Crawford." Jeannie then excused herself.

"Miss Pearson, it's a pleasure to finally meet you." Cat stared, puzzled. "I've been listening to your praises ever since Millie moved in." His brown eyes appeared magnified through his thick glasses. "I'd love to hear about your many adventures—Australia, China, Africa," he said, taking her by the elbow and steering her toward a small waiting area in the corner.

"Yes...of course," she replied, perching on the edge of the chair he indicated. "When I return in a few weeks."

"You're leaving us?" He settled in the chair opposite of hers.

Pulling her purse strap up over her shoulder, she smiled. "Yes. I need to leave for New York as soon as I can make the arrangements." At the doctor's frown, she asked, "Why? Is there a problem with Millie?"

"It shouldn't be," he said, pushing his glasses into place again. "Early this morning your grandmother suffered a slight stroke."

The coffee and cookies Cat had eaten on her way to town transformed into a rock in the pit of her stomach.

"As of right now, she has some restricted movement on her right side, and her speech is slightly slurred."

She felt sick. She knotted her fingers together on her lap as he continued.

"We ran some tests earlier, measured her limitations and I truly feel with physical therapy, she'll be back to her old self before we know it."

Cat searched his eyes. Was he sugarcoating Millie's condition? Guilt washed over her in waves. She should have been spending more time with her grandmother instead of hiking up mountains and falling through ceilings. "Can I see her?"

"Of course." Dr. Crawford stood and reached out a hand to help her to her feet. "Just be prepared. She's going to appear fragile and a little sluggish."

"Thank you," she said, unsure for what she was actually thanking him.

He placed a reassuring hand on her shoulder. "This isn't uncommon for a person of her age. She's strong. She'll respond well to physical therapy."

Cat nodded.

"If you need to see me before you leave, tell Jeannie," he nodded toward the counter. "She knows how to reach me." Then he strolled away.

She stood in the middle of the entryway, confused and frightened. She glanced around the room, searching for some kind of answer. When her gaze landed on Jeannie behind the counter, the little blond smiled and nodded toward Millie's door, silently reassuring her that it wasn't going to be as bad as she was expecting.

Drawing a deep breath, Cat crossed the foyer on stiff legs and opened Millie's door. The pungent aroma of several medications assaulted her as she entered. The room was uncomfortably warm, making it hard to breath. The shades had been drawn. Eerie shadows danced along the walls. Across the room, Millie lay swaddled in blankets. Her chalk-like skin appeared thin and transparent. The purplish-blue veins in her hands and arms were raised. A haunting vision of her mother on her deathbed flashed before her, and Cat stumble backwards.

"Catrina...Is that you?" A weak voice whispered from the bed.

Cat crept closer and forced a smile. "Hi! How are you doing?" Reaching out, she gently placed the old woman's hand in hers. "I hear you stirred things up a little this morning."

When Millie smiled at her teasing remark, only the left side of her mouth curved up. "They'll all get lazy if someone doesn't keep them on their toes," Millie replied. Though her words were slow and choppy, it was reassuring to hear that familiar edge in the old woman's tone.

"I talked to Dr. Crawford. He says with some physical therapy you'll back to your old self in no time." She tried to swallow the lump in her throat and hoped the tears building behind her eyes would stay hidden. Though the doctor stated that Millie would recover, Cat had her doubts as she stared at the frail old woman—the only relative she had left.

"What's the matter, dear? You've been into the pickles again?"

Chuckling at her grandmother's comment, Cat shook her head and placed a strand of loose hair behind her ear. There was no reason to worry; Millie would be back to her old self sooner than predicted. If they weren't careful, she would be running the show before the end of the week.

"Grandma, I dread telling you," she squeezed Millie's hand, "But I'm glad you're in such good spirits. I called my agent in New York this morning. I had no idea what I was going to say or do. But I explained about the flash flood and what happened to my photos and paintings."

"It's a dirty rotten shame. You worked so hard..." Millie said, her voice straining and quivering as she forced the words out.

"Yes... Well. She wants me to fly back to Los Angeles, organize my negatives and then fly them out to New York. There's plenty of time before the art festival to have reprints made, and even redo one or two of the oils." The old woman started to spit and sputter. "Do you need the doctor or a nurse," she asked trying not to panic.

Millie shook her head slightly. "No. I'm fine. I'm just surprised that you're leaving so soon. I thought we'd have more time together."

"I'll fly back as soon as the show is over. We'll have plenty of time, and you'll be much better by then." At the dejected expression on Millie's face, Cat said, her voice laced with enthusiasm, "It should be warmer then. Maybe the mountain roads will be open, and we can go for a drive."

Millie's eyes filled with tears and she shook her head. "It's not that," she gasped for air, "It's just... I saw..."

"You saw who, Grandma?" Cat leaned forward, and Millie strained to speak.

"Your mother's best friend..."

"Who? When?"

"Sandy Huset. She'd know..." Her voice trailed off.

"She'd know who?" Cat encouraged gently. Did she dare to hope this person knew her father?

"If you leave..." Millie gasped. "Miss her."

"Why, Grandmother? Please tell me."

"Tired. I'm so tired." As Cat watched, Millie drifted off to sleep. She rested quietly, one corner of her mouth turned up in a slight smile.

Cat tiptoed from the room and noticed Jeannie behind the desk. She approached her and asked, "Jeannie, do you happen to know a woman named, Sandy Huset?"

The blonde pondered the question then answered, "No. I've never met anyone by that name. Is something wrong?"

Cat smiled. "No. I've never met her either, but I heard she's been in to visit someone. I really need to speak with her."

"I'll keep my eyes open for any new faces," Jeannie replied, handing Cat a small piece of paper. "Write your name and number down. I'll post a note on the billboard for her to check in at the desk for a message."

"Oh. That would be great."

Cat left the medical center and drove to the motel to see if the woman was staying there. The answer was the same, but the man at the desk offered her a phone book. She searched through the white pages, but couldn't find the woman who held the secrets to the other half of her life.

The drive back to the ranch was long and torturous, a roller coaster of emotions. There was a chance the woman was here visiting someone since she wasn't listed in the phone book. If that was the case, and Cat left town now, she ran the chance of missing her completely. On the other hand, if she stayed, there was a good chance she'd be flushing her career down the toilet. Maybe Rooster or Cliff knew the woman, knew if she was married and still lived around here. With renewed hope, she pulled off the tar road and sped up the Circle D ranch road.

* * * *

An hour later Cat sat on the edge of her bed. Her head pounded with frustration. Neither Cliff nor Rooster knew anything about the elusive woman. Millie appeared to be her only connection to Sandy Huset, which lead Cat to believe that the woman was only in town temporarily. She reached for the phone and dialed the number.

"Hello, Crystal Robertson speaking."

"Hi Crystal, it's Cat." She raked her lower lip through her teeth. There was no easy way to do this.

"Wonderful! Give me your dates and times, and I'll have a car waiting to pick you up."

Cat rubbed one temple. "I'm afraid I have another problem. After we spoke this morning, I received a call from the medical center where my grandmother is staying. She's had a stroke. I can't leave her right now. Maybe in a few days..."

Crystal heaved a great sigh, and with a tone reserved for small children, she stated, "Catrina, I don't think I need to remind you that you are under contract. I went out on a limb to get you a *damn good* position on this spring art festival, as well as the cover of the brochure. Not to mention," she added, with an air of irritation. "All the money tied up in the event.

"I know, Crystal, and I really appreciate it, but I don't know what I can do. I just know I can't leave her right now." The line went silent; Cat held her breath and waited for the other shoe to drop.

Crystal's voice sounded flat and direct. "Both of our careers are on the line here. Even though you're prepared to throw yours away, I'm not. The window of opportunity is on the verge of slamming in our faces. You need to reassess your priorities. What do you really want?"

Crystal was a good friend, one who would go to bat for you in a heartbeat, but she wasn't one Cat wanted out for her blood. Cat reached into her purse for a bottle of aspirin, and her hand brushed against a small photo. Puzzled, she pulled the photo out and smiled. "Crystal! I have an idea."

Cat described the photo she found at Millie's house of Cliff dressed in his Native American regalia. She explained the saga of Cliff's existence and how he had chosen to leave one life for another.

"With branding coming up in a couple of day, I have the opportunity to capture him in his element. The guy's like a double sided billboard, like he's got 'A Foot in Two Worlds'".

"I like the concept," Crystal stated, though her voice lacked enthusiasm. "You'll need to produce top quality, Catrina."

"I need only a few days. I promise you won't be sorry, Crystal."

Once again, Cat's plans changed in a blink of an eye. Now she had two things to accomplish in a few short days. She needed to track down Sandy Huset and extract as much information from her as she could and then try to get close enough to Clifford White Fox to capture on film who the man really is, without raising his suspicions. Both aspects sounded intriguing and equally challenging.

Chapter Seven

Streaks of white light from the morning sun splashed across the wide-plank floor. Cliff half listened as Rooster explained between sips of coffee and forkfuls of scrambled eggs and ham, what needed to be done that day. The old man reported that most of the storm damage to the barn and trees had been repaired and cleaned up.

Cliff raised a cup of lethal brew to his lips. The scalding liquid burned a trail down to his empty stomach, yet did little to wash away the recurring visions. Cat sunbathing naked, her skin kissed by the sun, her rich brown hair streaked in shades of red and gold or barefoot, parading across his kitchen in shorts and tank top with her hair trussed up in pigtails. His favorite image was of her straddling his lap, her breasts pressed against his chest, her eyes glazed with desire.

Over the past week, he hadn't slept more than a few hours each night, and he had all but lost his appetite. If this kept up, by the end of the month he would be either dead or totally out of his mind.

"And then the corral will be finished," Rooster said. One curly gray brow rose as he studied Cliff. Setting his cup down, he shook his head, chuckling.

"What?" Cliff growled. "Sounds like you got it all figured out, old man."

"At least one of us has it figured out." Reaching for his cup, Rooster lifted it to his lips. Cliff caught the old man's smirk and scowled.

The chair scraped across the worn floor as Cliff shot to his feet. "You almost finished?"

The old man reached up and leisurely scratched his chest. "What's your hurry?"

"I don't pay you to drink coffee." Cliff's words hissed through clenched teeth. Maybe he should think about hiring someone younger. The old man had started to slow down. He was, in Rooster's own words, "pert-near" eighty.

He sensed Cat seconds before she entered the room. All hopes of avoiding her by getting out of the house before she came down stairs vanished. She sauntered into the kitchen dressed in jeans and a pink t-shirt. Not only did the t-shirt fit like a second skin, raised nipples pulled the material taut. Her silky hair hung loose around her shoulders, her full lips turned up in a wide smile, her eyes sparked with mischief.

"Good morning!" She stopped and eyed the old man with suspicion. "Rooster, you look like the cat that caught the canary."

"Morning, girlie. Aren't you a breath of sunshine."

She crossed to the stove, helped herself to a cup of coffee and joined them at the table. A frown marred features when her gaze met Cliff's. "You don't look like you slept too well. Are you coming down with something?" Rooster coughed and spit his coffee back into his cup, then wiped his sleeve across his face.

Cliff fought the urge to strangle the old goat right then and there.

"Are you all right?" She reached out a comforting hand.

Cliff retrieved his coffee cup walked to the sink and poured out the lukewarm remains. A light floral scent engulfed him, its sweet perfume making him feel light-headed. His groin tightened. Closing his eyes, he struggled to draw a steady breath. The best thing to do was keep busy and continue to avoid her. It wasn't like he didn't have enough work to keep him occupied through branding.

Rooster's voice sliced into his thoughts. "Spotted a mountain lion with two cubs up on the bluffs the other day. I wonder how the little family survived the storm."

The old guy felt more like visiting than working. Fine. Cliff crossed to the coat rack and grabbed his hat and jacket. He stepped out onto the porch and drew a deep breath. It was a new day ahead, and a new image to haunt him.

* * * *

Twenty feet from the back of the house, Cat paused to adjust her backpack and tighten the strap of her camera case around her waist. She didn't want any more close calls. Today she would capture something on film to prove to Crystal she was worth backing. If she got a few good shots this morning, she would still be able to make it into town to visit Millie and see if Sandy Huset ever returned to the medical center.

In the distance, the rocky bluffs loomed where Rooster spotted the mountain lion and her two cubs. She started out, but the image of Cliff's sober expression returned. What had he and Rooster been talking about when she entered the kitchen? The old man appeared quite pleased with himself, and Cliff had given the definite impression that he wasn't amused by their conversation.

The man was definitely an award-winning pain in the rear, yet each time she laid eyes on him, her insides started to bubble like a volcano. He had no idea how ruggedly sexy he looked with his dark hair curling around the collar of his worn work shirt and the way his faded jeans hugged his muscular thighs. That old, sweat stained, gray cowboy hat added the finishing touch to the whole package. He was the genuine article, a man's man, a real cowboy. With that look and his unapproachable persona, she could picture him modeling anything from work wear to tuxedos. He would be perfect in a cologne or pickup advertisement.

Cat smiled. Hell, she would buy anything the man was selling. Maybe it was a good thing he'd been avoiding her. She stopped in her tracks and shook her head to dispel the vision of Cliff leaning against the table, cradling a cup of coffee as steamy as the man himself. Was that it? Had he been avoiding her because he was attracted to her?

Her lips curled into a satisfied smirk. "What a beautiful day."

Off in the distance, snowcapped peaks towered above the majestic landscape. Keeping to the edge of pasture as Rooster instructed, she made her way along the deer trail, tripping and stumbling as she surveyed the sky and horizon for any impromptu photo-ops.

An hour later, she skirted a sea of miniature sunflowers and followed the yellow waves to the far edge of the field. As she approached a clump of trees, a frantic squirrel squeaked out a warning. The birds perched in the branches above took flight. Something rustled in the tall grass, and she froze in her tracks. Pivoting, she tried to locate the source of the sound. Several seconds passed before a porcupine lumbered from the weeds. Cat shuffled backwards, giving him ample room. The porcupine ambled along, ignoring the large intruder. Cat scanned her surroundings and then released a long breath. "Running into him would sure put a damper on a person's day!"

Wiping her damp hands on her jeans, she headed for a small clump of rock. The narrow path that led up to the bluffs appeared right where Rooster said it would be. Pulling out her water bottle, she removed the cap and took a sip. An outcrop of rocks loomed several yards up the incline. The trail was steep, and further up it disappeared around a clump of trees.

"No worries, mate," she said, then laughed. The familiar phrase brought to mind the trip she took to Australia three years earlier and the comical little Aussie who fearlessly guided her through the bush in search of a Tasmanian Devil.

With newfound enthusiasm, Cat fastened her loose hair into a ponytail and started up the rocky trail. The steep incline slowed her ascent, and more than once, rocks gave way, causing her to slide back down the craggy slope. "Ouch!" Cat blew on the back of her hand as little beads of blood boiled to the surface on a fresh scrape.

Glancing up, she studied the rocky outcrop then glanced back over her shoulder to the trail below. She closed her eyes against the sand and debris a sudden breeze stirred up. Blinking and pushing hair from her face, she resumed her ascent of the bluffs. Several minutes later, she reached a place where the path widened and flattened out. Standing, she brushed the dirt from her hands and clothes.

"What a beautiful view. You can see for miles." Her gaze swept across the rugged landscape below, the buildings of the Circle D Ranch were mere dots on the horizon. The giant trees around her swayed and cracked in the powerful breeze. Her hair had worked loose from its binder somewhere along the trail and flew around her head like a flock of black birds. She turned into the wind and brushed it away from her face. *If I can get further into the trees, I should be out of the wind.*

She ventured off the trail and came to an area where she was sheltered from the wind. She settled her tired body on a fallen tree and marveled at the rugged beauty of the wooded area. What an extreme change from the flat meadows below. Her senses felt overwhelmed with the contrasts of colors, textures and scents that engulfed her. She could have sat there forever just listening to nature and inhaling the earth's magnificent fragrance.

She removed her water bottle and took a long, cool drink. A noise came from the other side of a large boulder. Cat froze. Retrieving her camera, she crept toward the sounds. Without making a sound, she crawled up a pile of rocks onto a large boulder and peered over. Twenty-five feet away in a small clearing were two mountain lion cubs wrestling in some dried leaves. They purred and hissed like two house cats as they played. The scene reminded her of a Disney special she had once seen on TV. Experience told her the pranksters' mother wouldn't be far away. Her gaze swept the surrounding area. The cubs continued to frolic despite her presence and the lack of their mothers'.

Cat snapped several photos of the furry angels as they jumped and swatted at each other. The shots captured their reddish-brown undercoats covered in large black spots. The tips of their outsized ears, huge feet and tails painted black. One cub broke free and rolled a few feet away from the other. For a moment, it stood with its mouth partially open, panting. Lowering its head, it slowly crept toward its target until it was within a couple of feet and then it pounced.

Finishing one roll of film, she crawled down from the rocks and reloaded. As quiet as she could, she rounded the boulder and shot the two from a different angle. The lighting was perfect. She couldn't believe her luck; first to come across the cubs as quickly as she had, then to have them ignore her as she continued to photograph them. They performed and posed like seasoned professionals. Cat giggled as she caught their antics on film.

Something caught one cub's attention. Cat froze then turned her head until she saw the cub's mother perched on a rocky outcrop high above her. The mother's coat was reddish brown like a fox. Her underbelly creamy white, her intelligent green eyes focused on Cat. The large feline didn't roar, but offered a deep throaty frightening growl.

With slow and careful movements, she raised her camera and snapped a couple shots of the majestic animal. Without shifting her gaze, she took several slow steps backward. The first thing the guide in Africa had told her was never make quick movements and never turn and run.

The lioness growled again, then turned and disappeared into the trees. There was little chance that the animal was going to forgive her intrusion and let her walk away. Could she make it to the trail and escape? Shoving her camera back into her case, Cat spun around and ran. A scene she'd witnessed of a pride of lions closing in on a lone zebra flashed before her eyes.

"Mountain lions, pumas and cougars are all the same. They can weigh up to 200 pounds." A scream tore from her throat as she fell and slid down a steep rocky incline.

Cat scrambled to her hands and knees and shot a glance back up the hill. "I'd be just a snack for her!" She surveyed the rocky slope. She would never make it down the trail; the cougar would catch her in a second. It looked dangerous, yet it would be easier for her to continue down the rocky face than the mountain lion. Sliding down the steep slope backwards, she hoped to get down behind a larger boulder before the cougar spotted her.

"They like to hide in rocky places and are good climbers." Cat drew a deep breath and swallowed her rising panic. "They are seldom seen even though they hunt by day as well as by night. Mountain lions have large territories and cover many square miles in their hunt for prey."

A cry sounded overhead, and she glanced up, the agitated animal paced back and forth several yards above her. With its ears pinned back, it growled, its long white fangs gleaming in the afternoon sun.

"They live in North and South America, but have also been found in the tropical rainforests of the Amazon." She licked her dry lips. "They're considered to be a leaping cat because they slowly stalk their prey, then leap on it. They are an oversized small cat that can purr like a tabby." She glanced back up at the cougar. "Small cat, my Aunt Fanny!"

She continued to make her way over the rocks, stopping only to catch her breath. At last, she came to a large boulder. She scurried around behind it and hoped the animal would think she was gone and no longer a threat to her young. Below the ground sloped at a more severe degree. There was nowhere for Cat to go. She would just have to wait out the animal.

Panting, with shaky hands, she opened the water and took a sip. When she attempted to replace the lid the bottle slipped. It rolled and dropped over the edge. She heard the sound of twigs breaking and flinched as dirt, sticks and rocks rolled past her to join the plastic bottle below. Dropping twenty to thirty feet to the ground below would have been the quickest way down, but Cat didn't think it was the best. The mountain lion growled, and the threat sounded much closer.

A plan formed in Cat's mind. She took her hiking jacket, wrapped it around her backpack, and then tied the sleeves together. Easing forward, she threw the backpack off to the side into the animal's line of vision. It rolled several times then fell over the edge and disappeared. *The cougar should think I jumped or fell. Either way I hope she thinks I'm gone.*

She scooted back, wedged herself behind the boulder and wrapped her arms around herself. She didn't know how long she was going to have to sit there, but she was prepared to wait it out.

Curled up in a tight ball, she tried not to make a sound, although her body shook with fear. Terrified, her mind rewound and played back the past few days. Although she survived the flood, her artwork, vehicle and career hadn't. But those are all things that can be replaced. Millie however, had lost her home, and now was very ill. Her grandmother had looked so fragile, lying in the hospital bed. She must have felt so alone and been scared half to death thinking she was close to death. Cat shook her head in disgust. She had purposely put herself in danger. For what? To get the best photo? To prove to Crystal and the world that she was a great photographer? How pathetic.

The sun had moved on, taking its warm rays with it. Crouching behind the boulder, she rubbed the goosebumps on her arms. Her stomach growled, and she flinched. She should be sitting by Millie's side, consoling her. Learning as much about the woman and family history as she could before her grandmother was gone. Yet once again, she had put her own desires and feelings in front of someone else's. No one knew where she was, and by the time anyone found her—she'd be dead.

A lump of self-pity rose in the back of her throat, but her anger forced it back down. "Great. I'll be remembered as that crazy, mediocre photographer who climbed half way up a mountain, froze to death and then was eaten by wild animals."

She pulled up her knees and rested her chin. The beautiful, unyielding landscape spread out before her. *Even though a number of things have happened to me since I arrived, this place feels more like home then any place I've ever lived.* Her restless heart had found a sense of serenity. How ironic, she came back searching for answers and perhaps family, only to meet her demise—alone.

* * * *

"Looks like it's going to rain again," Cliff said, shutting off the tractor. He dropped a large round bale of grass hay in the middle of the corral for the mother cows and calves. Pushing back his hat, he scratched his head. Rooster had proven to be a big help; they managed to finish constructing the branding corral for the next day. Hungry and exhausted, the two men limped past the trucks and into a quiet house.

Strolling to the kitchen sink, Cliff washed his face and arms. He reached for a glass, filled it and let the cold-water sooth his parched throat. Rooster rummaged through the refrigerator behind him. "Where's that girlie hidden? My mouth has been watering for fried pork chops and gravy all day!"

A quick glance at the clock told Cliff it was 7:00 pm. He recalled seeing both trucks out front and wondered if she was upstairs napping or something. She had plagued his mind all day. The thought of sneaking up stairs and taking his time teasing her awake made him grin.

"Aren't you hungry?" Rooster asked, slamming the door.

"Yep. Sure am," he replied turning around. He was hungry all right, but it wasn't for pork chops.

The old man's face was creased with concern. "Where do you think she took off to?" Rooster limped to the table and lowered himself into a chair. "My knees are killing me." He stretched his legs out, wincing.

"She couldn't have gone far. Both trucks are still here. I'll run up stairs and see if she's there." Cliff rolled his sleeves down and snapped them as he headed toward the stairs. He took them two at a time, then stood and stared at her neatly made bed. An alarm buzzed in a corner of his brain. Spinning on his heels, Cliff raced back down to the kitchen.

The sound of his boots pounding on the bare treads echoed through the quiet house. "What the heck..." Rooster spat as Cliff entered the kitchen.

"What were you yapping about this morning?" Cliff demanded, staring at the old man.

Rooster frowned. "Huh?"

"This morning! What did you and Cat talk about after I left?"

The old man scratched his chin whiskers and pondered the question. Cliff wanted to strangle Rooster for his balky memory. "Nothin' really.

93

She did ask me where I'd seen those cougar cubs though."

No time to waste. Cliff grabbed his hat. "Which direction did you tell her?" He reached for the holster and revolver hanging by the door and strapped it on.

Rooster frowned and leaned forward in his chair. "Beyond the back pasture, up on the bluffs. You going to shoot her?"

Cliff paused and then glanced at the gun in the holster. "It's crossed my mind a time or two."

Sprinting toward the barn, he growled, "Fool woman. Why can't she tell a person where she's going?" He slid the side door open and whistled. Sonny tossed his head and trotted toward the barn.

Standing back, he let the horse into the barn then slid the door shut. "We've got our work cut out for us." He threw a blanket, saddle, and headstall on the horse and then led him out of the barn. He stepped into the saddle, and Sonny took off.

Cliff prayed he would spot her on the trail. He would look the fool for being so worried about her, but he didn't care. He would rather she thought of him as an idiot than for him to find her hurt. The thought twisted his gut as panic rose up and pooled in the back of his throat.

They dashed across an open field to where the narrow trail led to the base of the bluffs. Reining the big gray in, they continued at a quick trot. He stood in the stirrups and scanned the ground for evidence of Cat and possible hazards.

The faint smell of skunk brought Sonny up short. The gelding pranced in a circle and tossed his head. "That would be my luck," he said, collecting the horse and steering him back onto the trail.

Lightning flashed silently in the east. Cliff studied the sky. At the rate the storm clouds were moving in and darkness was covering the sky, it wouldn't be long before it was right over them. This area was dangerous enough during the day. At night and in the rain, the rocks and steep incline became deadly. She could slide on the wet rocks and fall into a ravine or slip and go over the edge. If she crawled into a shallow cave for shelter, she could easily find the space already occupied. If she was hiding, he might not be able to find her.

Cliff's heart slammed against his chest when he spotted a mound of black shiny material on the ground several yards ahead. He stepped out of the saddle at the base of a huge overhang. Reaching for the bundle, he found Cat's jacket tied around her backpack. His gaze swept his surroundings. Where was she? Turning his back into the wind, he cupped his hands around his mouth and yelled, "Catrina!"

Catrina held on to the edge of the cliff and her wits with a death grip. "Around 600 B.C. in the Mochica culture in Peru, the puma w-w-were worshipped as gods." Her teeth chattered, and she licked her chapped lips. "There's a sacred gold puma statue, decorated with jewels and a double-headed snake." Earlier she had tucked her bare arms inside her shirt to stay warm; though she was sure she would be frozen by morning, it had helped. "U-u-used in rituals."

"Catrina!"

She paused. The ancient Mochica Gods were coming for her; she could hear their voices in the wind. She wrapped her arms more tightly around herself. She didn't know how long she'd been huddling behind the boulder, but surly the mountain lion and cubs were long gone. She heard her name again. Rising up onto her knees, she glanced over the edge of the rock.

"Woman... Where the hell are you?"

Cliff! She gasped and smiled. Her heart swelled. "My hero!" Anxious to see him, she inched herself closer to the edge.

He stood in front of his horse with his hat pushed back, calloused hands resting on his hips. His intense stare washed across the rocks until he spotted her. "Are you all right?"

Placing her hands on her knees, she leaned forward and yelled, "Cliff! Help me!"

Cliff's heart pounded in his ears. "Stay there. I'll climb up." He removed the lariat from the saddle, slipped it over his shoulder and started up the steep trail.

The smooth surface of his boots slipped on the rocks, and he grabbed onto rocks and trees for leverage. He came down hard on one knee and scraped the side of his hand on a jagged rock. Cursing under his breath, he twisted to his right. Low branches clawed at him as he sidestepped up the sharp incline.

Thank God she hadn't met up with the mountain lion. He had visions of finding her mauled to death. His heart slammed against his chest, the pain threatening to knock him to his knees.

95

Reaching a flat area of the trail, Cliff searched the rocky slope until he spotted the tip of Cat's head several yards below him. Pulling the rope from his shoulder, he yelled, "Catrina, I'm throwing a rope down to you."

She appeared in the open and glanced up. Kneeling, she looked small and vulnerable. But something was wrong... Her arms were missing! His heart leapt into his throat. "Oh my God! Don't move," he hollered, trying to control the panic that threatened to overtake him. "I'm going to tie the rope off and come down for you!"

All of a sudden, Cat pushed her arms out through her sleeves, and yelled. "Just throw me the rope—I can climb up."

Clamping his mouth shut, Cliff stared down at the woman, who flapped her arms as if she could fly. He took a deep breath and sighed. *She's going to be the death of me yet.*

Wiping the sweat from his brow on his shoulder, he tossed the looped end of his rope down and then wrapped the knotted end around his hip. When the rope tightened, he leaned back, bracing himself to hold her weight. Gripping the rope hand over hand, she made her way up the rocky slope.

The hairs on the back of Cliff's neck stood on end. Something was wrong. Turning his head to survey the area, he saw an adult cougar studying him from a top a large rock. With its ears flattened against its head, it screamed, allowing a clear view of its flesh ripping fangs. Gathering the rope in one hand, he pulled his revolver out and fired into the air. The cougar jumped from the rock and fled.

"Did you shoot her?" Panting, Cat stood a couple feet away, her eyes round with concern. Although she shivered violently, her concern was for the animal that wouldn't have hesitated to devour her. Cliff glanced back over his shoulder. He couldn't condemn the cougar, as the same thought had crossed his mind.

"Did you?" She slipped the rope from around her and handed it back to him. The rolling clouds cast a shadow across her face, hiding her expression.

"Did I what?" Cliff asked, collecting his wondering thoughts.

"Did you shoot her?" Cat rubbed her hands up and down her arms, her gaze surveying the area.

"No. I shot over her head." He took a hesitant step toward her, his hands gripping the lariat for control. "You all right?"

Her eyes flashed bright, and she smiled up at him. "I think so."

"You're freezing. Come here." Gathering her into his arms, he stroked his hands across her back and arms. Her arms wrapped around his waist, and she pressed her cheek to his chest.

"I prayed you'd come," she whispered, her warm breath seeped through his shirt, sending heat throughout his body. Closing his eyes, Cliff held her trembling body tight to his. After a moment, his heart slowed to its normal pace. But he would stand there as long as it took to convince his soul that she was safe.

Thunder rumbled off in the distance, and rain clouds hovered overhead, waiting to make their move. "We'd better shake a leg. Think you can make it down the path all right?" She turned her face up toward him, grinned and then nodded. "Good. Let's get out of here before Sonny says to heck with us and heads for home."

Reluctant to let her go, Cliff squeezed Cat tight to him, then released her.

They worked their way back down the steep trail that proved to be much easier than going up. Cat slipped, but Cliff caught her before she fell.

Reaching Sonny, Cliff removed his oilskin duster from the back of his saddle and handed it to Catrina. "Here—put this on." Crossing in front of the horse, he tied the backpack and rope to the front of the saddle. Stroking the big gray's neck, Cliff circled back around and drew up short. With dirt smeared across her face and hands, she clutched the front of the huge duster. She had attempted to roll the sleeves back, but the stiff material prevented more than one turn. Loose, dark hair hung past her shoulders, one side tucked behind one ear. Lips slightly parted as she studied the approaching clouds. She was beautiful, a rancher's dream.

"Ready?" His voice cracked, and he cleared his throat.

"I guess." She offered a half-felt grin.

Cliff stepped into the stirrup and reached out a hand.

Hesitating, she gave him a sideways glance. "Where am I...? I mean...

He couldn't help but grin. "You have two choices. You can sit in front of me like in the barn or behind me." Rain started to fall. "But you'd better hurry up and make up your mind."

She glanced at Sonny's big hindquarters, her perfect brows gathered together. "He won't buck, will he?"

Holding a straight face, his gaze locked with her. "Only if he gets wet." Frowning, she reached up, and Cliff lifted her up behind him. "Hold on tight." She snaked her arms around his waist. Sonny spun around and headed toward home.

The sky opened up, and the rain fell in sheets, making it impossible to see. Pulling his collar up, he tilted his hat against the storm.

Once they reached the ranch, Cliff dropped Cat off at the house. She jogged up the stairs and disappeared inside. He rode to the barn as the strangest feeling came over him. A feeling like part of him had been removed.

Taking his time, Cliff unsaddled Sonny, wiped him down and gave him a handful of oats for his troubles. He couldn't shake the thought of how wonderful Cat felt pressed up against his back. Or how at Sonny's first jump, her fingers splayed wide across his chest before clasping together. Her hair had smelled like spring flowers. His groin tightened painfully. He needed to get this woman out of his house and out of his mind.

The kitchen was empty when Cliff entered the house. He heard the water in the shower running and wondered what she would do if he joined her. Instead, he headed for the stairs. He had been reduced to sneaking down the stairs to taking his showers after Cat went to bed. Tired and cold, he doubted he would get any real rest tonight. If he did happen to fall asleep, he would just dream about her like every other night since she decided to camp out in the middle of his life.

* * * *

Cat snuggled deeper under the blankets. The howling wind and rain pounded the thick windowpanes like vengeful banshees determined to get in. She couldn't sleep, couldn't stop thinking about Cliff and how he had rescued her. Flipping onto her side, she pinched her eyes shut against the haunting memory of how wonderful it felt to lean into his muscular back and breathe in his scent of leather, fresh air and hard work.

She sat up and flipped the covers back. "I'll make a cup of hot chocolate, curl up on the sofa and read the local paper. That should put me sleep."

Clad only in Cliff's denim shirt, which she'd confiscated for a nightgown, Cat crept to the door and opened it. Sneaking out into the hall, she headed toward the stairs. A noise coming from Cliff's room made her stop. She tiptoed over to his door then leaned close and listened. Muffled moans and groans came from within. Gently she opened the door and peeked in. The room was dark, but she spotted Cliff sprawled on his back across a huge, rugged pine post bed. His broad shoulders, chest and waist were bare. The blankets lay askew and barely covered his lower half. His hair looked wet and disheveled. Was he ill? What if he had a fever from riding back in the cold rain? She crept closer.

My God... He's gorgeous.

He moaned and whispered her name. A shiver slithered up her spine, and goose bumps broke out across her body. She took another step. He'd showered. He'd shaved and trimmed his thick dark mustache. With his piercing eyes closed, he appeared younger, vulnerable. The tough exterior he carried around like armor during the day had been washed away in the storm.

She stood next to his bed. Brushing the wet hair from his brow, Cat placed her palm gently against his forehead. No fever. She slid her hand down to his cheek. Cliff sighed, turned his head and kissed her palm. The action seemed so natural, yet the sensation that raced through her body was anything but natural.

Her fingers wandered to his bare shoulder and then lower to brush across the dark curls that carpeted his chest. Drawing in a ragged breath, he groaned and whispered, "My beautiful wildcat."

Cat's heart ricocheted off her ribs. With hooded eyes, Cliff reached out and ran his hand up her bare leg to her thigh. Sliding his hand up to her bare back, he pulled her down onto the bed next to him. His warm lips captured hers. His tongue coaxed hers into a primitive dance, and Cat was lost in the passion.

Chapter Eight

Cliff sensed something was wrong before he even opened his eyes. A soft, warm, naked body lay curled against his side. He peeked at her under half closed lids. Catrina's head rested on his shoulder, and her long dark hair flowed over his arm and down her back. A soft purr slipped through her lips, her warm breath washed across his bare chest.

Oh my God! What have I done?

Now what? Panic started to bubble in the pit of his stomach. There was only one thing he could do. He needed to get out of there before she woke up.

Making love to Cat had been a mistake. Yeah, he'd enjoyed every minute of it, but it never should have happened. After last night, she was bound to think they had a future together. He couldn't live through another relationship. And even if he wanted to, which he didn't, it could never happen.

Without a sound, he slid out from under the sleeping woman. Slipping the pillow under her head, she groaned and pulled it against her chest. The worn floorboards were cold against his feet as he slipped into his jeans. Grabbing a shirt from the chair, he snaked his arms into the sleeves. Reaching for the door, he shot a quick glance back to the bed and the amazing woman who lay curled around the disheveled blankets.

Too bad it could never be anything more than this.

* * * *

A couple of hours later, Cliff ushered the last calf from the protection of its mother, while Rooster closed the gate. Puffs of steam escaped from beneath Cliff's mustache, and he flipped his collar up against the early morning chill. His boots slipped on the muddy ground as he trudged to where Sonny stood tied to the rail. His mood was as gray and grim as the day ahead forecasted to be.

He could still taste the sweetness of Catrina on his lips, feel her curves pressed against him, see her eyes aflame with desire. He shook his head. What had he done? Each night she'd come to him in his dreams, and they made love. And each night the dreams became more vivid, more passionate. Then last night, in the midst of another dream, she'd materialized. And this morning, what he'd thought had been a beautiful, erotic dream had dissolved into a nightmare.

Reality had finally hit Cliff over the head, and like a reptile, he'd slithered out of the bed and slipped into the darkness. He'll never know what would have happened if he'd stayed or what Catrina thought when she awoke. Cliff glanced at the house, his empty gut twisted. *What did she think when she woke up alone?*

She was far too independent, always running off and getting into trouble. He didn't have time to keep an eye on her, much less keep her in line. One corner of his mouth cinched up in a lop-sided grin, and a warm feeling engulfed him. One thing he knew for sure, if he kept her around, she would drive him crazy all day and all night.

Cliff scraped the red clay off the bottom of his boots, grabbed the reins and stepped into the stirrup. Even though making love to her had been a wonderful mistake, he'd never let it happen again. Women weren't worth the pain and trouble they would eventually cause. Besides, he planned on being busy with branding all day, which would keep them far apart.

* * * *

Catrina awoke in a cocoon of warmth and security. She didn't want to move or even open her eyes. Rolling on to her side, she inhaled the familiar scent of the amazing man who'd made love to her several times during the night. His kisses were passionate, and his rough calloused hands had brought her to heights she hadn't experienced before. She had suspected a storm brewed under his sober exterior, but she had no idea the depth or magnitude of it. Even though every muscle in her body ached, she reveled in her exhaustion. The man had done things to her she had no idea were possible, let alone legal.

Sitting up, she swept her gaze around the cozy little room. It was definitely a man's room. A heap of clothes covered an old chair wedged in the far corner, and the dark antique dresser didn't match the rugged pine post bed. Leaning back against the headboard, Cat pulled the covers up under her chin. For the first time in her life, she felt like she belonged somewhere—to someone. This could be a true home for her.

Glancing around, she couldn't find a clock in the room, and she couldn't recall seeing Cliff wear a watch. She shook her head and laughed. "He doesn't know the time and doesn't care. He sets his own schedule, eats when he's hungry and sleeps when he's tired."

Throwing back the covers, she reached for the wrinkled denim shirt and slipped it over her head then stood. Taking her time, she made the bed and contemplated sorting and folding the clothes on the chair. But she wanted to see Cliff, so instead she wandered back to her room and dressed in the jeans, white-fringed shirt covered with big red flowers and the new red cowboy boots she'd bought in town.

After weaving her hair into two braids, Cat positioned her red cowboy hat on her head and smiled at her refection in the mirror. She could pass for a rancher's wife. Digging out the belt buckle she'd found in her mother's things, she attached it to her new belt, threaded it through the loops and hooked it. Cat rushed down the stairs, with her new sheep-lined denim jacket slung over her shoulder, her new boots tapping like wooden shoes on the steps. This was her first branding, and she couldn't wait to see Cliff and Rooster in action. She planned on taking lots of photos.

Reaching for the rotary phone that hung on the wall, Cat dialed the medical center.

"Black River Medical Center, Jeannie speaking. How may I help you?"

"Hi, Jeannie! This is Catrina Pearson. May I speak to Millie?" She twirled the cord impatiently around her finger.

"I'm sorry she's already over in physical therapy."

"Oh! Do you know if there are any messages for me from Sandy Huset?" Cat waited and heard papers being shuffled.

"It doesn't look like there is anything here. Sorry."

Frustrated, she sighed. "All right. Thanks for looking. Would you tell Millie that Cliff is branding today. I'll call her later and tell her all about it."

"Sure thing, Catrina. Goodbye."

Disheartened, Cat prayed the woman wouldn't leave town before she had a chance to talk to her. *Sandy Huset is my only hope of finding out who my father is.* After sliding her arms in to her coat, she snatched up her camera and headed out.

* * * *

Rooster stood in the open doorway of the International truck, retrieving a half-smoked cigar from the ashtray. Clenching it between his teeth, he flicked the end of a wooden match with his thumbnail and lit the well-deserved solace.

Down the ranch road, a cloud of red dust billowed into the sky as two vehicles emerged on to the Circle D. An old blue, four-door Suburban pulled up next to where Rooster stood by the barn. A handful of young men from the reservation jumped out. The driver grinned and nodded to Rooster. "Heard you were branding today. Need some help?"

The young guys always looked forward to branding and the chance to wrestle calves. At his age, Rooster welcomed their help. Limping around the back of the truck, white smoke circling his beat-up black Stetson, he greeted them. "Does a coyote have cockleburs?"

A stream of tobacco juice shot from the driver's mouth. He grinned, and then he and the other three wrestlers moseyed toward the holding pen where Cliff sat atop Sonny.

Ester White Fox, who was Cliff's mother, and a couple other women, immerged from the second vehicle. Ester smiled and waved. Carrying pots of food, the three little women, as round as they were tall, scurried toward the house like prairie dogs headin' for their hole.

Rooster turned to glance at Cliff. His hat shadowed his face, but Rooster could guess at his bewilderment. As far as Rooster knew, Ester hadn't come out to the ranch since Cliff divorced Nora and turned his back on his Native American life. In the past, it had only been Cliff, Doug and himself here on branding day, which made for a long day of hard work. But for some reason that neither he nor Cliff knew of, it looked like today there was going to be a party.

As the older women disappeared into the house, Cat shuffled out onto the porch. She looked like she'd just stepped out of a western magazine, all dressed up in her flashy new duds. By their hoots and whistles, he knew the young guys had spotted her, too. She didn't dare turn to see Cliff's reaction, but couldn't help but chuckle when the ruckus abruptly stopped.

Cat sauntered down the wooden steps of the ranch house and strolled toward him. When she reached him, she stopped, opened her jacket and twirled around. "Well? What do you think?" She beamed with excitement.

Rooster gripped the brim of his hat and shoved it back an inch. "Girlie, you're prettier than a field of flowering cactus."

"Thank you," she replied, but glanced beyond him. Her smile wavered at the sound of Cliff barking orders and the young men scurrying through the fence.

"So, what's put the hop in your step and that twinkle in your eye this morning?" he asked, hoping to distract her. She blushed and gazed at the ground.

So...they've slept together. By her shy smile, he guessed that she was pleased with what had happened between her and Cliff. Cliff, on the other hand, had been meaner all morning than a hungry grizzly in a creek with no fish.

With her hands in her pockets, Catrina flapped her jacket open and closed in a nervous and shy manner, drawing his attention.

Rooster's world stopped spinning, and he stumbled to one side. His chest constricted, his throat closed up, and he couldn't breathe. For a moment, he felt as if someone had punched him, knocking the breath out of him. Leaning against his truck for support, he blinked, not believing his own eyes.

"Are you all right?" Cat asked, moving closer and taking him by the arm. "Here sit down." She helped him onto the tailgate.

"I'm fine," he said, not wanting to draw any more attention. "I just need to sit a minute." *Could it be?*

"Stay here. I'll run to the house and get you a glass of water."

Rooster shook his head. "I don't need any water, but I'd like to know where you got that belt buckle."

"Oh!" Cat opened her jacket and tilted the buckle up with her hands. "I found it when I was going through my mother's things after she died. I don't know where she got it. I'd never seen it before." Gripping the cuff of her jacket with her fingertips, she wiped the shiny silver buckle with her sleeve.

She glanced up and smiled. "Here comes my car."

Rooster turned and saw Doug pull up in front of the house. "You go talk to Doug," he said, giving her a slight push. He needed a few minutes to figure everything out. "I'm fine now."

"Are you sure?" Her beautiful brown eyes were filled with concern, and she placed a hand on his shoulder.

"Yeah. Run along," he coaxed nodding his head.

Catrina trotted off toward her car.

August 31, 1965 hit Rooster like a bullet straight to the heart. Closing his eyes, the events that happened so many years ago replayed in his mind. The heat, the confusion, and the pain felt so real, so fresh. His heart slammed against his ribs, and white and silver spots danced in the darkness.

He stood behind the chutes and watched his nineteen-year-old son strap himself to the back of one ton of pure hate. Jim turned, smiled at his father, then nodded his head. The gate swung open, and everything changed forever.

The huge black bull named 'The Executioner' bolted from the chute, spun to the right and bucked. A rope of white snot flew from the beast's nostrils as he swung his massive head and horns attempting to connect with the young cowboy on its back. The enraged bull twisted back to the left. Losing his footing, the bull fell and rolled, taking his rider with him. Trapped by his rigging, Jim disappeared into the dirt beneath the massive killing machine.

The sound of the crowd's screams still echoed in Rooster's mind. He wiped his sweaty palms on his jeans. Twenty-eight years, but it seemed like yesterday. Every day the pain of losing his only son gnawed at his soul.

On the day of the rodeo, Jim's last ride received the highest score, which won him the All-Around belt buckle. The same buckle Cat wore today. The same buckle he'd presented to his son at the hospital.

A few minutes after Rooster arrived at the hospital to see his son, Cathryn Pearson had appeared. He recalled that Jim had dated her for only a short time. Amongst all the confusion in the emergency room and readying Jim for surgery, Jim must have given Cathryn the buckle. Cathryn disappeared a few days after Jim's funeral. Had she been pregnant when she left town?

He turned and watched Catrina. She walked side by side with Doug, her long strides easily matching the tall man's. She threw her head back and laughed at something he said. Did he glimpse a resemblance to Jim? At that moment, the portion of Rooster's heart that had died so many years ago flickered back to life. Could Catrina Pearson be his granddaughter, or was this just a cruel coincidence?

* * * *

What in the Sam hell's going on? Cliff slouched on the back of Sonny and watched as people converged on his world. His mother had taken it upon herself, though uninvited, to cross the bridge that had separated their two worlds for the past five years. She waved and smiled like she'd been expected to show up on branding day with a carload of food. His empty stomach growled.

He understood why Doug asked the four younger guys to come out and help; he and Rooster were getting a little long in the tooth. Cliff glanced over at Rooster. The old boy looked a little peaked, sitting there on the tailgate. He made a mental note to keep an eye on him today, make sure he didn't overdo it. Maybe it was a good thing Doug arranged for some help. Doug didn't mind hard work. If there was a way to get it done quicker, so he could get back to his favorite pastime of chasing women, he was all for it.

Just then, Doug slipped his arm around Cat's waist as they strolled toward him. She laughed and smiled at something he said. Cliff felt a sudden urge to rope and hogtie his cousin until the old boy cooled off. His jovial cousin helped Catrina up and into the back of Rooster's pickup. She stopped, rested her hand on the Rooster's shoulder and then whispered something to him. The old cowboy smiled, nodded in agreement and then patted her hand. Catrina straightened and pinned Cliff with her gaze. A slow, shy, yet seductive smirk crossed her full lips. Her eyes sparked with the secrets they shared.

Doug glanced up at Cliff and asked, "What's the matter with you?"

Ignoring his comment, Cliff growled, "About time you showed up. You got your irons?" Doug raised his arm to show that, yes, he had his branding irons. "Then get the fire started." As he urged his horse forward, another car pulled in. He pulled Sonny up and stared as Nora crawled out of her little yellow sports car. All smiles, she straightened her clothes, tucked her hair behind her ears and waltzed toward them.

"What the hell is *she* up to?" Cliff brushed his hand over his thick mustache as he studied Nora. The only reason his ex-wife would be here was to stir up trouble. She waved like they were good friends and then hopped up on the tailgate. After she planted a kiss on her grandfather's cheek, she turned and spoke to Catrina. No doubt, his ex-wife had found out that Catrina was staying with him, and she was here to check out the situation. If she had any idea of what he and Cat had done last night, she'd send up smoke signals and put a war party together. Even after five years, she had a crazy notion that one day he'd take her back.

With Nora's arrival, more hoots and hollers came from the four young Casanovas in the calf pen. Cliff turned and scowled. The ruckus ceased.

He eased Sonny toward the gate, yet before he could reach for the latch, one of the guys jogged over and opened it for him. The kid tugged on the tattered brim of his hat respectfully and then closed the gate. It set Cliff's teeth on edge that the four *boys* had clearly put him in the aged category with Doug and Rooster. Heck, he remembered when he thought thirty-two was old, too.

Sonny slowly edged along the fence, eager to get started on the day's work. Cliff glanced over the fence to Catrina. Her inappropriate outfit, topped off with a bright red, felt cowboy hat, no doubt, had been a figment of Nora's cruel imagination. Now he knew why his ex-wife had driven all the way out here. Her intention had been to embarrass Cat. As if knowing he was thinking about her, Nora turned and grinned sweetly.

Women. All they did was aggravate him and disrupt his world. Maybe it wasn't right to lump Catrina and Nora together, like he'd been lumped in with Rooster, but when it came right down to it, all women really wanted was to hogtie a man and either run his life or screw the whole thing up. He shot Cat another glance, and she winked. Growing uncomfortable, he shifted in the saddle and looked away.

Sonny tossed his head, and Cliff loosened his grip on the reins. He was irritated with himself for not wanting to admit that on some level he'd known he hadn't been dreaming last night. Not at first when he'd felt her soft hand roam across his chest, but when he pulled her down onto the bed and her lips touched his. The jolt had been like nothing he'd ever felt before. At that moment, he hadn't dared speak. He didn't want to stop what was building between them and give her a chance to come to her senses.

Turning his attention to the bawling calves, Cliff swung his rope a few times to build his loop. The four anxious flankers pushed each other, seeing who would fall into the mud first, while the scarred calves huddled together at the far end of the pen. This was turning into a three-ring circus. Cliff sighed. "Well, it can't get any worse," he muttered under his breath.

Then his brother Charlie pulled up in his black pickup.

* * * *

Cat stood in the back of the truck with her camera in hand, her denim jacket buttoned, the sheepskin collar turned up to protect her ears and neck against the cool breeze.

She studied Cliff through the lens and snapped several shots as he rode into the pen. Then something caught his attention, and he stared over his shoulder as if danger loomed close by in the bushes. The man had two sides like a coin. Today he was distant, rigid and unapproachable, yet last night he'd held her gently in his arms, their love making more passionate than anything she'd ever experienced before.

Cliff shot her a quick glance and the intense emotion in his eyes was unreadable. Her body shuddered, and a soft groan slipped between her parted lips at the thought of being in his arms again.

"This could be trouble," Nora stated from where she sat next to Rooster on the tailgate. The old cowboy patted the girl's leg with reassurance. Cat glanced up as a black pickup pulled in. A man she guessed to be in his late twenties slid out from behind the wheel. Despite the cool weather, he wore no jacket. His long legs were clad in faded blue jeans, which hugged his muscular thighs like a second skin. A tight fitting gray T-shirt encased his chest and dark walnut arms. With an air of confidence, he strolled, unhurried, toward the calf pen. He glanced at Nora and Rooster. Once he spotted her, a slow smirk softened his chiseled features. Cat shivered as his dark stare raked her from head to toe. He crawled through the fence, and she saw the long shiny black ponytail that hung down to the middle of his back.

"Who is that?" Cat whispered her voice cracking as she spoke.

Nora twisted to one side. With a smug expression, she said, "That's Charlie White Fox, Cliff's brother."

Charlie? But before Cat could question the girl's remark, Rooster glanced up and shook his head, as if to say that now was not the time nor place for explanations. Cat clamped her lips together and turned her attention back to Cliff. He regarded his brother's presence with a scowl, then turned and headed toward the calves.

With slow easy steps, he pressed his horse closer to the huddle. He swung the rope over his head twice before letting it fly. Cat captured each movement on film. The loop hit the mud, and the calf jumped through it and ran off. Cliff recoiled his rope. The calves bunched closer to the fence, but then one broke away from the rest and ran. Zooming out, Cat took several shots as Cliff twirled once, threw the loop and caught both of the calf's back legs. He dragged the bawling calf to the guys by the fire. Two of the men flipped the calf on to its side and removed Cliff's rope. Holding the calf down, Doug placed the hot branding iron on its side, and white smoke billowed up around the crew. Stumbling to its feet, the disoriented calf bellered and trotted off, not looking any worse for wear. Cat turned her face into her collar as the stench of burnt hair, cow manure, and mud drifted toward her.

"Wow! That was awesome!" Cat grinned, her heart hammering wildly in her chest.

The truck rocked as Rooster hopped off the tailgate and limped toward the fence. Stooping over, he crawled between the rails and hobbled through the deep mud to the men standing in the middle of the pen.

"That's different from what I've seen in the movies," Cat said, snapping photos of the old cowboy as he headed to make sure everything was done right. "On TV there are always two guys roping the calves."

Nora got to her feet and brushed off the seat of her pants. "When the calves are small like these," she said, "It's better to use one roper. When the calves are older and larger, then you have to have a header and a heeler."

"A header and a what?" Nora was speaking a whole different language.

Nora grinned and sat on the edge of the truck box. "Do you want me to explain what each guy's job is?"

"That would be great. You wouldn't mind?"

Nora waved a hand in the air. "No problem. Now watch, Cliff's called the roper. He moves into position nice and easy so he doesn't spook the calves. He'll wait until he has a clear shot before he even twirls his loop. See," Nora pointed, and continued. "He heeled that calf by catching both back legs. Now he's dallying the rope around the saddle horn, then he'll drag the calf to the flankers by the fire. It's more difficult to heel the calves when their feet sink in the mud."

"This is going to take all day," Cat said, bewildered. "There must be over 200 calves there."

Nora chuckled. "One man can rope and drag sixty-five to seventy-five calves in an hour. The flankers wrestled the calf to the ground and held it down. Looks like Charlie is the vaccinator today. He'll inoculate each calf."

"These calves are babies," Cat murmured, feeling sorry for the little calves separated from their mothers.

"The youngest calf should be at least two weeks old before branding. They'll be put back with their mothers until October when they're separated and sold or shipped."

Cat eyed the woman sitting on the edge of the truck. She needed to remember this wasn't the city, and this was the way things were done on a ranch.

"Doug's doing the branding today." Nora's voice cut into her thoughts. "He knows which brand goes on which calf and where."

"What do you mean by that?" Cat twisted around to face Nora.

"The Circle D brand goes on Cliff's calves on the left side, and the Double D goes on Doug's calves on the shoulder. Each year, Doug brands twenty-five to thirty of Cliff's calves with his own brand."

"Why would he do that?"

"These calves will be donated to the reservation in Doug's name. This is Cliff's way of helping his people." She laughed. "Cliff doesn't think anyone knows that they're his calves, but everyone does."

Although he'd cut his hair, grew a mustache, wore chaps, spurs and a silk bandana around his neck, deep down Cliff still thought of his mother, brother and others on the reservation as family. Cat wondered if he let himself in on the secret, or if he'd buried it along with all the other feelings he didn't want to deal with.

"Hey, Catrina," Doug yelled, drawing her attention. "Do you want to brand one?"

Wondering if she should, Cat turned and looked at Nora for guidance. "Go ahead," Nora replied. "I'll hold your camera." Handing over her camera, Cat jumped off the tailgate and crawled through the fence. Her heart raced with excitement. She was in the pen with all the calves, and she was actually going to brand one. *Oh my god, there's a woman in the holding pen,* she thought. *I wonder if the world is going to come to an end.*

Keeping eye contact with Doug, she approached the men gathered around the small fire. She didn't dare glance up at Cliff, knowing his scowling face would cause her to bust out laughing.

A moment later, he dragged another calf to the flankers, and they wrestled it to the ground. Doug walked up behind her, hot branding iron in his hand. "Here," he said wrapping his arms around her. "I'll help you, so we don't have to do it twice."

Cat ran her teeth over her lower lip. "Are you sure about this?" She shot Doug a glance over her shoulder.

"You'll do fine, darlin'." The calf cried out, and she glanced down at it. The two men holding the calf down nodded in encouragement. "Grab the iron like this." Doug placed it in her hand and then placed his hand over the top of hers. "That's right. Now press it firmly against the hide." He leaned into her and pressed the hot iron onto the calf's side. White smoke and the smell of burnt hair rose up around her. A circle with the letter D in the center replaced the calf's fur.

"That won't rinse off in the rain," Rooster said. The other men gathered around and laughed.

"You did good," Doug whispered close to her ear. "You're a natural."

"She's a chip off the ol' salt block all right." Rooster playfully nudged her. Cat stumbled backwards in the deep mud, causing both her and Doug to lose their footing. Their feet tangled together, and she screamed as they fell. Doug hit the ground, and Cat landed in his lap.

"I'm so sorry!" she said over her shoulder. Doug faked being dead, his arms flung out wide. Cat laughed and rolled off the man into the mud. "Are you all right?"

Doug looked up and then past her, his expression altering to one more serious. Her gaze shot up to Cliff's. He was not amused. With his eyes squinted, he had a look, like the one Clint Eastwood was famous for when he was about to draw down on some over-confident fool. At first glance, you're convinced Clint's a real bad hombre, but if you look deeper, you notice he looks more confused than dangerous. She waited, expecting to hear cheesy, spaghetti western music. Unable to control herself any longer, Cat burst out laughing, shattering the tense atmosphere.

Charlie reached out a hand and helped her up. Her smile faded. The intensity of Charlie's ebony eyes caused a chill to slither up her spine as they studied each other for several moments. Under his left eye, he sported an old, raised scare, about an inch and a half long. His strong jaw and cheekbones appeared as if an artist carved this masterpiece from a piece of rich, dark walnut. The man oozed strength and arrogance. He was magnificent.

Charlie turned away breaking the incredible hold he had on Cat and came face to face with Cliff. Cat held her breath as the two brothers stood no more than three feet apart. She shot an alarming glance around the group of men. No one uttered a word or moved.

Stubborn and proud, the two men struggled for control over an unspoken, unresolved battle. After several moments, a silent message passed between them, and at the same time, they both turned and walked in opposite directions.

Cat exhaled when Cliff stepped into the stirrup, spun his horse around and cantered off toward the calves.

Why was he so angry?

Cat offered Doug a hand. The older man stood, grinned and then winked. Several of the other men turned away, as if they were trying to hide their expressions.

She stared after Cliff. Could it be he was jealous of the attention she was getting from Doug, Charlie and the other guys? The thought that he might really care for her warmed her insides and set her heart to beat a little quicker.

* * * *

After standing in the back of the truck taking numerous snapshots,

Cat hoped she'd be able to use several of the photos for the Spring Art Festival in New York.

Rooster limped to the edge of the fence, pushed back his hat and scratched his head. "Hey, girlie, know what time it is?"

Cat shoved her jacket sleeve up and glanced at her watch. "It's almost 2:00."

"Well, no wonder I'm hungry enough to eat a flea-riddled saddle blanket." When he grinned, she snapped his picture. "What do you say we mosey up to the house and see what the ladies have for us?"

Cat smiled, then glanced past him to where the men branded another calf. "Sounds good to me, but what about them?" She pointed the camera toward the pen.

Without glancing back, he said, "They're going to come in after they finish with that one." He crawled through the fence and helped her down from the truck.

Cat walked in step with the weathered old cowboy. Halfway to the house, he slipped an arm around her waist. He looked melancholy and tired. "Are you doing all right?" she asked, hoping she didn't sound like she was prying.

His smile never wavered, but his eyes held unshed tears. "I'm as fine as frog's hair." Just before they reached the steps, he gave her a quick squeeze and then released her. An arthritic, twisted hand, weathered, and covered with age spots, gripped the railing behind her. They climbed the stairs in silence.

Once they reached the porch, Cat heard the men coming up behind them. She stepped off to the side, twisted around and held the door open. The hungry men filed into the house, yet Cliff and Charlie were still several yards back. They walked together, Cliff's battered and sweat-stained hat pulled low over his eyes, his chaps and shirt crusted in dried, red mud. She heard the faint sound of his spurs clinking as he crossed the drying ground.

Charlie's clothes were muddy also, and his long ponytail hung over one shoulder. Lifting her camera, she snapped several shots of the two men before they noticed her. Although they chose to live in different worlds, they weren't all that different from each other. Both were strong, proud, idealistic and most of all stubborn.

Cliff's gaze locked with hers, his mouth set in a firm line as he mounted the stairs. Both men reached the porch at the same time. For a split second, everything stopped, and Cat held her breath. Then Charlie took one step back, and Cliff entered the house. Confused, Cat glanced at Charlie. One corner of his mouth hiked up in a slight grin, he winked, and then motioned for her to enter before him. She imagined he'd taken a big risk by showing up today. Cliff had apparently accepted him on some level, and Charlie showed his respect by allowing Cliff to enter the house before him.

* * * *

Cliff and Charlie's mother Ester and a couple of her friends had put together a feast. The house smelled wonderful. Casserole dishes, platters of sliced meat, homemade breads, cookies and cakes covered the old round table.

Pausing, Cat raised her camera and took pictures as everyone helped themselves to the food. She enjoyed the great food and the easy conversation. She laughed and joked and even let herself pretend that she really did belong to this family.

As she watched everyone, she played the well-mastered game of "What if". What if she and Cliff got married? She already knew the sex would be great. She fantasized about the two of them having a family together.

Glancing around, she found herself sitting off in the corner alone. Once again, she was on the outside looking in. This wasn't her home, and this wasn't her family. She didn't belong here or anywhere for that matter. She'd done what she'd always done. As a kid, she'd wiggle into the middle of a friend's family, hoping to be accepted, and then pretended that it was her family. Except eventually she'd return to her own house, where it was only her and her mother, when her mother was there and not working one of her many jobs. Whoever said, "You want what you can't have" must have said it with Cat in mind. She'd grown up wanting what every other kid took for granted. A home with a mother and father, brothers and sisters and maybe a few cousins. Cat may have grown up and moved on, but her dreams of belonging to a family had never changed. She wanted this kind of family, where people talked and laughed, and after everything was said and done, they still loved each other.

She glanced over to where Cliff stood talking to his mother. He'd been on her mind all day, but he'd been avoiding her. If they made eye contact, he appeared angry, and then he would look away. It was obvious that he wasn't interested in any type of long-term relationship. That was okay. She'd be leaving soon, and until then she'd take whatever he was willing to give.

A long time ago, she'd learned that the only person you could really depend on, really rely on, was yourself.

She'd be wise to remember that.

* * * *

It was dark, and all the chores were done. Everyone had left except for Doug, Rooster and a couple of the younger guys. Cliff and the other four had come in to play the traditional-after-branding poker game, and he was itching to rake in a big pot.

"I'm going to take a quick shower and change into some clean clothes," Cliff said, placing a plate of sandwiches and several beers on the table.

He headed up to his room to gather up some clean clothes. Although he appreciated the extra help with branding, he hadn't liked the way Charlie, Doug and the other guys had been eyein' up Cat all day. Reaching the top of the stairs, he paused. Her bedroom door was closed. They needed to talk about last night, but now wasn't the time.

They played poker, drank beer and smoked cigars for several hours. Cliff was even ahead a few dollars. Then out of the blue, Doug said, "Well, guys, it's late. I think it's time to head out."

Cliff glanced up from his cards and saw Doug nudge the man next to him with his elbow. One by one the other guys looked up and nodded. Dropping their cards, they all stood and filed out without another word.

"What the heck is going on?" Cliff turned in his chair and saw Cat standing on the stair landing. She wore his faded denim shirt, the sleeves rolled halfway up her arms. Her hair messed as if she'd just made love, her high cheekbones flushed. One long, smooth, bare leg peeked out from behind the newel post.

He swallowed hard and wiped his damp palms on his jeans. Every muscle in his body tightened as the flowery scent of the shampoo she favored drifted across the room. Right then he knew, no amount of time would ever erase her sweet taste or rub out the memory of how

115

wonderful it felt to have her amazing body tangled around him.

Though it hadn't felt like it, and his body screamed that he was a fool, he reminded himself that last night had been a mistake. They needed to talk.

Cliff stood and crossed to her. "About last night—"

Cat stepped forward, laid a hand against his chest and gazed at him through heavily lidded eyes. She licked her lips and reached for his hand. "I'm leaving soon. Let's not waste the night talking." She turned and led him up the stairs.

Chapter Nine

Cat dialed the number to the nursing home, apprehensive about telling Millie her plans had changed and that she would be leaving for New York sooner than anticipated. Her car hadn't sustained as much damage from floating several hours in the ditch as she had expected, so she was free to leave whenever she wanted. Besides, Millie was receiving good care, and there really wasn't anything Cat could do right now to help her. *There isn't anything keeping me from leaving.*

An image of Cliff stretched out on his bed, the covers resting low over his hips popped into her head. She worried her lower lip once again. Even though they had slept together, he made it clear he didn't want to get into a serious relationship.

"Black River Medical Center, Jeannie speaking. May I help you?"

Cat smiled, thankful for a chance to speak with Jeannie. "Hi Jeannie, this is Catrina Pearson."

"Hi, Catrina. How's it going?"

"Fine, thanks. I called to speak with Millie, but I'm glad you answered." She mentally crossed her fingers, hoping the little blonde had some information for her. "I hate to be such a pain, but could you look and see if there are any messages for me?"

"Sure, just a second." Cat waited, and after a moment, Jeannie returned on the line. "Sorry, I don't see any."

Cat sighed. "That's all right. Thanks for checking."

"I'll take the phone to Millie. She just wandered back to her room."

"Thanks, Jeannie." There was always the chance that Sandra Huset had already left town. If so, then the secret of Cat's father's identity left

117

with her.

"Hello?" Millie answered her voice frail and soft.

A lump formed in the back of Cat's throat. Her grandmother sounded so fragile. "Hi. It's Catrina."

"Oh! Hi, dear. It's so nice to hear your voice."

"How's physical therapy going?"

Millie heaved a great sigh. "I guess it's going as well as can be expected." The line was silent for a couple of seconds. "Slow and painful, but it's coming along. I doubt I'll ever get around again without a walker."

Cat strained to hear Millie's words. "I'm so sorry. I wish there were something I could do for you."

"You are dear. It's meant so much just having you here with me. I wish your mother and I had been closer. I never understood why Cathryn felt she couldn't come to me when she found out she was pregnant." Cat overheard her shaky sigh. "But I'm sure she's pleased that we're finally together as a family."

Were they really a family? Cat knew her mother and grandmother hadn't been close, however, her mother had never given her a reason why. Although Cat had only been here for a short time, she felt guilty that she hadn't spent more of that time with her grandmother. *Maybe she'd like to go for a ride in the country? The fresh air would do her good.*

"I was thinking," Millie, continued her voice stronger. "With the insurance money I'm getting from my house, I thought I would move a new trailer house out on my land."

"That sounds nice, but shouldn't you wait and see how your recovery goes?" Cat asked, unsure if it was a good idea for Millie to live so far out of town by herself. What did Dr. Crawford think about this?

"It's not like I'm going to be out there all alone." Her joy was evident. "You'll be there to help me. It'll be so nice."

"Oh!" Cat closed her eyes and drew a reinforcing breath. "Well, don't rush into anything. You have plenty of time. You just concentrate on getting better." Cat rubbed at her throbbing temple. How was she going to tell Millie she was leaving? "We'll talk about it later, okay?"

"Okay, dear." Millie's voice grew weak, and she coughed, a pathetic cough. "I'd better rest now."

"We'll talk again," Cat said, hoping to pacify her.

"I don't know what I'd do without you, Cathryn—I mean Catrina. You're all I have left."

"You rest. I'll call you after lunch. Goodbye."

A black cloud of guilt hovered over Cat's head. She should have told Millie she was leaving, but the old woman had them living together in a trailer house, where her home had once been.

Maybe this wasn't the right time to leave. What if Millie's health took a turn for the worse, and she couldn't make it back in time?

She crossed to the door and walked out onto the porch. The clouds and cool weather from the previous day had moved on. A handful of birds dotted the blue sky, darting back and forth, competing for any unsuspecting insects. What a beautiful place; she could be happy living here. After her premier in New York, maybe she would come back and try to make a life for herself in Black River. There would always be opportunities for freelance work, although she couldn't be away from her grandmother for too long.

Across the yard, she watched Cliff lead a horse into the barn. Even though he was concealed in jeans, a long sleeved work-shirt and chaps, Cat had no problem conjuring up a more revealing and delicious image of him. Her heart started to pound, and she suddenly had to talk to him.

* * * *

More content then he had felt in years, Cliff positioned his saddle on the big gray's withers and reached for the girth strap. Thoughts of making love to Cat the past two nights filled his conscience with peace and other emotions he wasn't ready or quite yet willing to explore. Each night started with a frantic need to be naked, to feel skin against skin, then with slow deliberate moves, they took the time to explore each other. He grinned, recalling how she had stretched and purred when his mustache brushed from the back of her neck to the hollow of her back.

She'd showed this old cowboy a couple of new tricks.

Cliff slipped the headstall over Sonny's head and buckled it. He patted the horse's neck, tightened the cinch and led him out of the barn.

"Where are you off to?" Cat strolled toward him, her thumbs hooked in the belt loops of her tight Wranglers, hair loose around her shoulders. She ambled to the fence, leaned against the post and kicked the dirt with the toe of her boots.

"Nice shit-kickers," he said, nodding to her red cowboy boots.

She grinned and brushed her hair behind her ears. "Thanks."

"I'm going to take the cattle back out to the big pasture. Want to ride along?" He remembered the last time they rode double and chuckled when she gave him a suspicious glance. "Can you ride?"

"Yes, but it's been awhile."

"I've got just the horse for you. Here." He handed her his reins. He ambled back into the barn, grabbed a halter and lead rope and crossed to Jack's stall. He slipped the halter over the sorrel's head and led him out. "This here's Jack. He knows English, Ute and some sign language." Cat giggled and brushed her hand along the sorrel's neck.

"He looks gentle," she said, nuzzling the side of the animal's face. Jack closed his eyes and soaked up the attention.

Cliff's body stirred to life. He envied the old horse. But he couldn't blame the old boy; he would've done the same thing. "He's so smooth he'll rock you to sleep."

Once Jack was saddled, Cliff hoisted Cat up onto the horse's back and adjusted the stirrups. "How's that feel?" he asked, holding onto her ankle after he positioned her boot into the stirrup. The scent of flowers mixed with horse, leather and fresh air. She glanced down at him and smiled. Her beauty paralyzed him. How on earth had this crazy woman worked herself so far under his skin?

"Feels just right to me." One corner of her mouth hitched up in a saucy little grin.

Mounted, they followed the lead cow as she headed for the gate he'd opened earlier. "Hep. Hep. Let's go," he said, slapping his hand flat against his chaps. A sharp whistle sent the lead cow into a trot.

The calves jumped and bucked as they raced past their mothers, only to circle around and bellow as if to say, "Hurry up—we're almost free!" Cat laughed at their antics.

Old Jack ambled along behind the cattle as they crossed the large open field as if he had been set on autopilot. Cliff rode alongside Cat through the tall grass in silence. As she watched him from the corner of her eye, everything about him fascinated her. It was as if he were one of her childhood heroes sprung to life from an old western movie. He had the part down pat, with his weathered hat, dusty stained chaps and muddy spurs. Even his no-nonsense manner of speech, arrogant swagger and the way he stepped into the stirrup and moved as one with his horse paralleled the cowboys of the old west.

Cliff glanced over. With his head slightly tilted, he studied her with sharp eyes, then leisurely brushed his long mustache down with one hand and winked. Cat's heart raced, and she couldn't help but smile back at him. She responded to this man like no other, but her mind questioned, was it because of "who" the man was or because of "what" he was?

A slight breeze tugged at her loose hair, and she tucked it behind her ear. Approaching the opened gate, the cattle slowly filed through one at a time. After the horses walked through, Cliff dismounted and closed the gate. She watched him as he worked, every movement perfected by years of practice. The question rose again, and she shoved it aside. It made no difference what her feelings were, he had made it clear that this truce was only temporary, which would make leaving much easier.

Cliff turned and surprised her with a flower that had several light purple pedals surrounding a spiny, dark purple center. He handed her the flower. Though his lips never moved, his rich ebony eyes revealed the depths of his desire. He placed one hand on her leg then slowly slid it up to rest on her thigh.

Breathe, she told herself, bringing the flower to her nose, inhaling deeply. This rugged, half wild cowboy proved to be full of surprises. Did he plan to take her right there in a bed of wild purple flowers?

"Coneflower," he said his voice low and deep. "Indians have used it for coughs, sore throats and even for headaches."

"I don't have a headache," she stammered, and then realized she'd ruined the moment.

He turned away and glanced at the ground. "That's a good thing then, I guess." He reached down and picked up his reins.

Idiot! Why had she said that? Was he laughing at her? She couldn't tell? He mounted his horse, spun him around, and the old sorrel fell into step with the big gray.

They rode in silence for a couple minutes before Cliff said, "I heard that your mother died... I'm sorry."

Cat glanced his way, but Cliff continued to stare off into the distance. "She died in a car accident in Los Angeles a year ago last February." Without turning, he nodded his head, his hands once again

121

resting on the saddle horn. "She was cremated. There was a small service in L.A., then that April I brought her ashes back to Utah. We had another service and buried her next to my grandfather in the family plot behind Millie's house." Cliff pointed off to the left, and Cat found that they had come up on the old homestead from the backside.

Cliff studied her for a second and then asked, "Would you like to ride over to where they're buried?"

"I've been meaning to go." She paused. "I guess I've been putting it off. The time never felt quite right." Her words sounded lame, and though he never said anything, she hoped Cliff hadn't thought the same.

They rode through the deep spring grass stirring up insects, and the scent of the fresh grass engulfed them. A large gray rabbit shot out from behind a fallen tree and raced off in search of new cover. They rounded the tree line, and her grandfather's old barn came into view. The same barn where she had hung from the rafters. She shot Cliff a quick glance and found him watching her. She knew it was too much to hope he wouldn't comment.

"Want me to rescue you again?" He combed his mustache down with a quick swipe of his lower lip, his eyes alight with mischief. "I can guarantee it won't end the same way as last time."

The visual that surfaced in her mind was tempting. She gave it a second thought but then decided it was best to ignore his comment and change the subject. "I don't know who my father is. I was hoping that I'd find him on this trip." They stopped next to the white fence that surrounded the small cemetery.

A deep frown furrowed Cliff's brow. "He's from Black River?"

"He has to be. My mother was pregnant when she moved to L.A."

"Does Millie know who he is?"

"I thought so. When I received a letter from her saying that she was ill and asked me to come for a visit, I figured I'd better ask her." Cat's gaze washed over the weathered head stones. Cliff said nothing as he dismounted, and came around to help her down.

Her legs threatened to buckle. She toyed with the mother-of-pearl snaps on his shirt. "She said my mother never told her. But there is a lady in town named Sandra Huset." She glanced up; Cliff's intense eyes were filled with concern. "She was a good friend of my mother's, and she might know. She's my last hope, but I've been unable to contact her, and I'm afraid she might have already left town."

* * * *

Tears filled Cat's eyes. The shield of determination and confidence Cliff normally witnessed vanished. The softness of vulnerability replaced it, and the sudden urge to protect her overcame him. Reaching out, he squeezed her arm, and she moved into his embrace. Laying her head against his chest, she wrapped her arms around him. Her trembling body molded to his, and he brushed a kiss against her brow. He recalled when a simple hug and kiss could fix all problems. That had been a lifetime ago when his life had purpose, made sense. But holding Cat in his arms felt right. Had the spirits pardoned him? Had they given him a second chance at love and happiness? Did he dare hope?

Cat leaned back at arm's length and tried to pull away. Cliff placed a couple fingers under her chin and tilted her head back. "You all right?" She wiped away her tears, nodded and offered up a slight smile. "I don't recall ever hearing about this Huset woman. But I'll check with Doug. If a person wants to find the whereabouts of any woman, he's the man to ask."

They mounted their horses and started back. Realizing they were heading back, Jack picked up the pace. He moved ahead of Sonny, giving Cliff a chance to study Catrina. He wanted to wrap her up into a neat little package, but the truth was, there were too many aspects to the woman. She was strong and independent, yet vulnerable, and she desperately needed her own people. He had a strong feeling she felt she didn't belong, which he understood too well.

She twisted in the saddle and smiled. "Can I ask you about your father?" Curiosity had seemingly washed away her distress.

He urged Sonny to catch up to Jack. "What do you want to know?"

Reaching down, she stroked Jack's neck. "Well, I don't know. What was he like? What's his story?"

He thought for a moment. The best thing he could say about Hank was nothing at all. But he knew that wouldn't fly. "He was born Hank W. Dawson. He made everyone's lives miserable, and then in December of 1988 he died of pneumonia. End of story."

Stunned, she stared at him. "There must have been something good about the man. Didn't you get along with him?"

"No one got along with Dawson," he added, wishing she had never asked.

"But he took you in. Gave you a home."

He glanced over. A primal grunt escaped him. She obviously wasn't going to let it rest. "He took me on as a hired hand that he didn't believe he had to pay."

"The ranch must have been better than living on the reservation, right?"

Her question held a slight hint of sarcasm.

People just didn't understand the situation. Yeah, they might have meant well, but unless you lived with a foot in two worlds, you had no way of knowing what it was like. He shifted in the saddle, wishing he could change the subject. "I'd trade everything I own to have the acceptance and the sense of belonging that my brother Charlie has."

Her brows drew together. "What do you mean by that?"

"At least Charlie knows what he is and where he belongs."

"What does that even mean? It doesn't make any sense!"

"It means that I'm not white enough to fit in the white man's world and not Native American enough to fit in that world."

"But you have family, Cliff, and wherever *they* are is where you belong."

She didn't get it and probably never would. "Forget it. You don't understand." Looking away, he judged how far they were from the gate and how soon he could escape the rest of her interrogation.

"You have family, a mother you can go to and touch and talk to, who loves you. You have aunts, uncles, cousins and even a brother." She paused. "I guess you're right—I don't understand what your problem is."

"Just drop it!" he barked.

"No!" She twisted in the saddle toward him. "You grew up knowing your father and spent time with him." She spread her arms wide. "And you inherited all of this. Remind me again what your problem is!"

Like every other time he let himself think about his father, his hatred for the man surfaced. His guts twisted into knots. His heart hammered against his ribs, and his hands grew damp. "I worked hard to prove worthy of Hank's affections. And even though I was treated like one of the hired hands, I had his blood in me, so I was expected to be tougher, stronger and always smarter than the others." They reached the gate.

Cliff dismounted, opened it, and after both horses walked through, he latched it and remounted.

Cat continued to stare at him as if she expected him to go on. With one hand, Cliff settled his hat down tight on his brow and then cleared his throat. "Hank was a hard man. Nobody questioned him. Every day I strived to meet his expectations. But no matter what I did, he was always quick to remind me that for an *Indian* I was lucky to have his measly handouts. Nothing was ever good enough!"

"Your father would be proud of you," she screamed. "You've turned out just like him!"

"You don't know what you're talking about." He shifted in the saddle. Sonny strained against the bit and sidestepped.

"Are you kidding me?" she laughed. "You expect everyone to behave a certain way, and when they don't, you dismiss them. They're no longer worthy of your time or love. Love," she repeated and snorted disdainfully.

Jack pranced in place, shifting his weight from one leg to the other. Then without any warning, the sorrel bolted toward the barn. Leaning forward and giving Sonny his head, Cliff chased after Cat. He watched in horror as the old horse jumped a downed tree, and she struggled to stay in the saddle.

Reaching the barn, Cliff vaulted from his horse's back before the horse even stopped and ran to her side. "Are you all right?" His eyes searched for injuries.

Big brown eyes stared down at him, and she laughed. "That was amazing. I've never jumped anything before." She gasped, out of breath and then patted the horse's neck. "I want to do it again!"

"I can't believe you. You could have been hurt. He could have stepped in a hole and broke a leg." *Horses may be a dime a dozen, but women this reckless were worth only five cents.*

His entire body shook as he reached up, gripped her by the arms and pulled her off the horse. "You do whatever you want without consulting anyone else. You just take off and then wonder what happened when you get yourself into a predicament where you could get seriously hurt. Don't you have any common sense whatsoever?"

Her chin jutted out as her hands shot to her hips. "At least *I'm* not afraid to venture out and try something new."

Cliff's teeth ground together, his words, short and clipped. "Being cautious, alert and careful is a sign of good sense—something you could use a good dose of!"

"I've been all over the world, and I'm still in one piece." She pushed against his chest, broke his grip and marched away. After a few steps, she turned and snarled, "At least I'm not hiding out in my own little perfect world!"

* * * *

The sound of pounding hooves caught Rooster's attention. He looked out the driver's side window, fixing his gaze on the horse and rider racing toward the barn. Catrina's long dark hair flew wild in the wind, her eyes wide with excitement. A broad smile lit up her face. One hand gripped the saddle horn; the other clutched the reins in a white knuckled fist. The resemblance to his late wife, Fawn, in her younger and wilder days, astounded him, and he couldn't help but smile.

But his smile and good humor faded at the sight of the second rider gaining on her. Cliff rounded the fence and bolted off Sonny like he had done a hundred times when roping calves. Two swift strides took him to her horse's heaving side.

Reaching up, Cliff hauled Catrina out of the saddle. His angry voice carried across the yard to the truck. Rooster wrestled with his conscience. He had no idea what the problem was, but he knew Cliff. If pushed too far, he could be a hot head.

He watched, gripped with curiosity as Catrina placed her hands against Cliff's chest and shoved him backwards. She held her fists ready, squaring off with Cliff like a prizefighter.

"At least I'm not hiding out in my own little perfect world!"

"What the hell..." Rooster opened the truck door and trotted toward the couple about to do the fool's two-step.

Cliff stiffened, then lurched forward as Rooster stepped between them and threw out his hands. The weight of Cliff's chest pushed against his hand. He glared up at Cliff and said, "Go stick your head in the trough and cool off." Cliff stared at Rooster as if he had just noticed him. Cliff weighed his words of warning, then turned and walked away.

"He's lucky you stopped me," Cat spat. She held her fists at her side, her lips pursed in a perfect bow. "If he took another step I was going to let that arrogant SOB have it!"

Rooster relaxed his stance and pushed his hat back. He would put money on this girl against the best. "Come on, Killer," he said, slipping his arm over her shoulder and steering her toward the truck. She held her body stiff, and each step was taken with quick jerky movements. Then she took a deep breath and sighed.

"I've got to run home and pick up something. Why don't you grab your camera and come with me?" When she hesitated, he added, "Humor an old man. I don't get to drive through town with a pretty girl in my truck too often."

One corner of her mouth turned up in a crooked grin. Placing a finger to her lip, she pretended to ponder his request for a moment before agreeing, then sprinted up the steps and disappeared into the house.

Rooster glanced over his shoulder toward the barn. Both horses had been unsaddled and turned out. Old Jack lay down and began rolling in the dirt. Cliff was nowhere in sight. He was most likely working off his anger at the end of a pitchfork.

Climbing back into the truck, he retrieved a cigar from the ashtray, popped it in his mouth and rolled it around with his tongue. Though it wasn't any of his business, he wondered if Catrina would share what their argument had been about. He was concerned for Cliff. It had been some time since Rooster had seen him so angry.

Cliff had felt betrayed after finding Charlie in bed with Nora. But the beating he had dealt his brother that night changed several people's lives forever.

Striking a stick match against his thumbnail, the grizzled cowboy lit his cigar and squinted through the blue smoke. On the outside, it appeared that Cliff possessed much. Yet on the inside, his hardened heart and drained soul had left him a shell of a man, a man without compassion.

Every man has wounds. It just takes some longer to heal than others.

Rooster's mood lightened when Catrina walked out onto the porch. She skipped down the steps with her camera case slung over one shoulder. She jiggled the door handle several times, but it wouldn't open until she pushed the handle down. Tossing her camera case on the seat, she jumped into the truck and settled back against the cracked leather seat sighing.

"You finally ready?" he teased as he turned the key.

She nodded and smiled, but her eyes still glittered with anger.

They drove several miles in silence before she spoke in a guarded voice. "It's time for me to head for New York." Out of the corner of his eye, he viewed a master wall-builder at work. She hadn't turned toward him, only tossed the statement out into the air as if testing the way it sounded.

The '52 black International, his pride and joy, bounced as the dirt road switched to pavement. Rooster made no remark, merely sat with his elbow resting on the opened window and chewed on the stub of his cigar. Was she running to something or away from something? His guess would be away from Cliff, but why? They were two of a kind.

Rooster would be the first one to say he didn't know much about women. But the one thing he knew for sure was that if they had a captive audience, sooner or later they would tell you what was on their minds and then some.

"I didn't come here to only see my grandmother," she started, her voice low and soft. "I was also hoping to find out who my father is." She swiveled in the seat to face him.

Rooster's mind raced back to the night he found her perched on the hood of her floating car. She mentioned being Millie's granddaughter and a lot about floods, yet he couldn't recall anything else. "Does your grandmother know who he is?"

Cat shook her head. "I prayed she would, but she doesn't. She had a shoebox with some old snapshots and I thought there might be one with my mother and father together, but I never came across any."

Staring down at the truck's floorboards, she kicked the toes of her red boots together. "There was a woman who my grandmother said might know something."

"Who's that?" he asked, hoping he sounded casual.

"Her name's Sandra Huset." She shrugged her shoulders. "Except I haven't been able to contact her. I don't even know if she's still in town." Cat glanced out the window. "Besides, it'll have to wait. It's time for me to leave."

Rooster wanted to tell her about Jim and how much like him she was. He wanted to reach for her hand and call her granddaughter. And tell her that she had healed a hole in his heart he thought could never be

128

mended. Except this wasn't the time. There were things she needed to work out on her own. He wanted her to stay or come back because she felt a connection here, not out of a false sense of obligation to him.

* * * *

Nora sat behind the wheel of her yellow Camaro, about to place the key into the ignition when she saw her grandfather's truck. A cloud of red dust billowed up behind the rusty old scrap iron as it rattled up the dirt road. She heaved a heavy sigh. "I suppose I should wait and at least say hi to him."

She drummed her fingers on the top of the steering wheel and waited. He pulled into his driveway, and when the dust had settled, she noticed Cliff's new "squeeze" riding shotgun. Cat spied her, smiled and then waved. Nora smiled and waved back.

Great. Now she's sideling up next to my grandpa. Before I know it, she'll have Charlie sniffing around behind her.

Crawling out of the low riding vehicle, Nora strolled toward her grandfather's truck. She reached him as he stiffly maneuvered his arthritic body out from behind the wheel.

"Hi, Grandpa. You playing hooky today?" She offered him a big smile and returned his hug.

He tossed his cigar butt onto the grass and grinned. "I will from now on if it means being surrounded by pretty girls." Placing his weathered paw on the door, he leaned toward Cat and said, "I'll be right back, girlie."

With his arm still around her waist, he pulled Nora with him toward the house. "You be nice to Cat. You two have more in common than you know." He tweaked Nora's nose the way he had done since she was little, and she still hated it. Even after she and Cliff married, he continued to treat her like a child.

Just because Cliff and Cat are living together doesn't mean Cat and I have anything in common. She huffed out a breath. *Old coot.*

Nora plastered a sweet smile on her face and wandered back to the truck window. Crossing her arms over the driver's opened window she said, "How's it going?"

The other woman slid her knee up on the seat and placed her arm across the back. "As Rooster would say, 'fine as the hair on a newborn calf'."

They both giggled, and Nora replied, "Glad to hear it." She knew her suspicions that Cliff and Cat were sleeping together were justified.

Noticing the camera case on the seat, she asked, "Planning on taking some photos?"

Catrina glanced down at the case and shrugged. "If I come across something remarkable I will."

Nora shot a quick glance toward the house and back. "Have you taken in the sunset from up on Red Rock yet?"

"Red Rock? No. Where's that?"

"Oh, not far. It's just southwest of Circle D Ranch. I'm sure Cliff will take you up there if you ask him."

I'd be more than happy to show you where Rattlesnake Ridge is, Nora thought. *Nothing could scare this city girl back to where she belongs 'quicker than a herd of rattlers'.*

Nora leaned back when she saw Rooster hobble toward the truck with a big satisfied grin on his face.

"There's my two girls," he said, giving Nora a quick hug. "Glad to see you two gittin' along so well." He kissed Nora's cheek and then scrambled in behind the wheel.

"See you later, Cat." Nora waved. "Grandpa, you drive careful in that old piece of junk."

His arm shot out the window, and he patted the door. "Don't be saying anything insulting to the ol' girl. She'll start to bucking and spinning, and I'll be in hell of a fix."

Nora smiled and waved as her grandfather pulled away. It wasn't that she wanted Cliff back; heck no, he was way too boring for her. It was just that it still irked her that he had never put up a fight for her. He merely handed her over to Charlie like it was no big deal.

She strolled back to her car and climbed in. *All's fair in love and war, and having "Little Miss Fancy Boots" running back to L.A. where she belongs will even the score.*

* * * *

Cat stared out the side window. It was the right decision to leave Black River. It was crazy to think that she and Cliff could ever have a life together. She would never put herself in a position where she had to answer to a man—any man. She always did what she wanted, when she wanted and exactly how she wanted. *There's no way I'm going to start asking anyone's permission now.*

Cliff's ex-wife crossed her mind, and she wondered if he'd kept the woman on a short leash. Had that been the reason she cheated on him with Charlie? Although Cat didn't condone the woman's behavior, she sympathized with her on some level.

Glancing at Rooster, she longed to question the man about the kind of woman Nora had been and what their life had been like. But she let it slide. If Cliff had wanted her to know his business, he would have told her. Besides, it didn't matter; she would be gone in a day or two.

Seeing a rise southwest of the ranch, Cat swung around in her seat and asked, "Is that Red Ridge?"

Rooster squinted into the late afternoon sun. "Ayup."

"Oh! How far is it from the ranch, do you think?"

"Oh..." He scratched his whiskers. "No more than four or five miles, I'd say."

Not too far, she thought, eyeing up the red clay ridge. She could easily hike up there, get in a few shots and make it back to the house before sundown.

* * * *

The sun slowly slipped behind a far off ridge, casting the evening sky in shades of pink, orange and red. Cliff's spurs jingled as he and Rooster trekked in silence toward the house.

The day had been a whirlwind of emotions. Waking up two days in a row with a woman in his arms had done wonders for his mind, body and soul. Even now, bone tired, just the thought of her renewed his spirits, and he anticipated the night ahead.

Earlier she told him about her mother's death and her hopes of finding her father. Then when she cried and seemed so vulnerable, he wanted to hold and protect her.

They mounted the steps and entered the dark house. Cliff stopped, his senses heightened. The air smelled stale with no hint of Cat's scent. Her car was here, but her hiking boots and camera case were gone.

Rooster brushed past him, tossing his hat on the table.

Something was wrong. "Where did you and Cat go today?"

The old cowboy mumbled as he opened the refrigerator.

"Rooster," Cliff said, trying not to panic. "Where'd you guys go today?"

The fridge door closed, and the old man stared at him. "I took her with me when I went home. Why?"

"What did you talk about? Who else did she talk to?"

Rooster scratched his head. "She talked to Nora for a couple of minutes while I went in to the house."

"What did you talk about on the way back? Did she ask you anything?" Cliff's heart pounded in his head like a stampede. He held his breath as the old man searched his mind for an answer.

"She pointed toward a rise and then asked if it was Red Ridge. She also wanted to know how far..." His words trailed off as reality set in.

A dull ache wallowed in the pit of Cliff's empty gut. "Damn!" Cliff spun around and yanked the door open. But before he reached the last step, Rooster called out to him.

"Hey! You might need this."

Cliff turned and stared at the holster and pistol the old cowboy held in his hand. He gripped the gun belt and glanced up. "I just *might* shoot her," he said hesitantly.

The old man nodded in agreement. "You just might have to."

Chapter Ten

Cat tossed her backpack to the ground by a cluster of tumbleweeds nestled around a pile of rotted fence posts and coiled wire. The granite peaks of the Wasatch Range and the snowcapped Uinta Mountains loomed in the far distance. "This place is amazing." A cool breeze brushed her hair across her face. Taking a deep breath, her lungs filled with the crisp, fresh, mountain air. Cat sighed and turned in a slow circle taking in her incredible surroundings. A strange feeling washed over her, an unusual sense of peace and spiritual connection. She belonged here; her roots were here. Her heart ached at the thought of leaving this place to go to New York.

The late afternoon sun highlighted the bright red and orange vertical stripes of the granite peaks extending up from the dark green tree line. The field below held scattered patches of Quaking aspen, Douglas fir and Engelmann spruce.

"Heaven," she murmured, retrieving her camera. "A photographer's paradise." She snapped several landscape photos before spotting a small herd of Mule deer grazing in a meadow. Lifting her camera, she brought the deer into focus. Then one lifted its head, its ears perked to an invisible danger.

The roar of an engine fighting against the terrain assaulted the silence, and the old black International truck came into view. Red dust billowed behind it and clung to the vehicle. The growl of the truck matched the expression of the man behind the wheel, his face, pinched with rage. The engine died, Cliff bounded out from behind the wheel and slammed the door.

Now what did I do? she thought as he marched toward her.

"What the hell do you think you're doing up here?" Cliff's arms flapped around his body as if he thought he could fly. "You can't keep running off into the wilderness by yourself. It's too dangerous—what were you thinking?" Two large calloused fists finally landed on his hips. His feet were planted a shoulder width apart. A muscle in his clenched jaw jerked, and his snarl matched a Tasmanian Devil's.

Cat stared in disbelief. The man had more audacity than anyone she had ever met. Why did he continue to treat her like a child who didn't have any common sense?

"Where do you get off telling me what I can and cannot do?" She matched his stance. "I can take care of myself. I've been on assignments in Africa, Australia and China. Sometimes I need to take chances to get the best shots. That's my job!"

He would shake some sense into her until her teeth rattled loose if he had to. Cliff stepped in front of Cat, kicking her backpack aside.

The unmistakable rattle sounded seconds before Cliff felt a sharp pain in his leg just above his boot. Shocked, he jerked away and looked down in time to see the oval, yellowish brown spots of a Midget Faded Rattlesnake slither back under the tumbleweeds.

He pushed Cat behind him.

"Was that a rattlesnake?" Her eyes were large and round. "Did it get you?"

Cliff drew in a ragged breath. He needed to keep them both calm. He'd seen first-hand what could happen to a person after being bitten, and he didn't need her going all hysterical on him. "Don't panic."

He scanned the ground before moving, then retrieved her backpack and handed it to her. "Listen to me." He limped a few steps and guided her toward the truck. "Get your stuff together and get in the truck."

"But...But..." she stammered. Her face was distorted in fear, but she slipped her arm around his waist to help him walk.

"Cat," he said, slipping his arm over her shoulder to steady himself. "You need to take me to the hospital." She nodded, and they hobbled to the passenger's side of the truck.

She reached for the door handle, pulled the handle up, but the door didn't open. "Come on! Open up, you stupid door." She tried several more times without any luck.

"Push the handle down," Cliff said, his head starting to pound. The door opened, and she helped him onto the seat.

"Are you okay? I'm so sorry." Her eyes pleaded for his forgiveness.

"I'll be fine. Just get in and drive." Pain shot through him when she slammed the door. She ran around to the other side and grabbed the handle. Once again, the door wouldn't open. After several tries Cliff glanced over, a frown creased Cat's forehead. "Push it down."

The door swung open, she hopped in behind the wheel and turned the key. Closing his eyes, he rested his head back against the seat as the old truck roared to life. She popped the clutch, and the truck hopped several yards and died. "I don't believe this," she spat, hitting her palms against the steering wheel.

A cold sweat covered Cliff's body. In the calmest voice he could muster, he said, "Relax. Let the clutch out slow."

"I know, I know. I'm sorry." She turned the key again, and they set off down the narrow trail toward the main road.

The truck lurched sideways, and Cliff bounced his head off the side window. He groaned and fought the nausea that was quickly rising within him.

"I'm sorry. Maybe I should stop, take your pulse and check your leg for bruising or something like that!" The pitch of Cat's voice was slightly elevated.

"I'm fine." He swallowed. His throat felt dry, his tongue swollen. "Keep driving."

"You're not fine." She sounded close to hysterics. "You've been bitten by a rattlesnake." The truck lurched and bucked on the rough path, causing every muscle in Cliff's body to ache.

"Slow down. We've got plenty of time to get to the hospital."

She wrestled for control of the wheel as the truck bounced onto the pavement. The engine roared as they picked up speed. The sound of grinding gears echoed through the cab of the truck as she attempted to shift gears. "What if you pass out, and I need to do CPR on you?"

"Don't stop. Keep driving."

"Undo your belt..."

He shot her a sideways glance. "Not now..."

"No! You can't have anything tight on, unless it's a tourniquet!" She down shifted for a sharp curve. "Maybe I should stop?"

"Don't stop. You do know where the hospital is, don't you?"

"Yes, it's at the other end of the nursing home." She glanced toward him, her face etched with distress.

Closing his eyes, Cliff slumped on the tattered bench seat beside her. His pulse stampeded in his chest, and he would kill for a cool glass of water.

"Rattlesnakes are found in almost every state in the country. Copperheads are most common in the Eastern U.S., and they have much milder venom than the rattlesnakes. Water moccasins, on the other hand, live in the Southeast where there's a lot of water, which is where they get their name from, and their venom potency is somewhere between the rattlesnakes and copperheads."

Cliff forced his eyes open when he felt the truck do a bank shot around a curve. The speedometer gauge glowed bright green in the dark and read seventy-five miles an hour. *No need to worry about getting to the hospital in time, she's gonna' kill us long before we reach the edge of town.*

Closing his eyes again, Cliff drifted off, only to be awakened by the high-pitch voice of a hysterical chipmunk narrating a scene from "Wild America".

"The Anaconda, on the other hand, lives in the Amazon. They're a constrictor and kill by wrapping their victims up and drowning them. There's a Green anaconda that is camouflaged with a yellow underside and big black blotches on its back. They've been known to get up to thirty feet long.

"Cobras are very poisonous and live in the jungle. They hunt during the night, and they'll even eat other snakes. They seize their victims with their fangs and then inject their venom. If a person was to get bit by a cobra, their poison goes right to work on the person's nervous system.

Where's my pistol? He sighed and placed one arm over his eyes. *If she keeps this up, I'm gonna' shoot myself.*

"But in South America, most people die from the Southern Fer-de-lance snake. It searches for its victims by using its heat-sensitive pits, which are located between its eyes and nostrils. When it wants to strike, it opens its mouth, and two long fangs swing out and stab its prey, injecting its lethal venom.

"The Boa Constrictor," she drew a deep breath. "Will lay motionless until its prey comes along..."

"Woman," his voice sounded as dry as sandpaper against stone. "Would you shut the hell up?"

They drove the last several miles in silence.

Cat pulled up to the emergency entrance of the Black River Medical Center. "Stay here. I'll be right back!"

The door slammed. Cliff peered out from under heavy eyelids as she disappeared through the automatic doors. He managed to chuckle. "No problem."

Cat raced to the counter where a heavyset woman with curly black hair and silver framed glasses hung up the phone. She glanced up. "May I help you?"

"He was bitten by a rattlesnake," Cat yelled, though she fought for control. The stone-faced woman push a buzzer on her desk, and two men in white uniforms appeared with a gurney. They exited through the automatic doors toward the black truck.

Cat turned to follow.

"Miss?" the woman called and Cat twisted back around. "I need your name, please."

"Catrina Pearson," she said, staring at the automatic doors.

"The name and age of the person you brought in?"

"Cliff... Clifford White Fox...He's about thirty?" It dawned on her that she really didn't have any idea how old he was. It didn't matter. Her head swivel from the reception desk to the automatic doors and then back. *Dear God, don't let him die.*

The doors opened, and the two orderlies entered with Cliff stretched out on the gurney. They passed the desk, went fifty feet and then disappeared behind a big green curtain.

"Excuse me, Miss Pearson?" Cat heard the woman, but wanted to follow Cliff to make sure...of what she didn't know, she just wanted to be with him. "Miss Pearson?"

"Yes. I'm sorry." Cat's stomach leaped to the back of her throat. She had a strong urge to cry and throw up. She pressed a hand to her stomach and wondered which would happen first?

"You'll have to fill out some forms for me," the curly haired woman said, handing Cat a clipboard with several sheets of paper and a pen clipped to it.

She scanned the top sheet, but didn't know any of Cliff's information. Checking her pockets, she realized her cell phone was in her backpack in the truck. "Is there a phone I can use?" she asked, setting the clipboard on the counter. "I need to call his family." With her pen, the woman pointed to a phone at the end of the counter. "Thank you."

The phone rang three times before Rooster's beloved voice came on the line. "Rooster? Thank God you're there."

"Catrina? Where are you?"

"It's all my fault." She choked back her tears.

"What happened?" His voice sounded so far away.

"Cliff was bit by a rattler. We're at the hospital."

"Sit tight, girlie. I'll call his Ma, and then I'll be there quicker than two shakes of a...Just sit tight."

* * * *

From the few seconds that Cliff caught a glimpse of Cat, she looked worse than he felt. She must be frightened half out of her mind, he thought as people converged on him.

A woman dressed in blue scrubs, with a long blond ponytail asked, "What is your name, sir?"

"Clifford White Fox," he said, as a man removed his boots and socks.

"Did you see what bit you?"

"Snake–a Midget Faded rattlesnake." He winced at the pain when the man cut his bloodstained sock off.

The woman kept scribbling on her paper. "Where were you bitten?"

"On the outside of my right leg, just below the knee."

People milled around him. Someone took his blood pressure, while the man cut his jeans away from his swollen leg. Two streaks of dried blood on his bruised leg resembled a double river brand.

"Can you tell us what your symptoms are?"

"Right now, I'm having difficulty breathing, my vision's sort of blurred, and my leg feels sort of numb. I need to speak to Cat." When the woman frowned, he added, "Catrina. The woman who brought him in."

Another woman walked toward him, holding a syringe. "Your chart has been ordered, but we need to know if you have any allergies to any medication, particularly to penicillin?"

"No, ma'am." He turned back to the blonde. "I want to talk to Cat."

"We're going to give you Ceftriaxone. It's an antibiotic," the second woman stated.

After a couple of shots, they removed the rest of his clothes and then slipped a hospital gown around him. He pushed the thermometer in his mouth to one side. "Where's Cat?"

"Just relax, Mr. White Fox." Someone removed the thermometer and patted his shoulder. The bed lowered, and several warm blankets were placed over him.

He fought the weariness. Voices echoed around him. *Cat...I need to make sure she's all right.*

"His blood pressure is 60/40, his pulse 160, temp's 102."

"Mr. White Fox," a male voice said. "I'm Dr. Holcomb."

Cliff forced his eyes open. A sober little bald man with large round wire rimmed glasses studied a metal folder.

"We're going to do some tests." He glanced up and shoved his glasses up to the bridge of his nose.

"What about Cat?" Cliff's voice sounded thick in his head.

"We'll check into that for you. There's always a chance of complications with snakebites," the doctor continued. "We're going to keep you overnight for observation. But there's no need for you to worry. It's all routine."

He turned to leave, but Cliff's hand shot out and grabbed the front of man's lab coat, sending the doctor's glasses askew. The metal folder crashed to the floor as Cliff hauled the doctor close to the bed. The man's eyes bulged, and through clenched teeth, Cliff demanded, "Get Cat. Now!"

Chapter Eleven

Cat's mind reeled. What on earth were they doing to Cliff in the emergency room? Since he'd disappeared into a room down the hall, she had learned nothing about his condition. Several people rushed in and out of his room, carrying covered trays, but no one would stop long enough to brief her on his condition.

A severe pounding threatened to split her head wide open. She glanced around the small blue and beige emergency waiting room. Headlights from passing vehicles flashed across the tinted windows. Cat collapsed into the closest chair and covered her face with both hands. *Oh God, what have I done? Please don't let him die!*

The two-foot round clock, which hung above the registration desk clicked the seconds away with ear piercing precision. She glanced up at the squeaky sound of nurse shoes on polished linoleum floors. A young woman with long blond hair pulled into a ponytail, wearing blue scrubs, glanced toward Cat as she approached the nursing desk. Cat held her breath as the two women whispered across the Formica countertop.

Just tell me he's going to be all right, Cat begged in silence.

The whoosh of the automatic doors drew her attention. Cliff's mother, Ester, entered and marched toward the desk. The shy little woman who never spoke more than two words on branding day vanished, as she demanded to know the condition of her son.

The doors slid open again. Charlie and Rooster entered. Charlie headed for the counter, while the grizzled old cowboy lumbered toward her. He offered a sympathetic grin, sank into the chair next to her and slipped his arm around her shoulder. "How you holding up?"

140

Cat's throat tightened, the tears she'd been holding back threatened to finally escape. "It's all my fault. I'm so scared." She reached out and gripped his hand. "They won't tell me anything..."

"It'll take a lot more than a little ol' snake bite to keep that Cayuse down," Rooster offered in his rough manner that she was growing to love.

She twisted to face him. "I need to speak to Charlie. He and Cliff have to clear things up between them before it's too late."

Rooster frowned and glanced up at the young man standing at the counter.

"Can you help me make him understand?" she asked. "It's important that Charlie knows how Cliff really feels about him."

Ester and Charlie turned to follow the blond nurse. In a calm but serious voice, Rooster called out, "Charlie. Come here, son. Catrina needs to speak to you."

Charlie said something to his mother and then motioned for her to follow the nurse. He strolled over to where they sat and pulled up a chair.

Not quite sure where to start, Cat jumped in with both feet and prayed she wouldn't make matters worse. Glancing from one man to the other, she took a deep breath and started. "Cliff told me that he'd trade everything he had to have the acceptance and the sense of belonging that you have." She stared into Charlie's eyes. Eyes so dark they were almost black. Eyes that reflected your feelings yet concealed his. "He said that at least you knew what you were and where you belonged." Neither man offered a comment. "He stated that he wasn't white enough to fit in either the white man's world, or Native American enough to fit in your world."

Something so small flashed in Charlie's eyes that she couldn't grasp it or name the emotion. She'd hit a nerve, hopefully in a good way. "I tried pointing out that it didn't matter. He has family, and that's all that truly matters. He had also stated that he grew up hating his father." She still couldn't understand how anyone could say that when all she ever wanted was to find out who hers was.

Rooster patted her hand and nodded his head, his eyes glowing soft and kind like those of the old horse she'd ridden. Yet Charlie sat rigid, offering no hint to his thoughts or emotions.

"He said that no matter how hard he'd work to prove himself worthy of his father's affections, he was still treated like one of the hired hands. And no matter what he did, his father was quick to remind him that for an *Indian* he had it pretty good."

Charlie's chair scraped across the floor when he stood. A silent conversation passed between him and Rooster. Then without a sound, he withdrew and headed off down the hall.

Confused and weary, Cat cradled her head on Rooster's shoulder. "Why do people say and do things to intentionally hurt each other?"

She gripped the front of his faded western shirt for emotional strength then let him pull her into the comfort of his strong arms. Seconds later, his weathered cheek rested against the top of her head.

* * * *

Once Cliff was moved to intensive care, Rooster positioned himself in the hall to keep an eye on Catrina. An endless cluster of relatives took turns visiting Cliff, but in a drug-induced state, he rambled on about Cat and ordered people around. Though she couldn't enter his room because she wasn't family, she stood in the hall and peeked through the window.

The girl's pain soaked into Rooster's soul. He ached for her, *his granddaughter*. One corner of his mouth curled up in a slight smile. His heart soared like an eagle at the mere thought that a part of his son still lived. Catrina had her mother's almond shaped eyes, but her high cheekbones and the shape of her full lips had come from her father. Her adventuresome and strong-willed personality had come from her father, too.

She came to town looking for answers, anticipating meeting her long lost father. However, since she hit town, her life had been turned upside down. First with her grandmother being far more ill than she expected and maybe dying, and then almost drowning in a flood that completely destroyed her family's home. And now, the poor girl was in love with a man she didn't have any idea how to halter break.

Rooster scratched at the stubble on his chin. *It would do them both good to spend a little time away from each other. Maybe they'd figure out what they really want out of life.*

He didn't like butting into other folks' business, but sometimes you just had to push the horse's head into the water tank before he realized he was thirsty.

"You look tired." Rooster sidled up next to Catrina. "Go home, and get some rest. I'll call you if there's any change." She wrapped her arms around his neck, and he couldn't help but pull her close. She had no way of knowing what her acceptance of him meant.

Cat leaned back. "You sure you'll call me?" The apprehension in her voice reflected the dark smudges underlined her red eyes.

"Don't fret. If his condition changes, I promise I'll call, and let the phone ring until you answer," he teased as he ushered her toward the elevator. "Just make sure you drive careful." He pulled her into his arms and held her for a long moment. He sighed when she returned his hug. He just found her; he couldn't afford to lose her now.

Cat promised herself that she could hold it together, yet her lower lip quivered as she walked away. Her pounding head made her sick to her stomach. It was her fault Cliff stepped into the snake's path, and it would be her fault if he died. Hot tears trickled down her cheeks.

Even though her body ached with exhaustion, she dreaded going back to an empty house. She didn't want to be alone. She needed someone to talk to. Someone to hold her and tell her that everything was going to be all right. *Mom, I wish you were here. I miss you so much.*

If she couldn't talk to her mother, she would go to the next best thing. The clock hanging in the corridor read 10:35 p.m. "I hope she's still awake." She proceeded through the small hospital to Millie's room on the east side. Wiping the tears from her face, she raked her loose hair back into a ponytail and straightened her clothes.

No one stood sentry at the desk, and a faint light shown under Millie's door. Cat glanced around the deserted hall. *I'll just check to see if she's still awake.* She leaned against the door and it quietly opened.

The first thing she saw was Millie, squatted on her hands and knees rifling through the bottom drawer of her dresser, while her wheelchair and walker sat parked across the room. She sat back on her heels, placed her hands on her hips and cursed in a stronger voice than Catrina had heard since Millie's stroke. Apparently locating what she was digging for, the old woman stood and turned. Her contented smile faded.

"Catrina! I...I know how this must look." She tossed the thick crossword puzzle magazine on to the bed. "But there's a logical explanation."

Cat's pulse quickened. Millie had sounded so ill and fragile during their earlier phone conversation when she shared her hopes of living together as a family. Now she caught Millie getting around as if she hadn't been sick a day in her life.

Cat's knees weakened. With this revelation coming on top of everything that had happened to her today, she feared they were going to give out. Leaning against the doorframe, she heard her voice shake, "Have you been faking all along?"

Millie crossed the room to stand in front of her. Reaching out, she grasped Cat by the shoulders. Their gaze locked. "I did it for you. I figured it was the only way to get you to come home."

Shocked, Cat shook loose of the older woman's hold and lurched further into the room. "Home!" she spat, spinning around to face Millie. "I could never live with a person who would straight out lie to me about something as important as her health." Too irate to look at Millie any longer, she gazed around the cozy little room, searching for a way to make sense out of everything that had taken place that day. But when she noticed just where she was, she spun back around and pinned Millie with her stare. "Sandra Huset—Mom's supposed best friend. Did you make her up, too?" Waiting for Millie to answer, she prayed that the last possible link to finding her father hadn't been another one of her grandmother's lies.

Millie's rigid stance would have made a general proud, yet her eyes begged Cat to understand. "Catrina, listen to me."

Cat closed her eyes for a second and sighed. "No! No more lies!" Millie reached out a weathered, aged spotted, olive branch of an arm, but Cat raised a hand to ward her off. "I worried about you." A lump rose in the back of her throat, yet she managed to continue, "I feared that this would be our last time together, that I wouldn't have enough time to get to know you." Her head threatened to explode at any moment. She rubbed at one pounding temple. "I agonized over putting my career on hold and staying here instead of fulfilling my commitment in New York." She shook her head in disbelief. "Why would you do this to me?"

"I wanted to see you happy," Millie said, matter-of-factly. "To stop gallivanting all over the world." She waved her arms wildly. "You should be married. Settled down with a whole herd of kids running around."

"Married!" Cat gulped in a deep breath. "To who?"

Millie's brows shot up. "Who do you think? Clifford White Fox!

You're perfect for each other."

Cat's hands flew to her hips. "That's why you were so adamant about me staying at your house. You set me up. You knew sooner or later we'd cross paths." Well, they had crossed paths all right. She'd been enjoying the early spring weather by sunbathing *naked* when he rode up and demanded she move into town.

"He's a good man," Millie insisted, folding her arms across her chest, her brows pinched together in frustration. "You could do worse."

Cat's mouth opened and closed twice before her words found their way out. "Do you realize if I'd been in that house during the storm I would have been crushed? It would have collapsed right on top of me—tree and all!"

Millie turned, strolled over to her bed and perched on the edge. "I was only trying to help you get a husband," she mumbled, her comment laced with sarcasm. "You sure weren't catching one on your own."

"When I decide it's time to *catch* a husband, I won't need your help or anyone else's!" Cat pulled the door open, then stopped. Sadness gripped her heart, and she glanced back over her shoulder. Suddenly, the only feelings she had for the lonely old woman who no longer had any family or a home to go to…was pity. "Did you do this to my mother?" Her voice wasn't much louder than a whisper. "Is that why she left and never wanted to come back?" She took one last look at her grandmother, before walking out and letting the door close behind her.

Chapter Twelve

Cliff sat propped up in the hospital bed. It had been a long night, and all he was able to think about was Catrina. She was probably worrying about him, and he wanted to reassure her that he was fine. But demanding to see her and grabbing the doctor's shirt had only gotten him a hefty dose of a sedative.

Recalling their wild ride and her nervous chatter on their way to the hospital made him chuckle. He shook his head and smiled. She quoted every poisonous snake and how they killed their prey all the way to town. It seemed comical now, but at the time he hadn't found it very amusing.

"It's nice to see a feller who thinks almost dying is so pleasurable," Rooster said, strolling into Cliff's hospital room. He placed a rain soaked paper bag on the bed at Cliff's side. "What's tickled your craw this mornin'?" The old cowboy limped over to an empty chair and then gingerly lowered himself into it. With one finger, he pushed his wet black Stetson up and then sat back and sighed. "How you feelin', son? You look pert near alive today."

"Accept for the bedsores I'm gittin on my backside from sitting around not doin' nothing, I'm dang near perfect." Cliff fiddled with the buttons on the side of the bed, raising himself up. "Doc won't tell me when I can get out of here," he said, embarrassed for being in the hospital in the first place.

Rooster hoisted one booted foot across his opposite knee. "You're one lucky Cayuse. Doc said you received a pretty hefty dose of venom from that rascally reptile."

146

"Was my own stupid fault." Cliff drew in a frustrated breath and sighed. "I was so scared for Cat's safety that I raced up there, then carried on like a lunatic. If I'd been paying closer attention, I wouldn't have gotten bit in the first place." He scratched at an imaginary itch above his left ear. "How's she doing? She didn't show when I said I wanted to see her," he tossed out, but kept his eyes averted, to hide his disappointed thoughts from the old man.

"They wouldn't let her in to see you. Said she wasn't *family*." The old cowboy huffed, his eyebrows pinched together with disgust. "She was pretty upset last night, so I sent her home."

Cliff nodded in agreement. "I figured as much. But she's tougher than she looks." He felt an admirable grin hitch up one corner of his mouth. "She'd been close to losing it," he admitted with an amused snicker. "Yet she kept it together, got me into the truck and drove us into town."

"She called me at the ranch." Rooster shook his head. "Told me what had happened. She was pert near out of her mind. You scared her half to death."

"That woman is something else." Since she charged her way into his life, his emotions spun and bucked like a mad Brahma out of a chute. And he had jumped on a ride he couldn't get off. At the moment he wasn't sure he wanted off. If he learned anything from all of this, in a blink of an eye, your life could be over, and he didn't want to spend the rest of his alone anymore.

Reality slapped him hard up alongside of the head. He loved Cat and wanted her with him. Love was something he never thought he would let himself feel again. His heart raced as if he was facing a killer bull; he scoffed at the thought. *I know how to handle a killer bull. Cat, on the other hand, is a whole different creature, soft and cuddly, but with claws guaranteed to make life with her intriguing.*

A warm sensation washed over Cliff, and he longed to hold Cat in his arms right then. He would whisper in her ear what he planned to do to her the next time they were alone. He could hardly wait; he had something he wanted to ask her.

* * * *

Cat stopped at the reception desk and asked for Cliff's room number before cautiously proceeding down the corridor. Her plan was to beg for his forgiveness and tell him how sorry she was. She realized that his yelling and berating was his way of trying to protect her.

Her stomach rolled with nausea as the strong odor of antiseptic engulfed her. She rubbed at the throbbing pain in her temples. *I'm so confused about our relationship at this point. There's so much we need to iron out before I leave for New York.*

She was up all night worrying about Cliff's condition, and how upset he had been with her. Even after Rooster phoned to tell her Cliff was out of danger and resting well, she had tossed and turned. *Maybe now isn't the right time to tell him what Millie's been up to. How's he going to feel when he learns she lied to everyone and set us up?*

Approaching Cliff's door, Cat paused to collect her thoughts. After wiping away the imaginary wrinkles on her shirt, she pressed a firm hand against her tumbling stomach and took a deep breath to control her frazzled emotions.

Male voices came from within the room. Not wanting to interrupt the conversation, Cat glanced around the hall for a place to sit and wait. But then Cliff spoke, causing her to stop in her tracks.

"She's been a pain in the butt ever since I first saw her. I told her to move into town, and the next thing I know she's moved into my house."

He's talking about me! She leaned closer.

"Every day she cooks up some cockamamie, harebrained idea and wanders off into the wilderness, *and then* when she finds herself in a dangerous predicament, she can't figure out what happened. The woman's crazy! Hell! She's driving *me* crazy!" Cat sucked in her breath and placed a hand over her mouth.

"She's a huge distraction," Cliff continued, the rumbling of his deep voice grew louder. "When she's around I can't concentrate or get a damn thing done. If she's not around, I worry about where she is and what kind of trouble she's getting in to."

Both men chuckled, and then Rooster asked in his low raspy voice, "Why did you sleep with her?" Cat's stomach rose to the back of her throat, and she held her breath waiting for his answer. The room grew silent. Just when she thought Cliff wasn't going to answer, he said, a hint of exasperation in his voice, "To be honest, I dreamt it so many times, I thought I was dreaming again that night until I woke up the next morning and found her curled up next to me. She had the sweetest expression on her face. I didn't have the heart to tell her it had all been a mistake."

Cat felt like one of the small calves on branding day, desecrated and confused. *Millie lied to me about everything, and I've been nothing more to Cliff than a mistake.* A sharp pain burned deep in her soul. She had been branded a fool.

Cat's heart skipped a beat, and her breath lodged in the back of her throat. She spun around, groping for the cool, tiled wall as black spots swam around in front of her eyes. *I should have never come to Black River.*

"Are you all right?" A woman's voice asked from somewhere in front of her. A hand reached out and grasped Cat's arm.

Cat blinked, and the woman came into focus. Nora held her steady, her brows pinched in concern. "You're as white as a ghost."

"I just need some fresh air," Cat said, staggering along the wall in the opposite direction of Cliff's door.

Nora glanced over her shoulder. "Were you visiting Cliff?"

Glancing up, Cat saw alarm flash in Nora's eyes. "No. I never made it. I started to feel funny before I could walk in." Cat glanced back towards Cliff's room. "I don't think I should go in right now. But..." Her gaze met Nora's. "When Cliff's released, would you tell him that I won't stand in his way to buy Millie's land."

Nora nodded and said, "Why don't you tell him yourself?"

Cat felt winded and swallowed hard. "I'm leaving for New York. My original plans were to stay only a couple of weeks, but now I need to leave as soon as possible."

"That's too bad," Nora stated with a smug grin.

Feeling much stronger, Cat pulled herself up straight. "It was nice to meet you, Nora."

Nora released her arm. "You, too. Are you sure you're okay?"

"I'm fine. Thank you." Cat forced a pleasant smile, hoping the woman wasn't able to deduce her true feelings. Taking a couple steps backwards, Cat waved. "Good-bye, Nora."

She turned and with controlled steps walked toward the exit. She hoped she wouldn't lose total control before reaching her car.

The twenty miles back to the ranch passed in a blur of dark clouds and dust. Cat's life hadn't really changed from what it had always been.

She was still on her own, and she still couldn't count on anyone except herself. But at one point, just for a moment, she felt like there might have been something more, that she belonged and was actually wanted. Except, as usual, it had been only wishful thinking on her part.

Turning onto the ranch road, she swerved around deep ruts, praying she wouldn't slip and end up stuck in one. She parked her car and ran up the steps into the house. Once inside, an eerie silence filled the empty rooms, and Cat shivered before running up the stairs.

Tears blurred her vision and ran down her checks as she crammed her possessions into two paper bags. Funny how at home she felt here, and yet in less than ten minutes she had gathered and packed all of her meager belongings.

She spotted the blue denim shirt she had used as a nightgown laying on the bed. Closing her eyes, she lifted it to her nose. Cliff's intoxicating scent filled her senses. For a moment, she contemplated taking the shirt with her. *It was all just a mistake,* she reminded herself, tossing the shirt on the bed.

When she reached the threshold, she stopped and twisted around, taking one last look at the room. Tightness gripped her heart and throat at the thought of never returning to this house again. A heavy sigh tore from her lungs as she turned and walked out leaving it all behind her.

* * * *

Cliff picked up the paper bag that Rooster had tossed on the bed, containing a pair of jeans. He threw back the covers and stood. He'd been in bed long enough. Plenty of work at the ranch needed his attention. Work that he didn't want Rooster to feel he had to do.

He stripped off his hospital gown and tossed it on the bed. Naked as the day he was born, Cliff reached into the bag and pulled out the jeans. He shook them out and was about to slide one foot into the pant leg when the door opened behind him.

An older woman in dark purple scrubs stopped in her tracks. "Just what do you think you're doing?" The sharpness of her voice reminded Cliff of his third grade teacher, Mrs. Peppercorn. The woman stood with her hands fisted on her ample hips, waiting for his reply.

Cliff stepped into the jeans and pulled them up over his naked body. "I'm skinny-dipping with a blonde, brunette and a red-head. What does it look like to you?"

Red-faced and disgusted, the nurse pivoted on her heels and left. Rooster chuckled and shook his head. "You're more trouble than a young bull on the wrong side of the fence from a pasture full of horny heifers."

Not in the mood for one of the old man's colorful comments, Cliff replied with a grunt. He stepped barefoot into his boots, then slipped his shirt over his head and tucked it into his jeans.

In silence, they trekked out of the hospital into the pouring rain and headed across the parking lot to the red Ford pickup. As Rooster drove, Cliff gazed out the window. He looked forward to nightfall and being alone with Catrina. It surprised him how much he missed her after being away from her for only two nights.

A vision of her lying on his bed, dark hair spread across his pillow, eyes shining in anticipation, overwhelmed him. It was true; Catrina was beautiful, talented and sexy as hell. Yet he also admired her independence, her ability to pick up, go anywhere in the world and fit in. Even confessed to himself he was a little jealous of her strong sense of freedom.

He would never be free to come and go as he pleased because he knew he would never be able put himself into a position where strangers would judge him.

The old man pulled up to the ranch house and parked next to the International truck. Glancing around, Cliff noticed Cat's car was gone. He wondered where she needed to be that was more important and when would she be back.

Hours later, after the chores were finished and Rooster had headed home, Cliff slouched in an old, wooden, rocking chair on the porch. He'd taken a shower and warmed up some leftovers, but his plate sat next to him untouched. The empty crate that doubled as a table bore stains and burn marks from years of abuse. The rain moved on, leaving behind a light cool breeze. A patch of clouds swept across the dappled sky, allowing a glimpse of a yellow moon.

He rubbed a hand across the back of his neck. Soft tones from the grandfather clock drifted through the open windows, informing him it was the end of the day.

He glanced at the denim shirt he held then brushed it against his cheek. Burying his nose into the worn material, he took a deep breath and savored her lingering, feminine scent.

The chair creaked as he rose to his feet. He stretched, his muscles cramped from hours of sitting and waiting for someone who wasn't coming back.

He entered the dark house. It felt large and empty without Cat's constant chatter and the way she banged around the kitchen, trying to find pots and pans.

Forcing his weary body to do his bidding, he stepped onto the stair landing. Placing a calloused hand on the newel post, he rubbed the worn surface. He would always picture Cat standing there with nothing on except his denim shirt. Her bare legs and feet half-hidden, her hair tousled as if they had just made love. He knew that everywhere he looked, whether in the house, the barn or outside, he was going to see her and smell her intoxicating scent. He knew it would be years before the woman who tortured him with her presence stopped torturing him with her absence.

Cliff climbed the stairs, not sure if the pounding in his head hurt worse than the emptiness in his chest. He crossed to the bedroom at the top of the stairs and peered in. The room stood empty; she had removed every trace of herself. It was as if she had never really been there. Like she had been a figment of his imagination.

You're a fool, just a dumb cowboy. Face it, she's gone, and you'll probably never see her again.

Cliff closed the door to the empty room and to a future based upon empty dreams.

* * * *

In a tiny motel room off Interstate 80, Catrina lay curled up on the hard lumpy mattress, the faded and snagged bedspread pulled up high. The bar sign from across the street flashed off and on in orange and green neon. She ran out of tears somewhere around Kimball, Wyoming, and after driving 600 miles became too weary to continue on. She had pulled off the highway a couple hundred miles into Nebraska.

The burrito she picked up at a fast-food drive-up lay like a brick in the bottom of her stomach. Rolling over, she punched the firm pillow a couple of times, then flopped down, hoping to get comfortable enough to fall asleep.

The small room held a bed, a few mismatched pieces of blond furniture and a small round table and folding chair. The space was neat, dust free and smelled of disinfectant. She was sure the decor hadn't been updated since the late 60's. A faded watercolor of drakes and mallards frolicking on a lake, enclosed in a tree branch frame, hung over the bed. She figured it was worth more now as an antique than when it was first painted.

A clock radio on the nightstand read midnight. She pinched her eyes shut and off in the distance heard the soft rumbling of thunder. She wasn't going to get any rest as long as Cliff and Millie continued to invade every thought. She was angry with her grandmother for luring her to Black River by lying to her about being sick and then making up a fake person who possibly knew her father's identity. What made a person do something so despicable?

And then there was Cliff. She rolled over again. Had he been using her all this time for some sick game? Was he still laughing at how gullible she was and how easily she crawled into his bed?

They both deceived her, tricked her into believing just what they wanted her to believe. The idea of Cliff not having any real feelings for her hurt the most, and she couldn't help but wonder if he'd known all along about Millie's deception.

A crack of lightning startled her, and she flinched. She didn't want to admit it to herself, but she was scared and alone. Stranded again, like when she was trapped on the roof of the car floating in the ditch.

Yeah, her heroes had always been cowboys, but she wasn't a scrawny kid parked in front of the boob tube or in the front row of the Saturday afternoon picture show, anticipating the wild romantic adventures of the Old West. This was reality, and no wrinkled, weathered old cowboy who spoke in funny riddles or dashing hero on a white horse was going to show up and save her.

She was on her own again, remembering that the only person she could depend upon was herself. Rolling over, she kicked the blankets then pulled them up tight under her chin.

The rumbling thunder intensified as it rolled across the dark sky, and neither the pouring rain nor Cat's tears could wash away the awful pain that filled her empty heart.

She sighed. Her eyes filled with tears, and the image of her mother came to mind. *You must have had a very good reason for leaving home.* "What's so terrible about my father that you felt you couldn't tell me?"

I'm strong. I'm used to being on my own. And if I never find out who my father is—well, I guess that's the way it's supposed to be.

Chapter Thirteen

The horse shied as Cliff flung the saddle blanket onto his back. Picking up the saddle, he hurled it into place. Sonny flinched when the bulky, leather stirrups slapped against his sides.

"Stand," Cliff growled, reaching under the horse's belly for the girth strap. He hadn't slept much the night before, and when he did, he dreamt about Cat. This morning he had awakened alone, the spot where she'd curled against him in her sleep was empty and cold.

After dragging himself out of bed, he downed a pot of strong coffee and sorted mindlessly through the stack of mail. He soon discovered that the silence of the house had become deafening and realized he would go crazy if he didn't get out of there. He hoped going to work would help get Cat off his mind. Yet he couldn't help wondering where she went and if she was all right.

He grabbed his cowboy hat from its hook by the door and headed for the barn.

The sound of tires crushing gravel, and the purr of a car engine near the barn caught Cliff's attention. His heart leaped. Was it Cat coming back? Yet his stubborn pride caused him to take his time threading the latigo strap through the front rigging dee and tightening the cinch. He would hold his ground. She would have to come to him and apologize.

A car door slammed, and footsteps approached the barn. He turned and glanced at the woman who stood framed in the doorway. Dressed in black, knee-high, *city boots*, black jeans and a pink t-shirt that clung to her like a second skin, Nora flashed him her *I've got the afternoon free*

155

smile. Her raven hair hung loose to her slim waist where a pink and black bandana sufficed as a belt.

"Think it's a good idea to work after just getting out of the hospital?" The voice that had once sounded as sweet as honey droned around his head like a swarm of ornery hornets.

He turned away, grabbed the headstall and slipped it over the horse's head.

"Cliff?" she purred, resting her manicured hand lightly on his arm. "I've said I'm sorry for what happened between us several times already. Are you ever going to forgive me?"

Cliff felt the muscles in his jaw tense. He had no desire to stand around, now or ever, and rehash their past with her. Stepping forward, he started to pass her, but she stepped into his path, bringing him up short, forcing him to acknowledge her. Planting her hands on her hips, she stared at him and waited.

He closed his eyes for a couple seconds, drew a deep breath and prayed for patience. "I've forgiven you, Nora, but every time I lay eyes on you, I see *my wife*—naked in my brother's arms."

"Cliff..." She broke off when he raised his hand.

"Listen. I've found there are consequences to everything we do," he said, thinking back on how he'd yelled and berated Catrina at every turn. "Sometimes the price is too high to pay or too painful to ever get over." It would be a long time before he recovered from the loss of Cat. He had pushed her away, and along with her went any chance they might have had together.

Nora's lips puckered into an inviting little pout. She placed a hand against his chest and said, "Give me a couple of hours, and I could make you forget your name."

He recoiled as if she slapped him. "What the hell's the matter with you, woman?" The sound of his raised voice caused Sonny to toss his head and take a step back.

Nora's brows knitted together, her full lips stretched into a firm, straight line. "I don't even know why I try to be nice to you. I just thought..." She brushed her hair behind her ear. "Since she left town and all..."

Before he realized it, he reached out and grabbed her by the arm, pulling her closer. "When did you see Cat? What did she tell you?"

When she flinched, he released her.

"Gee, Cliff," She rubbed the spot where his hand had just been. "You're such a smooth talker. No wonder the women are lined up to the road."

"Quit stalling, and spit it out."

As if taking a cue from his horse, she took a step back. "Maybe I don't want to tell you now." She turned away from him as if she found something more amusing out the window to look at.

Cliff's blood started boiling, pounding in his head. He was going to wring her neck. "Nora! Tell me what you know or so help me..."

"Okay, okay." She turned to face him, and although she had a smug expression, she kept a safe distance away from him. "I ran into Catrina at the hospital yesterday. She was standing outside your door, crying."

"What was she crying about?" he asked, knowing Nora just loved having the upper hand on him. She would drag this out as long as possible, just to watch him squirm.

"How do I know?" Her tone indicated her frustration. "She told me to tell you that she wasn't going to stand in your way of buying her grandmother's land. Then she said she was leaving for New York."

"If you were outside my room yesterday, why didn't you come in and tell me this?"

Nora shrugged. "I don't know. When I looked in, you were sleeping. I didn't want to wake you up, so I just left."

So, that's where she went. Why didn't she say good-bye? What was she crying about? None of this makes any sense!

"Hey, lover boy?" Nora's sarcasm pulled Cliff out of his wool gathering. "So? What did you do that made her cry and leave town when her grandmother's on her death bed?"

Gritting his teeth to keep from yelling, Cliff led Sonny out of the barn and tossed the reins up over his neck. With his back to her, he said, "It was her decision to leave. I didn't do or say anything." He stepped heavily into the stirrup and Sonny danced in place.

Nora glanced up at him and shook her head. "Maybe that's your problem." She replaced the sarcasm with a serious tone.

He knew she was probably right, but he wasn't going to give her the satisfaction by telling her so. Instead, he growled, "My problem right now is that I've got work to do, and I've already wasted too much time."

With a slight move of his boot, Sonny spun to the right and launched into a gallop across the field, leaving Nora behind. After a few moments, he slowed his horse to a fast-paced walk.

Well, he had gotten what he wanted. Cat finally out of his life, and nobody stood in the way of him purchasing Millie's land. So...why wasn't he deliriously happy?

Catrina had taken up root in his home and then proceeded to turn his serene little world upside down at every chance she got. He was better off without her.

If she was such a burr under his saddle, then why did he feel like he just came off a four-day bender? Besides recovering from snakebite, his guts were twisted in a tight knot. His head pounded as though a herd of buffalo had run in one ear and out the other. *Why the hell had she just stood out in the hall at the hospital and not come in and explained why she had to leave?*

For the life of him, he couldn't think of what he did or said that would cause her to get so upset that she would leave town. *Sure, I yelled at her. Damn it, I thought the fool woman was going to get hurt or kill herself.*

"Well, good riddance. She'll be somebody else's problem soon." He snorted. "She'll get into all kinds of trouble in a big city like New York." He yanked back on the reins as Sonny broke into a fast trot. *If she's driving all the way to New York, she could run into trouble along the way. Who'd be there to save her? Any number of guys, that's who! They'd love to step in and help a pretty little thing like her. They'd look deep into those dark hypnotic eyes and fall for her just like I did.*

The big gray gelding sidestepped a large rock. Surprised at the horse's quick movements, Cliff pulled him up short and headed him in a different direction. "What the hell's wrong with you today?" he growled and cursed at the horse. "Pay attention to where you're going!"

Some degenerate's going to come along and...and what? One of two things...he'll either take advantage of her, or he'll do the same thing I did. Take one look at her and be lost. Think about her every moment of the day, so he can't get a damn thing done and then dream about her every night so he doesn't get any rest.

"Maybe it's better that she's gone," he said aloud, hoping to convince himself that it was true. However, no matter how much he told himself she was out of his life, it was going to be a long time before she totally vanished from his mind. He knew once she reached the big city, she'd forget all about him and everyone else in Black River. She'd start a new life in a new town.

A new life... Another man's hands and lips touching her! Making love to her! Cliff's stomach churned. Bile rose to the back of his throat. Sinking his spurs into the horse's sides, he urged him into a faster lope.

Sonny slipped on some slick rocks and stumbled as he started across a shallow creek, causing Cliff to almost lose his seat. "Watch what you're doing, you stupid Cayuse," he yelled. His heart slammed against his ribs. Pulling back on the reins, he spurred the horse, and Sonny vaulted onto the other bank.

"I'll kill anyone who lies..."

Without warning, Sonny dropped his head, cut loose and started bucking. Unprepared, Cliff hit the hard ground with a thud. A loud "Ohff" escaped as the air rushed out of his lung. With his butt in the dirt, he pulled off his hat and slapped it against one knee as his horse ran off. He wasn't hurt. He'd landed on his pride. Although it had already been pretty bruised, limping back to the ranch wasn't going to help it much.

* * * *

Cat reached for a map and travel booklet by the checkout at the gas station while she waited in line. Opening the colorful brochure, she glanced over the information. Suddenly she jammed it back into the holder, realizing that anything she read might one day pop out of her mouth during some catastrophe. How could she have ranted and raved about snakes and how they killed their prey all the way to the hospital? No wonder Cliff had thought she was crazy.

She paid for her gasoline, a couple bottles of water and a bag of individually wrapped Bit-O-Honeys. When the young girl at the register smiled, Cat asked, "Do you know where I can get some film developed close by?"

"Yeah! There's a one-hour photo shop in the Northside Shopping Center. It's about a mile and a half up the service road on the left. You can't miss it."

"Thanks." Cat grabbed her stuff and headed out the door.

She pulled into the Northside Shopping Center's lot and parked in front of the photo shop. After dropping off several rolls of film, she headed to the large craft store where she could stretch her legs. She would shop while she waited for her photos. The shelves in the colorful craft store were filled with everything a creative person could dream of. There were rows of tubs filled with beads, every color of yarn and tons of paint supplies and wood working materials. Grabbing a cart, she wandered around. Although Crystal had sent some items to her, she searched for additional things she needed.

Two hours later, she pushed her cart, filled with painting supplies, sketching supplies and extra canvass to the counter. Pulling her teeth over her bottom lip, Cat felt giddy about everything she purchased. The total came to one hundred and thirty-five dollars, but she didn't care. She had everything she needed to replace the paintings that were ruined in the flood.

She loaded the bags into her car and headed back into the photo shop to pick up her pictures. She couldn't wait to go through them and pick a second photo to paint, which would show the cowboy side of Cliff and what his life consisted of now. She had already decided she would paint the photo she found of him dressed in his Native American regalia.

Back in her car, Cat ripped open the packets. When it came to viewing her photos for the first time, she had no patience whatsoever. Nervously, she thumbed through the scenery and animal snap shots, anticipating the photos of Cliff. She came to the ones she took while in the haymow. They were of Cliff casually moving a small band of cattle. Snow-capped mountains and towering pines loomed in the background. She flipped through the stack and remembered that this was the same day she fell through the rotted wood. *I must have looked like a fool, my body dangling through a hole in the floor!* Her pulse raced, and her breath caught. A shiver ran up her spine, and she could still feel his rough hands grip her hips then slide up her sides to help her down.

She shook the feeling off, flipped the next photo and froze. She gazed at Cliff atop his big gray horse, his wrists crossed and resting on the saddle horn, his collar turned up against the wind. With his hat pulled low over his eyes, his face held no expression. But his dark, brooding eyes, revealed that he studied something off in the distance.

The man was a mass of contradiction. She wished things had been different so she could have taken the time to peel back his many layers to see what was hidden beneath.

This was the perfect photo to do in oils as the second painting. The deep lines etched on his face and his thick mustache made him look much older than the Native American snapshot. It showed the man he had become.

She continued and came across several pictures of Doug, showing her how to brand. In the first one, she held the branding iron with both hands. Doug towered over her from behind, his large calloused hands covered hers. Her face held a serious expression as she concentrated on her task. She smiled. On the ground behind them in the shadow, the couple's embrace could have told a story of intimacy. "What a great shot!"

In the second photo, her face was scrunched up as she pressed the hot iron to the calf's thick hide. "Nora must have taken these." She laughed out loud as she flipped to the next one. Doug lay flat out on the ground with Cat sprawled on her back on top of him. "Oh my God, that was funny!"

Tears filled her eyes as she continued laughing, however, the next photo was sobering. She drew in a deep breath. Cliff stood over her as his brother offered to help her up. His hands were planted on his hips, his expression murderous. It was the same expression he had the day they had that terrible fight and he pulled her off her horse.

She closed her eyes and cringed. Cliff had opened up that day and shared with her how his father treated him and how he had hated the man. She'd taken his troubled relationship with his father and mixed it with her own fears of never having a family. He had confided in her, expected her to understand and be compassionate. But what had she done? She'd thrown it back in his face and accused him of being a monster just like his father.

Bile rose in the back of her throat. It would have never worked out between them. Her independence and her adventurous spirit threatened him. He would have locked her up in his world where she wouldn't be exposed to any new stimulation. That would have only staunched her creativity, and she would eventually grow to hate him for it.

She may have felt a small connection between her and Cliff that day, but now all she felt was another loss. She had never minded being by herself before; she actually enjoyed traveling alone. Yet she never felt more lonely and isolated than she felt at this moment.

* * * *

Perched on the tailgate of his truck, Rooster sipped his beer and watched Cliff limp toward him. Cliff had stepped in all those years ago and took up the slack where his son James had left off. Rooster didn't think he could have loved the boy more if he *had* been his true son. But today he saw a man with both boots overflowing with heartache and troubles.

The passion that danced between Cliff and Catrina had been like watching a lighting storm. There was a thin line between love and hate, but he would bet his '52 International pickup that it was love. He scratched the stubble on his chin and then spit a stream of tobacco juice on the ground. He just might have to bang their heads together to make them understand and accept it though.

Cliff didn't look any worse for wear as he hoofed it toward the barn. Rooster had caught Sonny, unsaddled the lathered horse, rubbed him down and then turned him out in the small paddock. Rooster chuckled when horse and rider spotted each other. Cliff glared through squinted eyes at the beast. Sonny merely turned away and swished his tail. Cliff may have been the one who got the worst end of it today, and Rooster was itching to find out why, but he was pretty sure the other one was gonna pay the next time they rode out.

"Why the hell didn't you drive out and pick me up?" Cliff growled, as he approached him.

"Figured if you made Sonny mad enough to buck you off, you needed the walk back to cool off." Rooster opened a small cooler and handed him a cold beer.

Without a word, Cliff twisted the top off and downed half of the bottle in one gulp. After the younger man released a heavy sigh, Rooster felt safe to ask. "So where is she?"

Cliff stared off into the distance. "By now, half way to New York."

"Did you two have another fight? Why'd she leave?"

"How the hell do I know?" Cliff shook his head and nursed his beer.

"Do you love her?" He knew the answer; he wanted to hear Cliff admit it.

"It doesn't matter. It's too late to do anything about it now." He removed his hat and scratched his head.

"Buffalo chips!" Rooster spat. "It's never too late! You just have to have faith in love."

Cliff turned his head. "Faith? Yeah, that worked out well for me the last time!"

Rooster wondered if he should tell Cliff that he was convinced Cat was his granddaughter. He lost his wife and his only son. Nora's mother Anna moved to Oregon years ago, and she hardly ever wrote or called him. Cat seemed to feel a strong connection to everyone she met on the reservation, and he knew she was happy there. He also saw love in the girl's eyes when she looked at Cliff. *Damn it! This is where she belongs! I'm not going to let him screw this up!*

Cliff was looking at him with a puzzled expression. "What are you cooking up in that hard head of yours, old man?"

"You've been running long enough, boy. It's time you look to the spirits…figure out who you really are."

Cliff shook his head. "I know who I am and *what* I am."

Rooster worked his way off the tailgate. He adjusted his dusty old hat and pushed it back. "I'll build a sweat. You'll come, and find the answers you seek."

Cliff pulled his hat down low and started, "I don't think…"

Rooster waved his hand in the other man's face. "Get off my truck."

With a stunned look, he hopped off the tailgate.

"You leave the thinking to me." Rooster started toward the driver's door and then glanced back. "You're going to do this *my* way." He held Cliff's gaze for several seconds as he opened the truck's door. His aching legs protested as he climbed inside. The engine roared to life, and he drove away.

I'm done pussy-footin' around!

Cliff stared at the cloud of red dust that billowed up behind Rooster's truck. That old cowboy had been more of a father to him than Hank had ever been. He learned everything about both worlds from the patient, old Ute.

Hank had expected him to know things, and when he didn't, he had given him a hard time. *You'll never be more than an Indian.* His father's words still stung after all these years.

He turned and headed toward the house. He had learned a lot of things growing up with a foot in two worlds, and he learned them well. He learned to fight for what he had and what he wanted. Until what he had walked away and left him, then he learned to hate.

When he had the money, he decided to build up *his* ranch. So he built a world of his own, a world where he belonged; where he was the boss and where he could be and do whatever he wanted. Yet, no matter how big his world got, how many acres he owned, Hank's words hunted him down and haunted him. He would always be that *lucky* Indian boy Hank had taken away from the reservation and a life doomed to poverty. And although he cut his hair, changed his clothes, and he was far from being poor, he still carried the weight of what he was. He proved he was strong enough to carry that burden, but he wouldn't put Cat through the same humiliation.

He opened the door and walked into the empty house. A house filled with things Hank had owned, a house that had never felt like a home. "She deserves so much more than this. So much more than me."

The ringing of the phone pierced the silence.

Chapter Fourteen

Millie reclined in a chair in the corner of her room, perusing the next clue in the crossword puzzle book while waiting for Cliff to show up. "Fourteen down. A nine letter word that means positive." She smiled and scribbled the word *confident* in the small boxes on the page. She had confidence that White Fox would be able to straighten out this little misunderstanding between her and Catrina.

Last night she had called to tell him she needed to talk. She snickered at the thought that he had been bothering her for years to sell him her land. If she dangled it just right in front of him, there was no telling what he would do to get his hands on it.

The door to Millie's room swung open, and Cliff's frame filled the opening. Removing his hat, he swaggered into the room. His deep voice sounded like gravel when he spoke. "So, you've heard from her? Where is she?" he asked, one thumb hooked casually in the front pocket of his worn jeans.

Millie snapped the crossword book shut and tossed it aside. "What do you mean? She's supposed to be with *you.*"

"Well, she's not," he growled, slapping his hat against his leg. "She left town."

Rising to her feet, Millie began to pace across the floor. Sure, Catrina had been angry when she left here, but she didn't think the girl would leave town. Millie turned and frowned at the sour expression on Cliff's face. "What's the matter with you?" she said, placing her fists on her hips.

Cliff's arm raised, and he pointed his hat at her legs. "What the hell

165

is going on here? You're walking like nothing's wrong with you."

Feeling like she had just been caught *again* with her fingers in the cookie jar, Millie stammered and glanced around the room for some sort of diversion.

"You better tell me what's going on, old woman."

He stalked forward, and Millie motioned to the empty chair. "Sit down before I get a crick in my neck, staring up at you."

When he didn't move, Millie pointed toward the chair again. "Park your sorry ass, and listen up." Shaking his head, he settled onto the edge of the cushion and fiddled with the brim of his hat.

"I had good reasons for wantin' my granddaughter here with me." Millie scratched the back of her head and ambled aimlessly around the room. "But she didn't want to come, not right away anyhow. So... So I fibbed a little and told her I was sick." She shot him a glance, seeing his scowl, she said, "Don't be looking at me like that. It's time that girl stops running all over the world, getting into who knows what! She's not getting any younger. It's time for her to settle down and get married!"

Cliff shot to his feet, his face contorted with anger. "You stuck her out in that rundown shack knowing I'd find her out there all alone. She could have been killed in that storm. She almost drowned in the ditch as it was!"

"Well, she didn't, did she? It was the only way I could get her to stay. Besides she's tougher than you think. That's why she's perfect for you."

He stared at her in total disbelief. "That's why she left town. She figured out your little scheme, and you got caught in your own trap." He stepped toward the door, then stopped and turned to face her. "How could you do that to her?"

Anger surged through Millie. This wasn't over yet. "Me? How could you let her slip through your fingers after I literally dropped her in your lap?"

"Why you old crow... If you knew anything about Cat, you'd know that she wants family more than anything."

"So what the hell do you plan on doing to get her back?"

"What can I do?" His arms flapped at his sides.

She shook her head. "Go get her, and bring her back."

"I wouldn't know where to even start looking for her in New York.

After everything that's happened since she came here, why on earth would she ever want to come back?" He turned and reached for the door handle.

"Cliff. Do you still want my land?" A smug smile crossed her face when he stopped in his tracks. *All I have to do is reel him in.*

"Keep it." He tossed over one shoulder. "I don't give a damn about it anymore."

Chapter Fifteen

This is just going to be a waste of time.

The thought of being cooped up for hours in a cramped sweat lodge stampeded through Cliff's mind like a herd of wild mustangs.

He turned his Ford pickup off the highway onto the reservation road, heading toward the small lake hidden within a forest of quaking aspen. He expected to feel something spiritual take place when he crossed onto the reservation, but since he no longer believed in the old ways, he wasn't surprised when nothing changed.

He shouldn't have come, but Rooster hadn't asked him. He had *ordered* Cliff to come. The old man expected Cliff would have a vision telling him Cat's whereabouts. But he had already locked his feeling for her away and made up his mind to get on with his life.

The truck bounced along the rough road, then onto a patch of tall grass. He parked next to Rooster's International and snorted at the sight of Doug's '72 green and white pickup, known as the "Love Truck". It had twin, chrome stacks, a sprayed in bed-liner and a stereo system most guys only dreamt about.

Giving the door of his truck a satisfying slam, Cliff headed toward the woods and the small clearing by the lake. Over the years, he'd participated in several sweats, and he knew Rooster preferred a traditional ceremony, so he had fasted for twenty-four hours.

Cliff stopped on the edge of a small clearing and surveyed the scene before him. It was like looking through a window into time, to another era long ago. Dressed in nothing but a loincloth, his cousin Doug milled around the campsite. He tended the ceremonial rocks, which were placed in a large fire for hours until thoroughly heated. The small round wigwam structure covered in animal skins had been constructed of two-dozen or so, thin willow saplings.

Rooster appeared from behind the lodge. In a loincloth, the elder Ute looked twenty years younger. He stood straight, shoulders back, with his head held high.

Cliff's stomach twisted and turned. Since the beginning, his people entered the sweat lodge for healing sessions, before hunting trips, when going into war or for a vision quest. Experiencing a sweat was equivalent to being reborn. A man emerged with a clean soul, forgiven of past wrongs, ready for a new life.

I don't need a new life. I just need people to stay out of mine.

Although Cliff had his doubts, he stripped down to his loincloth. Leaving his clothes and the world he built for himself behind, he meandered into camp.

When Doug spotted him, he reached down and retrieved a clump of sage that had been placed over the hot coals. Without a word, Doug passed the smoking sage over Cliff's body to purify him before he could enter the lodge. Once inside the sweat, no words would be spoken except for prayers and chants.

Cliff entered the lodge and sank down onto one of the many furs spread over a bed of fresh sage. The familiar scent of smoke, animal fur, spices and rich earth engulfed him, taking him back to a time when his life had been happier. A time when he thought he knew who he was and where he belonged.

Rooster entered next and moved to one side. When Charlie entered the lodge, Cliff drew in a deep breath and glanced toward Rooster. The elder Ute averted his eyes, and both men settled down on the furs.

Through the opening, Cliff watched Doug fish out a rock with a pitchfork and rake, making sure to leave the coals behind. He entered the lodge and placed it in the hollowed out spot in the middle of the lodge. Seven rocks were placed in the hole. After each one, the three men leaned forward and sprinkled cedar over them. Cliff knew Doug's job for the next five hours would be to beat the ceremonial drum outside the lodge, tend the fire and every forty-five minutes pull back the heavy hide door and add more rocks.

The flap closed, and the ceremony started. Rooster poured water from a bucket, which had been placed by the entrance, over the glowing rocks. The stones hissed and whispered incoherent words of wisdom as steam rose and filled Cliff's lungs. The hot, damp air bathed his face.

As the orange glow of the rocks subsided, the small space was engulfed in total darkness. Closing his eyes, Cliff let his mind open, and one by one his worries escaped and mingled with the rising smoke. Tension he didn't realize existed began to drain out of his shoulders and tense muscles.

Rooster began to chant and pray in a mixture of ancient dialect and his native language. He thanked the Grandfathers and prayed to the spirits and the four winds.

The hours passed in a haze of dreams as Cliff chanted and prayed. In his first vision, he saw himself and his younger brother Charlie as small boys. Wind and leaves whipped their bare arms as they laughed and ran through the woods. Once they reached the lake, they sat on the bank to fish, and Cliff showed his brother how to place a worm on the hook while they soaked their feet in the cool water. That vision faded, and Cliff smelled the warm, familiar scent of horses as he taught Charlie to ride a pony. Determined to ride like his brother, Charlie kicked the pony's shaggy sides, but the small boy fell when the pony bucked and ran off. Cliff placed the boy on his own pony and then led them back to the corral.

Similar visions played out in his mind, and he soon realized that in the absence of a father, he had taken on the responsibility of protecting his family and teaching his brother. But then somehow things changed, and his brother challenged everything he said and did. Life became a competition between them to prove which boy was stronger, faster, and smarter. Whatever one boy had or found the other wanted.

Then Cliff remembered the day Hank Dawson, his father, drove up in a new pickup. Hank had come for his thirteen year old son, to take him back to his ranch. He had promised to give him a better life and make a man out of him. Cliff had been proud to have a father and went willingly. But now for the first time, he saw the tears in his mother and brother's eyes as he drove away. His heart ached at the thought that his mother had no choice in the matter and that he had abandoned his little brother.

Perspiration covered Cliff's body. His head felt light, and his eyes burned when the sweat dripped into them. He licked his dry cracked lips and wished he hadn't come.

Sinking deep into the vision world again, Cliff saw himself wandering in the wilderness, alone with no food, no water and no shelter. He wandered aimlessly without seeing another person. The days turned into weeks, then months and then years. His thin, wilted body was burnt from the searing sun, his feet blistered and bleeding. He felt hollow, as if he was nothing more than an empty shell of a person. He was an outcast with no people, direction or purpose.

Cliff heard the screech of an eerie cry as a huge shadow blocked out the sun. A giant eagle swooped down. Its sharp talons dug deep into Cliff's flesh, and the enormous raptor snatched him up. The massive bird carried him far away, then ceased its hold and dropped him from the sky. Arms and legs flailing, he fought to grasp something real, something solid and dependable that could save him. Panic ripped through Cliff's chest as he watched himself fall. If he continued as he was, he would certainly plummet to his death.

But then he landed unhurt, and Cat was waiting for him. She smiled and reached out to him. He inhaled her breathtaking scent of wild flowers. Peace and happiness replaced all his fears and the loneliness he lived with for years.

The mystery of life became clear. Man was never meant to be alone. He was meant to have a partner, a second half to make him whole. Someone who offered love and understanding and gave life purpose, because without those things life wasn't worth living.

Cliff knew if he continued to flounder, going through the motions of living, that at the end of the day, he would still have exactly what he started with—nothing. He was tired of being alone. He loved Cat and wanted to make a life with her. All of a sudden, a sense of calm and forgiveness washed over him. In the past, others had told him that they felt liberated or reborn after hours in the sweat lodge. Now he knew what they meant.

Rooster's voice broke through his thoughts as he murmured the ending prayer. The flap was opened, and the three men exited the lodge. Cliff stood and stretched his cramped muscles. He drew in a deep breath of fresh air and marveled at the countless stars that lit up the night sky.

Charlie stood off to his right. With his lean, muscular build and his arrogant stance, he resembled an ancient warrior. His long raven braids hung down over his smooth, sweat-soaked chest. Dark brown, brooding eyes studied him as Cliff turned to face his brother. The hate he carried for five years had fled from his heart. Cliff reached out and extended his hand. Charlie followed his lead, and the two men clasped arms in a symbol of brotherhood.

Turning toward Rooster, Cliff embraced the man. "Thank you, Father." His voice strained as he spoke. "I'm thankful that you stood by me all these years."

Rooster nodded his approval, and then cleared his throat. "What will you do now?"

Cliff shook his head. "I have no idea, but if I have to, I'll turn the whole state of New York upside down and shake it 'till she falls out."

* * * *

Cat rolled onto her side and gathered the covers tight to her chest. Blinking, she heaved a heavy sigh as her gaze lifted and the colorless room came into focus. The bright morning sun seeped through the plastic blinds of the room's only window, casting streaks of white light across the yellowed ceiling and faded panel walls. She stretched and winced in pain. She hadn't slept well on the motel's lumpy mattress, and now she would pay the price.

She threw the covers aside and swung her feet to the floor. Standing, a weary groan escaped her lungs as her stiff muscles stretched. She trudged toward the bathroom, her feet dragging as though they were encased in concrete. Passing a small table in front of the window, Cat reached into a bag and pulled out a day-old donut. She bit into the dried treat and tried to ignore the loud protest from her growling stomach. "I get the message," she said, knowing her habit of not eating well while on the road. "I'll find some *real* food today."

She shoved the rest of the donut into her mouth, entered the bathroom and kicked the door shut. Settling onto the stool, she glanced over at the empty toilet paper roll, then fished in the plastic grocery bag next to the sink but came up empty. The dry donut protested against being swallowed, and Cat started to gag and cough. The next thing she knew, she was heaving into the toilet and sobbing for no reason.

"What's wrong with me?" she muttered, turning on the shower. "I need a good night's sleep and good meal."

Twenty minutes later Cat sat defeated on the edge of the bed. The shower had cleared her head and helped her sore back, but she still felt exhausted, as if someone had sucked the life and creativity out of her. She desperately needed to talk to her friend and agent, Crystal. Grabbing the phone next to the bed, she dialed the number.

"Hello?" The redhead's voice sounded like an angel to Cat's ears.

"Crystal? It's Catrina." Her voice cracked, and she fought to clear her throat.

"Catrina, honey, what's wrong?"

"She lied to me about everything. She really wasn't sick, and there was no mysterious woman who knows who my father is. And I'm out of toilet paper," she sobbed.

"Honey, calm down. Where are you?"

Catrina glanced around the dull and depressing room. "I crossed over from Ohio into Pennsylvania a couple of days ago."

"Are you hurt? Is it your car?" The pitch of Crystal's voice rose in panic.

Cat struggled, but drew in a calming breath. "I'm fine—I think. I'm just worn-out and hungry. I haven't been sleeping very well." She grabbed the box of tissues, pulled one out and blew her nose.

"I know how you get when you're traveling," Crystal scolded. "You don't eat well. You stay in cheap motels, and before long you come down with a cold."

"I know," Cat said, rubbing her temples.

"Take a breath and start over. Who lied to you?"

Cat settled back against the headboard and sighed. "Millie, my grandmother. She lied to me about being sick so I'd come to Black River and see her. Then she lied about knowing a woman who was supposed to be my mother's friend. She said this woman would know who my father is."

"Well, that stinks. I'm sorry. What did Cliff think about all this?"

"I was on my way to the hospital to see him..."

"The hospital?" Crystal's voice rose into a shriek. "Why was he in the hospital?"

"I had to drive him there after the rattlesnake bit him."

"Oh my God! How the hell did that happen?"

Cat bit her lip in shame. "I hiked up to a place called Red Rock to take photos of the sunset, and Cliff followed me. He started stomping around like a wild man and yelling that it wasn't safe..."

"Obviously, he knows what he's talking about."

"Yeah, I guess," Cat said, wishing she hadn't called Crystal after all. "Well, that's when he was bitten by the snake."

"Is he going to be all right?" The line went quiet for a few seconds. "Catrina?"

"I guess he's going to be fine," Cat muttered and gnawed on one fingernail.

"You guess? Haven't you seen him or talked to him?"

"That's what I was saying before you interrupted me. I was walking down the hall to his room to tell him that I walked in on my grandmother and found out that she'd been lying to me. That's when I overheard him talking to Rooster."

"Rooster? There are chickens in his hospital room?"

"Crystal, shut up and listen to me!" Cat shook her head. Couldn't the woman pay attention for two minutes? "Rooster's the man who saved me from the flood and took me to his ranch. Well, I thought it was his ranch, but it turned out to be Cliff's ranch." She took a deep breath and continued. "I heard him tell Rooster that I had been nothing but a pain in the butt since I arrived. That I spent all my time dreaming up cockamamie ways to get into trouble," she scoffed. "That mountain lion was only trying to scare me away from her cubs."

Cat heard Crystal gasp. "Mountain lion?"

"Never mind that. He said that I drove him crazy, and I was a huge distraction. He couldn't get anything done with me around. Then, when Rooster asked him why he slept with me..."

"You slept with him?"

"Just twice."

"Twice?"

"Crystal!"

"Sorry. I think I should be taking notes."

"He actually told him that he thought he was dreaming."

"Who was dreaming?" Crystal asked confused.

"Cliff thought he was dreaming, and the next morning he didn't have the nerve to tell me that it had all been a mistake."

"A mistake?" The line went quiet again then Crystal's voice became calm and soft. "Honey, do *you* feel it was a mistake?"

Cat tried to stay angry with Cliff, but she missed him so much. Each day took her further away from him, and she was making herself sick thinking about him.

"Catrina? Are you still there?"

"I'm still here," she sniffled and blew her nose again.

"With everything that has happened to you, no wonder you're exhausted. It sounds like Cliff was only concerned for your safety. He must care for you. If he didn't, why would he come looking for you? And even though you might not think so, you've taken some pretty stupid chances over the years trying to get that million dollar shot."

"Wait until you see some of the shots I got," Cat added, moving to where the photos were stacked on the table. "You're going to flip when you see the ones from branding day. Not only the ones that I took, Nora took some nice photos, too. She has a pretty good eye for photography."

"Nora? Who's...? Never mind. When do you think you'll arrive in New York?"

"That's the problem," Cat said. She crawled back onto the bed and sat cross-legged. "I arrived in Pennsylvania and checked into a motel in what appeared to be a quiet area. I was so tired of driving that I decided to stay here for a few days before arriving in New York."

"Have you done any painting?" Crystal asked.

"Some. I started on the first painting, but spilled some color on the carpet. So I decided to go outside for better light. It was a beautiful day, no wind, sunny with a few scattered clouds-perfect for painting. I set up my easel in a small park area next to the motel."

"I don't think I'm going to like where this is going," the redhead grumbled.

"But then I heard banging from a machine shop and the sound of road construction vehicles. The icing on the cake was the wonderful smell of fresh tar being laid."

There was a pause, before Crystal asked, "Did you get any work done?"

"In my room I finished the first painting. Mixed a little glaze in with the oils, so it should be dry by the time I get to New York."

She slid her hand in long slow strokes across the bed, remembering how just a glance from Cliff could make her feel all warm and secure.

"Catrina?"

"I love him. I can't stop thinking about him. I want to be part of his world."

"What about your career?" Crystal asked in a subdued tone.

"I'd gladly give up all the traveling, everything to settle down and make a life with him. I could be happy in Black River."

"Wow. I never thought I'd ever hear you say that. You're pretty independent," Crystal said. "You've been able to do whatever you've wanted without checking in with anyone for a very long time."

"I know," Cat murmured, picking at the worn bedspread.

"You'd have to learn to take Cliff's feelings and concerns into consideration. Is that something you think you can do?"

"After all the trouble I've been to him, leaving town the way I did, he won't want anything to do with me now." Cat brushed her thumb over a photo of Cliff, and her throat tightened up. It was best to just leave the poor man alone.

"I'm sure if he knew how you felt about him, he'd react differently."

Cat snorted. "Right about now he's thinking good riddance."

With a lighter tone, Crystal changed the subject. "When do you think you'll arrive?"

"If I leave early tomorrow morning," Cat said. "I should be to your apartment around 8:00 tomorrow night."

"That's great," Crystal said. "Take care of yourself, and don't take any chances on the highway. Call me at the office if you can't find my building."

"Thanks, Crystal. Talk to you soon." Cat hung up the receiver and glanced over to the oil painting drying on the table. The three paintings that were ruined in the flood were from her Africa collection. The photos had been fabulous, the oils done in rich vibrant colors. And although the subjects had been inspiring, none of them touched her like the snapshot of Cliff dressed in full regalia. Even before she'd known the man's true identity, something in his intense, stern expression sent chills slithering up her spine. The photo depicted a man who was dangerous, defiant and most certainly domineering. Although she had only seen the cowboy side of Cliff she had no problem picturing him emerging from a tepee shirtless, his long raven hair flowing down his back.

"Damn him!" She flopped back against the pillows. "I miss that pigheaded man and everything about him." The way his face scrunched up when he was cross, the way he settled his sweat-stained, old gray cowboy hat on his head, but mostly, the way it felt when he held her in his arms and loved her.

Cat's eyes stung with tears. Dashing the tears away, she sat up and swung her legs over the side of the bed. She had been all over the world, met dozens of wonderful people. What was it about him and that "nothing" little town in Utah that she couldn't get out of her head?

Trudging into the bathroom, Cat stopped and studied her reflection in the cloudy mirror. It was different this time. She liked Black River and the people who lived there. Most of all she felt like she belonged there. Then it hit her; she was homesick for the first time in her life.

Chapter Sixteen

Cliff slapped his hat on his head, stepped into his boots and reached for the backdoor. The phone shrilled, making his head pound. He hadn't slept much and was in no mood to speak to anyone this early in the morning. Scowling, he marched across the room and scooped up the receiver.

"Yeah?"

"Cliff? It's Charlie..."

I don't need this right now. "I'm just heading out to do chores. What's up?"

"Rooster's had a heart attack. We're at the hospital. He's asking for you."

Cliff's stomach rolled. *Oh my God.* He didn't need to hear more. In three strides, he was out the door. The crisp morning air stung his face as he bounded down the steps. He stopped short when he noticed the left front tire on his pickup had gone flat. "This whole day is going to hell in a hand basket," he shouted, leaping into the box of the truck for the jack and spare.

Within minutes, he changed the tire, flung the flat tire, jack and tire-iron into the back of the truck and headed for town.

This was his fault. He worked the old man too hard, expected too much out of him. When Rooster insisted that he build the sweat lodge by himself, which was the custom, Cliff should have ignored his request and helped him.

He slammed the palm of his hand against the steering wheel. "If he dies..." The thought of losing Rooster sent a sharp pain shooting across his forehead. Checking the dashboard clock, Cliff hoped he would make it to the hospital in time. There was so much he needed to tell the old man before... Why hadn't he waited to hear what else Charlie might have told him?

Cliff's head pulsed with every rapid heartbeat. He rubbed his temple, trying to keep his panic at bay. The pickup ate up the pavement like locust clearing a field. He braked as he approached a sharp curve. The tires spun, spraying dried gravel into the ditch.

Just as he recovered, five mule deer bounded across the road, forcing him to stomp on the brakes. "What the hell's wrong with you, White Fox? You drive like that crazy woman," he berated himself.

The truck eased forward, and he glanced toward the passenger side, wishing a certain crazy woman sat beside him, her brown eyes and gentle touch reassuring him that everything was going to be all right.

"If you don't start paying closer attention, you're never going to get to town in one piece." He shook his head in disgust. *God help me. Now I'm talking to myself.*

The pickup roared onto the empty streets of Black River. Upon reaching the hospital, he pulled in and parked by the emergency entrance, then jumped out and ran for the door. He was forced to pause for a moment at the electronic doors. When they slid open, he rushed in and then skidded to a halt. He glanced down one corridor and then the other. At last spotting Charlie and Nora, he bolted toward them. Nora approached Cliff, her eyes swimming with tears, her arms reached out for him.

"Oh, Cliff..." Her voice wobbled. Grabbing her by the arms, he handed her off to Charlie.

"Take care of your woman, little brother."

Charlie took Nora into his arms and nodded his head toward an opened door across the hall. Cliff froze. Panic rose, tightening his chest muscles as he wondered what he was about to learn. How would he ever get along without the only real father he'd ever known? His knees felt weak, while his boots felt like they were filled with concrete.

Taking a calming breath, he hoped his expression masked his trepidation. The smell of antiseptic and beeping machines engulfed him as he entered the room. Rooster lay propped up in the hospital bed, tubes protruding from both arms. An oxygen mask covered his weathered face, making him look frail and vulnerable. Yet a faint smile quirked his lips when he spotted Cliff.

Swallowing a lump the size of a new salt lick, he trudged toward the bed. "I suppose this means you're not gonna be out to help me with chores today?"

Rooster motioned for him to come closer to the bed. Cliff leaned over as Rooster pulled the oxygen mask to one side and whispered, "She's my granddaughter. She's Jim's daughter," his voice a mere thread of sound.

Cliff shook his head. "I don't know what you're talking about." Rooster gave a weak gesture at a small brown paper bag on the bedside table. Confused, Cliff picked up the bag and handed it to Rooster. Nora and Charlie, who had followed Cliff into the room, moved in closer on the other side of the bed.

Rooster reached into the bag and pulled out a stack of pictures. With a shaking hand, he picked up the top photo. "My son, Jim." Cliff nodded; he'd seen snapshots of the old man's family before. What was he trying to convey? Rooster reached for another photo, one of Jim and a pretty girl with light brown hair. He struggled, but then murmured, "Cathryn, Catrina's mother."

He twirled his finger slowly, indicating Cliff should turn it over, and he did so. Printed on the back of the snapshot was the phrase, "I love you. C. July 7, 1965."

The old man reached out a trembling, arthritic hand to Cliff. His eyes filled with tears, he managed to say, "Go, bring our girl back home."

Cliff opened his mouth, then closed it. He felt as if a calf had kicked him in the head. He wanted to reassure Rooster that he would find Cat, but had no idea how he would ever do so. Besides, what if the old man was wrong about this?

"How can you be sure that she's Jim's daughter? These pictures aren't really concrete evidence..."

Rooster smiled, pulled the oxygen mask down to his neck and took a gasping breath. "Belt buckle...I saw it on branding day."

Cliff glanced over to his brother, but Charlie shrugged his shoulders as Rooster continued. "She wore the belt buckle Jim won the day he died. Then in the sweat lodge, Jim came to me." Rooster's eyes sparkled as he recalled his vision. "He handed me a small bundle. Inside the blanket was a baby. He told me to care for it always."

Grief burned the backs of Cliff's eyes, but he held it in check. He no longer believed in the Ute ceremony when he'd entered the sweat lodge, but hadn't his own visions shown him what he needed to do to find happiness? Did he have the courage to search for Cat, only to dash her dreams by telling her that her father was dead? What if she refused to return with him?

Cliff's gaze met and held Charlie's. His brother appeared older as he held Nora close to his heart, comforting her as she wept. But then, as if answering Cliff's unasked question, Charlie nodded.

"Don't worry about the ranch," His brother reassured him in his unhurried deep voice. "I'll take care of everything while you're gone."

* * * *

Cliff rolled up a pair of clean socks and shorts in a T-shirt and shoved them into a small leather bag along with his razor and toothbrush. He gave his room a quick glance and decided if he needed anything more he'd buy it in New York. He wondered how long it would take to find Cat, considering he had no idea where to begin looking.

His guts knotted up like a bundle of twisted barbwire. Searching for Cat would be the easy part. He didn't look forward to leaving the security of his ranch and getting on a plane for the first time in his life. He wiped his sweaty palms on his jeans.

The cordless phone on his bedside table rang. Cliff's heart tightened into a hard ball. Had Roster's health failed? Could Cat be calling? His hands clammy, he fumbled to snatch up the receiver.

"May I speak to Catrina Pearson, please?" a pleasant sounding voice asked.

"Who's this," Cliff growled, then took a deep breath and wished he hadn't sounded so gruff.

"Crystal Robertson. I'm Catrina's friend and agent. Is this Mr. White Fox?"

Crystal? He rolled the name around in his head. *Right! Cat's friend who lives in New York.* Cliff's heart slammed against his ribs and tore off like a spooked colt. "She's not here. Darned woman took off for New York a few days ago. Do you have any idea where I can find her?"

"Oh! Well, let me think..." The line went quiet, while Cliff held his breath. If anyone knew where Cat was headed, it would be this woman, he thought.

"Were you planning to come to New York for the Spring Art Fair?" she asked, seemingly unaffected by the news that her friend was missing.

Closing his eyes, he rubbed his temples with his right hand, struggling to control his apprehension. "Lady, I'm catching a flight to New York, and I'd appreciate it if you could tell me where I can find her when I get there." He paused, and then added, "There's something important I need to tell her."

"Wonderful! Which airport are you flying into?"

He tucked the phone under his chin, zipped the leather bag shut and headed down the stairs. He needed to stay on this woman's good side. She was his only link to finding Catrina and finding out why she left town in such an all-fire hurry. By damn, he'd get some answers, and then he'd drag her back to Utah by the hair if he had to.

"How many are there? I mean I haven't made any reservations yet." He wouldn't admit he didn't know where he was going or that he didn't have a plan when he got there, but it sounded like this woman would be able to head him in the right direction.

"Get a pen and write this down," she said. "Your best bet would be to fly into LaGuardia Airport."

Cliff dropped his bag on the kitchen table, grabbed a piece of paper and wrote down Crystal's instructions.

* * * *

All Catrina wanted was to make it through this day, then crawl back under the covers in Crystal's spare room and sleep for several months. She glanced around the small space designated for her display on the second floor of the Silverton Building. The old brick warehouse had been renovated into a beautiful art gallery with marble floors and gigantic crystal chandeliers, but the strong odor of floor wax was wreaking havoc on her sensitive stomach.

She worked all these years to build her career and knew she deserved the recognition she would be getting today. However, she didn't feel like celebrating. As a matter of fact, she didn't want to be there at all. That morning after complaining about being exhausted and feeling sick again, Crystal had insisted Catrina take a pregnancy test. With fate as it were, the test came up positive.

Yesterday she thought she had everything figured out. She loved Cliff and wanted to go back and try to rectify some kind of relationship with him. But the baby changed everything. He had told her straight out he wasn't ready for anything serious. If she told him about the baby, he would feel obligated to do the right thing, and she wasn't going to force him into something he didn't want. No, she would wait until the child was born, then sit down and write him a long letter and pray he would at least be willing to play a part in their child's life. She couldn't ask for anything more than that.

"How are you holding up?" Crystal's cheerful voice shattered Cat's private brooding. With her optimistic attitude, Crystal seemed more annoying than the cartoon character, Marge Simpson.

"Wonderful, considering my insides feel like two pigs fighting over the last corncob in the trough."

Crystal laughed and shook her head. "Your vocabulary has become so colorful. What's gotten into you?"

Cat's brows pulled into a deep frown. "Is that supposed to be a joke? Because if it is, it's not funny."

Crystal pulled Cat into an affectionate hug, whispering, "Everything is going to be all right. I know the buyers and the critics are going to sit up and take notice of your work. It's astonishing how you captured the true essence of the Wild West. It's almost as if time has stood still for the past hundred years."

When Crystal leaned away, her eyes sparkled like green-fired emeralds. "I loved the sample photos you sent from your trip to Africa, but these," she waved her hand toward Cat's display. "These photos are fantastic. And the title, 'A Foot In Two Worlds'… It's perfect." Crystal chucked Cat under the chin. "Smile! When this is all over, we'll both have a lot to celebrate. I promise."

Cat grunted in response. Crystal had always been a drama queen.

Her friend rubbed her hands up and down Cat's arms and flicked the fringe on her white blouse before cupping Cat's dark chocolate curls. In the worst southern accent Cat ever heard, Crystal said, "Your cute little cowgirl clothes and your hair curled is a nice touch. You look like a country-western singer fresh off the farm in Tennessee."

The redhead, who Cat had once thought of as her best friend, sashayed away, but Cat restrained herself from sticking out a booted foot and tripping her.

Glad I decided against wearing my red cowboy hat today.

Crystal had been right however. This was her big break. A chance to prove she had talent as a photographer and a painter. She'd worked her whole adult life for this day, except now that it was here, it no longer seemed important.

In the space of a moment, her entire life had changed. She had the future of her baby to consider. She didn't want her child to grow up like she had, moving from one rundown apartment to another as her mother found work nor left alone at night while she worked two and three jobs to make ends meet. Mostly she didn't want her child to wonder who its father was or question its own worth like she had.

Cat recalled asking her mother several times why she didn't have a father like her friends, but her mother would skirt around the question. After a while, Cat gave up and quit asking. Things were going to be different this time. No matter what Cliff's feelings for her were, she was going to make sure he stayed a part of his child's life, even if it was from several states away.

Last night she poured her heart out to Crystal. To her surprise, when she had finished, Crystal agreed with Millie that she and Cliff were perfect for each other.

Too bad he doesn't feel the same way.

All she wanted was for the next eight to ten hours to speed by without a hitch and without throwing up.

Chapter Seventeen

Cliff lumbered out of La Guardia Airport into the early evening light, his head buzzing and senses reeling. Cooped up for six hours on a plane with a quick stop-and-dash in Denver to catch a connecting flight wasn't his idea of a good time. His shoulders felt stiff and ached from being wedged into the miniature airline seat. The wound on his leg throbbed in time with the severe pounding in his head.

A man dressed in a business suit trotted past him to the curb and held up his hand. When a cab pulled up, the man crawled into the backseat, and the cab drove away. Cliff watched as others around him did the same, so he followed suit. Raising his hand, a yellow Crown Victoria pulled up and stopped next to him. He ducked his large frame into the backseat, and as he closed the door, the driver pulled away from the curb.

"Where to?" the heavy-set man asked as he maneuvered the cab into the fast pace traffic. The driver rested his elbow on the open window and nodded when Cliff rattled off the Manhattan address he had scribbled down as Crystal dictated.

Cliff wondered how long it would take to get to the Art Gallery; he didn't want to sit a minute longer than he had to.

Fidgeting, he tried to stretch out his long legs and kicked the back of the front seat. He couldn't wait to see Catrina. During the few days she was at his place, she and Rooster had become quite close, and he worried about how she was going to take the news of the old man's heart attack, let alone his request that she return to Utah.

The driver glanced in the mirror. Cliff knew his western clothes made him look out of place. He stared out the window, taking in the strange sights. He winced at the blare of a car horn when the cab abruptly changed lanes, feeling stifled by the buildings crowding the road. How could anyone stand to live in this God-forsaken place!

As they approached an enormous eight-lane suspension bridge, the driver said in a Sylvester Stallone accent, "This here's the Williamsburg Bridge. It's like over 7000 feet long, and the two towers alone are 335 feet high. They started this sucker in 1896, but it didn't open until right before Christmas in 1903."

Cliff couldn't care less if it had opened that morning, but the guy was just being helpful so he responded with a single nod.

The traffic slowed, and Cliff watched pedestrians and bicycles pass by above them. Two railway tracks ran between them and the oncoming traffic. He opened his window and almost gagged. It wasn't the smell of fresh air, tall grass or cattle that hit him, but a mixture of trash, restaurant odors and exhaust and oil fumes from the industrial buildings.

As they crossed the bridge the lights from the traffic reflected off the dark river far below. Cliff realized he could never live here. He wouldn't be able to handle the sound of traffic all day or the bright lights at night.

Yet this was Cat's world, just like the ranch was his. Could she give it up? He had only been here for twenty minutes, and he longed to be back home where the only thing a person would hear was the bawling of calves and a few howling coyotes. Industrial buildings, a combination of brick and glass, some old, some new, seemed to swallow up the landscape around him, making him feel trapped.

"So you an actor?" the driver asked, eyeing Cliff in the rearview mirror.

"Nope."

"You a real cowboy or something?"

"Or something," Cliff grunted.

"Here to visit someone?" The man persisted.

"Gonna find a woman and take her back home."

The driver smirked. "You have one in mind or is this sort of a shopping trip?"

Cliff closed his eyes, but couldn't keep himself from confiding, "She ran off while I was laid up in the hospital."

The driver's smile faded into a frown. "What were you in the hospital for?"

"Rattlesnake bite." Cliff returned the man's stare in the rearview mirror.

The driver shifted his gaze back to the road, and silence filled the vehicle for several moments before he hopped back into tour guide mode.

"Since you get to know beef on the hoof, ya might be interested to know that further west is the meatpacking district. Runs from about West 14th Street south to Gansevoort and east of the Hudson River up to Hudson Street."

Cliff groaned. *This guy's a wealth of worthless information.*

To his relief the taxi finally pulled up in front of a large brick building. The driver turned and glanced over the seat. "Well, here you go, Tex."

Cliff shoved a handful of bills in the guy's direction, grabbed his leather bag and then worked his way out of the backseat. At last, he stood on the sidewalk feeling like a jackrabbit in the middle of a herd of hungry coyotes as a constant stream of people brushed past him.

"Take it easy on that woman now," the driver said as another man bumped against Cliff and crawled into the back of the cab. "I don't wanna read about you in the paper tomorrow." With a farewell wave, the cabby pulled away from the curb.

Cliff glanced around again in amazement at the never-ending stream of people before turning to study the old brick building in front of him. A painted sign at the bottom of the wide stone steps read, "Silverton Spring Art Fair".

Gulping for air, he coughed at the harsh tang of automobile exhaust. *Okay, White Fox, all you needed to do is mosey on in, tell Cat about Rooster and that he needs to see her. Bring her back to Utah like you promised, but only after you find out why she snuck off in the first place.*

"Shouldn't take too long."

* * * *

Cat wondered whether anyone would notice if she slipped out the side door for some fresh air. Way too many people milled around the small room, and the walls were closing in on her. Being the last on the art fair's itinerary, newcomers drank champagne, mingled and appeared reluctant to leave.

She glanced longingly once more toward the door.

"Don't even think about it," Crystal purred, placing a restrictive hand lovingly on her arm. "Whether you realize it or not, you're a success. Everyone loves your paintings and photos."

She waved the young waiter away when he approached them with a tray of champagne. "The "buzz" is you've caught your subject's inner soul." Placing a hand against her chest, she sighed in dramatic effect.

"I'm glad everyone likes them," Cat mumbled. "But I think I'd rather be outside in the fresh air taking the photos or painting than stuck in here showing them and listening to this shrill babble of people talking over one another."

"I'm proud of you, champ! Despite everything that's happened, you've held up all day."

Crystal grinned, and Cat swore she saw little yellow canary feathers sticking out of the woman's mouth. Glancing at her wristwatch, she tugged at the neckline of her blouse. "I'm glad it's almost over. It's so warm in here." She glanced around and murmured, "I feel kind of light headed again."

A slender black clad woman in her late sixties approached. "Congratulations on your show, my dear."

Cat forced a smile. "Thank you." *God, I wish everyone would just get out, so I can leave.*

Crystal poked Cat in the rib as she stepped forward and reached for the woman's hand. "Mrs. Warrington. How lovely to see you again." Crystal's eyes sparkled with excitement, her smile triumphant. "May I introduce Catrina Pearson? Catrina, Mrs. Warrington is one of the original organizers of the Manhattan Spring Art Fair and quite the outdoors woman."

The woman beamed at the compliment. "In my youth I spent some time on a ranch in Montana riding horse, fishing and hunting." She treated them to a nostalgic giggle. "I guess one never really gets over that sort of experience."

Cat knew just how she felt, yet could only offer a lame smile in response.

"I'm really impressed with your work," Mrs. Warrington continued, strolling closer to the row of large black and white photos displayed along one wall. "Each of your photos demonstrates the simplicity of your subject's lifestyle, in addition to the hardships they've endured." She shook her head. "Truly amazing."

With a touch of melancholy in her voice, she added, "Makes me wish I was riding across the open range against a warm breeze laced with a hint of sage blowing across my face."

"Thank you, Mrs. Warrington. Although I spent only a brief time on the Circle D Ranch, I'm quite sure I'll never forget the experience." Crystal placed an arm around Cat's shoulder and gave her an encouraging squeeze.

"I have to admit I'm quite intrigued by the man in your two oils." The older woman winked at Cat. "Will he be making an appearance today? I'd love to meet him."

Cat's heart fluttered painfully in her chest. She had no idea when she would see Cliff again. She didn't know how she could face him, let alone confess about the baby.

She would stick to her plan about contacting him after the baby was born. That way, at least she wouldn't have to witness his reaction first hand, though she could guess. He'd made his feelings clear. She couldn't just show up and drop the news in his lap.

Yes, better wait and tell him later. That would also give her time to get her emotions under control and forge some sort of plan for her and the baby's life.

Cat realized that Mrs. Warrington still waited for an answer. She inhaled a deep breath and willed her nerves to settle down.

"No. I'm afraid Manhattan really isn't his kind of town."

An eerie silence spread throughout the room, as though someone had chucked a stone into a pond, then wild applause erupted.

Cat twisted to one side and peered toward the doorway, searching to see the cause of the commotion. She gasped. There he stood, black hat pulled low over his dark intense eyes.

Then his gaze locked with hers. Cat blinked first, searching his familiar features with an eagerness that shocked her. God, he looked good. Long dark hair curled around his collar, his thick mustache recently trimmed, exposing most of his full lower lip.

Another gasp ripped from Cat's lungs before she could contain it. She swayed and took a step back, but Crystal pressed a strong hand against the middle of her back in support. "Good Lord. Is that *him*, Clifford White Fox?"

The air buzzed with eager voices. People surged forward, all wanting to shake Cliff's hand.

Cat stood on her toes in an attempt to see every inch of him, thinking the guy cleaned up really well. He looked like a movie star in new jeans with a sharp seam pressed down the front, a dark tan, long-sleeved western shirt adorned with shiny black onyx snaps and a thin black bolo tie.

He even sported a sexy looking black cowboy hat and a shine on his old boots. Cat couldn't help but wonder if his spurs and pearl-handled pistols were tucked in the small leather bag he carried.

But Cliff continued to press forward, struggling to excuse himself from his group of fans. Removing his hat, he raked his fingers through his disheveled hair.

Little white dots flashed before Cat's eyes. *Oh God–don't let me faint or throw up.* "What are you doing here," she asked when he stopped mere inches from her.

He towered over her, voice growling deep and low. "You owe me an explanation for taking off without a word."

Those eyes blazing into hers, the edge to his voice gave Cat the energy to fire back. "I don't owe you anything, least of all an explanation."

Unwilling to stand and hash out their personal problems in front of a crowd, Cat turned to leave, but a strong, calloused hand engulfed her upper arm. No painful pressure, but she knew he wouldn't let go until he was good and ready.

"Tell me why you left, or I'll throw you over my shoulder and haul your pretty little ass out of here right now!"

Cat tilted her face up until her nose almost touched his chin. *"Now* who's acting crazy?" She wished everyone in the room would disappear, including her.

"What the hell are you talking about?" His eyes squinted into thin lines. Crow's feet creased his high cheekbones.

Shooting his hand a quick glance, he released her. Cat heaved a heavy sigh and squared her shoulders. "I'm sorry I caused you so much trouble. I'm even sorrier you think everything we had...was a mistake."

Out of the corner of his eye, Cliff saw the relentless colorful crowd inch closer. "We need to talk," he said, lowering his voice. "There're a few things I need to set straight, but not here."

"I've already heard enough of your rationalizations to last until the cows come home." Anger snapped in her eyes like fireflies.

Shaking his head, he blurted, "Damn it, woman. You're as stubborn as your—"

"Me!" She scoffed and placed her hands on her hips. "That's the pot calling the pail round!"

Cliff closed his eyes. This wasn't turning out like he had planned at all. "I didn't come here to fight with you. There's something you need to know."

"What's so important that you came 2000 miles to deliver a message?"

Cliff paused. "It's Rooster...He has something important to tell you."

"I'll call him next week."

"You have to come now." If she wasn't going to listen to reason, he would force her to come back with him.

"In case you haven't noticed," her eyes widened with sarcasm, "I'm a little busy right now. It'll have to wait."

"No." His voice thundered in the small room. "It might be too late."

"What are you talking about?" Her tone changed, her brows pulled in a tight frown.

"He's in the hospital. He's had a heart attack."

She swayed, her eyes rolled back in her head, and she fainted dead away. Cliff lunged to catch her, scooping her up before she hit the floor. Turning, he discovered a roomful of people staring as if he had done something wrong.

A redhead stepped forward. "Follow me," she said, "There's a lounge right down the hall."

He nodded and trailed behind her, his boots clicking on the polished marble floor. Opening a door, she led him to a small cream colored sofa.

"I'll get some water," she said then disappeared.

Cliff placed Cat on the sofa and knelt beside her. Taking her ice cold hands in his, he rubbed them gently. Her precious face had turned as pale as chalk.

God... What have I done? I love this woman more than life. If anything ever happened to her...

His heart swelled with love. He never felt accepted in either the Native American world or the white man's world. But when he walked in, he'd been accepted in Cat's world, and that's where he wanted to be.

The little redhead was back and shoving a plastic cup at him. "How's she doing?" She smiled and placed a gentle hand on his shoulder.

He turned back when a soft moan slipped from Cat's lips.

Thank God. "Are you all right?" His head pounded like a herd of stampeding cattle on the loose.

"Tell me what happened to Rooster." Cat pushed his hands away when he offered the water and struggled to sit up.

"I'm sorry," Cliff said, leaning forward to prevent her from standing. "I didn't want to break the news to you quite that way."

Her eyes filled with tears. "How severe is it?"

Cliff wished he could pull her into his arms and tell her everything was going to be fine, but this wasn't the place, and they were wasting precious time. "I never got the chance to talk to a doctor. As soon as I walked into that hospital room, the old man ordered me to find you and bring you back."

"Why should I believe anything you say?" She looked away as if she could dismiss him completely.

"Remember what you told me?" He rose and sat on the sofa beside her. "You said wherever there was family, that's where I belonged. Well, that goes for you too, Cat. You have family in Black River. They love you and want you to come back."

He placed a hand on her knee. "Cat...I love you. You're the only thing that matters to me. Not the land or the ranch. Just you. More than anything, I want to try, see if we can make a life together.

Cat's gaze swept from his to the woman standing off to the side. Was she going to bolt? "If you don't feel the same..." He shrugged and put his hands up in surrender. "I won't try to fence you in."

"Tell him, Catrina," the redhead urged. "Tell him now."

Color stained her delicate skin, and she avoided his gaze.

"Tell me what?" he demanded, his arms slipping around her slim shoulders.

"I'm sorry." Cat chewed on her lower lip. "I didn't want to break the news to you quite this way," she said, using the same words he'd just said. "If I go back with you, you'll be getting more than you bargained for. I'm going to have your baby."

The old brick building barely held its foundation as Cliff's roar of delight rattled windows and threatened to break masterpieces.

Chapter Eighteen

Cat paused outside Rooster's hospital room. What on earth did he have to tell her? The scent of disinfectant caused the butterflies in her belly to tumbled and fight like tiny Ninjas.

She wiped her damp palms on her jeans. Could it possibly have something to do with her father? Does he know who he is? What if it has to do with the old man's health? Nibbling on her lower lip, she glanced up at Cliff. He gave her shoulder a gentle squeeze. "It'll be alright," he said and reached for the door handle.

She hesitated at the threshold, surprised to find Cliff's mother, Ester, along with Doug, Charlie and Nora in the cramped little room. Rooster sat propped up against a half dozen pillows.

His face lit up when he saw her, and she returned his wide smile, relief flooding her soul.

Rooster patted the mattress and motioned for her to come and sit next to him. Thrilled to find him sitting up without tubes sticking out of him, she wrapped her arms around his neck and hugged him.

Leaning away, Cat searched his weathered face. "Are you feeling all right? What did the doctor say?" she asked, settling on the edge of the mattress.

"I'm better now that you're here," he reassured in a scratchy, dry voice. "Course they've been fussing over me like a bunch of old hens. Ran a bucket full of tests. All came back fine." His red-rimmed eyes twinkled with joy. "The warden's letting me out tomorrow."

"But he can't be alone for the first week," Nora piped up. "So I'm moving in to make sure he behaves himself."

194

Rooster reached out and engulfed Cat's hands with his bent fingers. His rough calloused hands warm against her own made her feel loved and protected. "How did your big art show go? Sell any of your pictures?"

Unsure of how to respond, Cat glanced around. Ester sat in the only chair, a pleasant expression warming her round face. With a flick of his tongue, Doug flipped a wooden toothpick from one side of his mouth to the other and winked. Nora and Charlie stood arm in arm, both smiling.

Why does everyone appear so relaxed like nothing happened? she wondered.

"Well, actually several sold." Cat paused, "Rooster..." Part of her wanted to know what he had to tell her, though she didn't think she could handle any additional changes to her life right now.

Rooster nodded toward Ester. Cliff's mother reached over to the window ledge to retrieve a small brown paper bag and handed it to him. His arthritic fingers wrestled the bag open, and pulled out several old, wrinkled snapshots and handed them to her.

Cat blinked in disbelief as she studied photos of her mother, Cathryn, along with a very attractive Native American man. They appeared young and looked very happy.

Rooster tapped the corner of a snapshot with his finger. "That's my son, James." He swallowed hard. "Died when he was only nineteen."

"I'm so sorry for your loss," Cat murmured. "But I don't understand." What was the old man trying to tell her?

Rooster gazed into the distance as if searching for another time, another place. The room grew quiet. "August 31, 1965. I remember it being too danged hot for a rodeo, so much noise and confusion. I stood behind the chutes and watched my son being strapped to the back of a ton of pure hate. Jim turned, smiled at me and then nodded his head. That kid loved the rodeos."

Rooster's hand tightened around Cat's. "Then the gate swung open, and a huge black bull, "The Executioner", bolted into the arena. He spun in tight circles and bucked. I can still see the rope of white snot flying from his nostrils as he swung that massive head and horns, trying to connect with Jim's body.

"Then somehow when he twisted, he lost his footing. Went down. Son of a gun rolled and crushed Jim beneath him." Rooster's eyes filled with tears. "Twenty-eight years...seems like yesterday." He patted her hand.

Hot tears rolled down Cat's cheeks, and her chest ached, making it hard to breath.

"Jim's ride got the highest score that day, giving him the All-Around belt buckle. I followed the ambulance and handed him the buckle before they took him for x-rays. That was the last time we spoke." Rooster cleared his throat and made a brave effort to smile. "Never laid eyes on that buckle again till you sashayed out sportin' it on branding day."

Cat struggled to draw in a breath, to concentrate on every word and to make sense out of what he was telling her.

"Lot of confusion in the emergency room that day. I'd forgotten your mama was even at the hospital till I stopped and thought about it. He must have given her the buckle just before going into surgery." Rooster shook his head. "She left town a few days after the funeral."

"You're saying your son is…was my father? She never told me any of this."

"I'm sure she had her reasons. They were both kids."

A lump formed in the back of Cat's throat. Her mother must have felt so alone after Jim died, so unsure of *both* of their futures. She had almost been in a similar predicament, but she had Cliff, and he loved her. She turned and smiled up at him.

"You know what this means, don't you?" Rooster said, cutting into her thoughts. "It means you're my granddaughter." He grinned, showing off big square teeth.

"And we're cousins," Nora said, pleased with the notion. "I hope you can forgive me for sending you up on Red Ridge. I never meant for anyone to get hurt." She shot Cliff a sideways glance.

Cliff's ex-wife is my cousin? Cat had a hard time grasping that, but remembered he had told her that Nora's mother, Anna, was his daughter.

Cat continued to shuffle through the pile of photos until she came to one of her mother and father standing in front of an old wooden fence, their arms circled around each other. She held the photo up to show Rooster.

"That's my favorite one," he said, wiping a tear from his cheek.

The search for her father was over. She would never get a chance to know him, but she had found family—a grandfather who she already loved and a cousin, with whom, it seemed, she had a lot in common.

Cat glanced at Cliff. One corner of his mouth hitched up to a lopsided grin. He nodded his head and winked. They had discussed everything on the flight back, from what she overheard outside his hospital room to Millie's scheme to get them together.

"Now's as good a time as any," Cliff said, stepping close behind her and resting his hands on her shoulders. "They're going to find out sooner or later."

"Find out about what?" Rooster asked, leaning forward in the bed.

Cat tried to hide a smile and said in a serious tone, "Maybe we should wait until he's feeling better."

Rooster's chest puffed up, and he started to throw back the covers. "I'm as fine as the hair on a new born calf. Don't go forgettin' who pulled you out of that cold wet ditch!"

Cat's hands shot up to hold him back. "Okay! I'll tell you. Your heart should be strong enough to handle good news." She felt the heat rise up from her collar. "You're going to be a great grandpa."

The old man's face paled, his mouth gaped open, and he fell back against the pillows.

"Get the doctor!" Cat yelled, but Rooster shook his head.

"I'm fine," he muttered. "No man ever died from getting good news."

The room erupted into shrieks of joy.

* * * *

Millie drove past what was once her home and headed toward the family cemetery hidden behind the deteriorating barn. She cringed. "Guess I'd better get used to livin' in town. Could live pretty comfortable on what the insurance company sent me."

She pulled up next to the three-foot high wrought iron fence and switched off the engine. Climbing out of the truck, she swung the gate open and hobbled into the small area. The space felt much larger when there had only been one grave. Richard, her son, had died in 1950 at the age of five. With three gravestones in the enclosure, it felt a little cramped.

"Grass needs trimming," she murmured aloud, brushing twigs and leaves from the rickety, whitewashed bench before she sat down. "Well,

Alfred, I did it again."

A warm breeze brushed her back, plucked at her thin gray curls. "I poked my big old nose into Catrina and Cliff's lives and ended up driving her off just like I did her mother. She's left town, and I have no idea where she went. I doubt I'll ever see her again."

She stared at her daughter's headstone. "Cathryn, I'm sorry you thought I was smothering you and prying into your life. I loved you so much. I just wanted you to be happy." She wiped a flowered handkerchief across her tearstained cheeks.

"I know my apologies are too little, too late, but I truly am sorry I made you feel you couldn't confide in me or stay here with me. Now I've done the same thing to Catrina. I swear I really believed she and Cliff were right for each other. All they needed was to cross paths and let nature take its course."

Millie shook her head. "It all backfired on me. From now on I'm going to mind my own business."

Standing, she crossed to her husband's headstone and ran a gentle hand across the rough worn stone before kneeling. Reaching out, she pulled up the dried, wilted flowers and tucked them into the pocket of her sweater. Albert had been a gentle, soft-spoken man, and the love of their forty-eight years together still filled her heart. "I guess I deserve to spend what's left of my life alone."

The snap of a twig caught Millie's attention. She twisted around and found Catrina and Cliff standing by the gate. How much had they heard? Wiping her hands on her trousers, Millie started to stand. Cliff reached out a hand. His lopsided grin caused her to pause before accepting his help.

"Do you really mean that?" Catrina asked, still standing by the gate.

Millie grasped Cliff's hand, and he hauled her to her feet. "Thanks, son."

She patted his hand before turning to Catrina. "I'm glad to see you. Wasn't sure I'd ever lay eyes on you again. Yep, I'm done trying to help people." She waved both hands in the air. "Everyone can make their own mistakes in life and live with the consequences."

Her granddaughter glanced at Cliff, and he nodded.

"Well, in that case," Cat said, in an even tone. "We have something we'd like to share with you."

Millie dreaded what was coming, yet she deserved the tongue-lashing she was going to get. She braced herself for the worst as Cliff cupped her elbow and helped her back to the old bench.

Catrina sat down next to her. "If you hadn't interfered in our lives, we probably wouldn't have met," Cliff said, standing behind Cat.

"You mean to tell me you two worked everything out?" Millie asked, hope filling her heart.

Cat nodded her head. "You were right. He is perfect for me." She squeezed Cliff's hand. "And because you went out of your way to make sure we got together..." Cat's cheeks flushed a bright pink. "You're going to be a great-grandmother some time next February."

"Oh, child. That's the best news I've ever heard." Millie slapped Cliff on the arm. "You old fox, don't ever think you can out smart this old hen!"

* * * *

Cliff settled back into the wooden rocker on his front porch, propping one booted foot on his knee. The night air surrounded him, sweet with spring flowers, tall pasture grass and a promise for an interesting future. A coyote howled somewhere off in the distance, and a yellow moon hung over a silhouette of the barn.

His chest rose with a contented sigh. Rooster and Catrina both back home where they belonged gave him a sense of order, of peace and quiet and normalcy. He rocked back and forth. Of course, he knew it wouldn't last for long, not with Cat around, but that was fine with him.

It still amazed him how one woman could invade the serene and secure world he'd built for himself and in just a few days turn it upside down. A chuckle slipped between his lips. *Just goes to show, no matter how firm a handle you think you have on your life, an unexpected package of total chaos could show up at any time.*

The screen door squeaked, and Cat strolled barefoot out onto the porch. "What are you smiling about?" she demanded.

In response, he tugged her down on his lap and kissed her hard, a sample of what was to come.

"I was just thinking how much my life has changed since I came home and found you standing in my kitchen with hardly anything on, and how you've turned this old house into a real home."

She giggled. "I love this place, but to be honest, I didn't know what to think when you barged in that night, dripping wet. You looked half-crazed. Frankly you scared me to death."

"I felt half crazed. I rode to Millie's to check on you. When I found the roof caved in, but your car missing I was relieved. Then I came across your car floating in the ditch. I searched for you, but when I couldn't find you, I decided to come back here and get the truck and head for town."

She kissed his forehead, his cheek, then brushed the corner of his mustache down with the back of her finger.

"I never thought I could be that scared again until I realized you'd left me. I didn't know where you went or if I'd ever see you again." He locked his gaze with hers. "Don't ever scare me like that again." He placed a hand on each side of her face and kissed her.

"I love you," he breathed. "I don't know what I'd do without you."

"I love you, too," Cat whispered, her eyes half closed, her breath warm against his neck. "So where does this leave us?"

"Woman, I told you before that I'd never fence you in."

"So you don't mind if I keep working?" She sat up with a jerk, a slight grin on her lips.

"You can go anywhere you want." He rubbed a gentle hand across her flat stomach. "As long as you take us with you. Oh, and this old blue denim shirt," he added, slipping a large calloused hand up under the hem.

Cat fell into his kiss, her promise to him sealed with love. Her roaming days were over. She'd found her home and her cowboy.

About the Author

The saying, "You can take the girl out of the country, but you can't take the country out of the girl" describes this author. She likes to herd cattle on horseback in Montana, snowmobile in Wyoming, garden and write romance novels.

Her tales stem from a combination of past experiences and a lot of wishful thinking. She's written since 1996, but has been dreaming up wild adventures her whole life. She resides in east central Minnesota.

The women in her novels are country girls, who find themselves in strange predicaments with men, who definitely have the makings of true heroes.

Email: Lfnies1@yahoo.com
Website: www.luannnies.com

Other Works by the Author at Melange

Bearly Christmas Darling in Christmas Wishes 2012